IT'S A WONDERFUL DOG

EASTER EGGS

MERIVELLE HOUSE INC.

*It's a Wonderful Dog – Easter Egg*s is a work of fiction. References to real people, events, establishments, organizations, or locales are only used to give a sense of authenticity and are fictional elements. All characters, dialogue and incidents are drawn from the author's imagination and are not to be construed as real.

It's a Wonderful Dog – Easter Eggs
Copyright © 2024 Keri Salas. All rights reserved.

Thank you for purchasing an authorized edition of this book. Please comply with copyright laws and reach out to the author for permission of use including reproducing, scanning or distribution.
Kerisalas.com

Library of Congress Control Number: 2024915544
ISBN 978-1-965265-00-0 (hardcover)
ISBN 978-1-965265-01-7 (paperback)
ISBN 978-1-965265-02-4 (ebook)

Cover art and Formatting by Damonza
Interior illustrations by Author

Also by Keri Salas

It's a Wonderful Dog-A Christmas Tail

Book One

IT'S A WONDERFUL DOG: EASTER EGGS

KERI SALAS

In memory of the real-life Henry.

Who wandered right into our hearts.

We're all just walking each other home.

-Ram Dass

Home of a Gentleman with Wealth

The day was calm, and all hearts were happy after scores of humans had crossed over the Rainbow Bridge to meet the pets from their lifetime. With the sunrise, a full spectrum of prismatic colors spanned above the horizon bringing humans to the dogs they loved on Earth by way of an enormous bridge. As the morning hours passed, the colors faded from sight and each newly reunited family found their way across the Golden Meadow, a place where each dog had passed time waiting for their human. Grass blew with a perpetual gentle breeze as groups of humans and dogs walked onward. As they disappeared, small visions of scenery appeared for a moment to show the human's dream of heaven. Snow-capped mountains, flower-filled valleys, sunset painted deserts and breathtaking cliffs above oceans would flash as the souls walked to their eternities.

Josephine, the chief guardian angel for dogs, stared down at Earth. The light of the afternoon shined through her, causing thousands of tiny sparkles to surround her.

"You're always looking down these days," Lea said. The angel had been at Josephine's side for centuries and was unaccustomed to such melancholy emanating from her friend.

Josephine gazed in Lea's direction. "I miss Bear Bailey," she said. "And sometimes I like to check in and see that he's still safe."

"Would you believe I do the same thing? When it's quiet around here. During the dog's afternoon nap time."

"How does he seem to you?"

"The same Bear Bailey that we've always known." Lea's attention trailed off for a moment as two dogs in the distance tussled in play on the far side of the Golden Meadow.

"Bear is the very definition of a canine gentleman," Josephine continued. "He makes everyone in his world feel valued. He's kind, loving and loyal. With a wealth of friends who love him."

"Yes, that sums it up," Lea said, turning back to Josephine.

Though it had been rare for the pair of angels to send a dog from the Rainbow Bridge to Earth, a majestic Labrador named Jiff had been waiting for his human to cross over for decades. As time passed, and though he wasn't supposed to be able to feel sadness while waiting, he mourned his human, Franklin. The two angels had agreed that a visit to Earth one Christmas season to help a despondent Bear Bailey would be the thing to help keep Jiff occupied while he was waiting. And true to their prediction, Jiff's willingness to help set things right ensured Bear Bailey didn't cross the Rainbow Bridge before his time.

"We have dogs crossing the Rainbow Bridge each sunrise, and still, Jiff and Bear hold a special place in my heart," Lea said. "Even though Jiff is in heaven and Bear is still helping on Earth."

Josephine scanned the horizon where Franklin and Jiff had walked into Franklin's idea of heaven three years before. "They're passing the time in the mountains, walking every stream, crossing immense bridges spanning mountain passes and eating popcorn at every opportunity."

"Isn't it interesting? Franklin was terrified of bridges."

"How wonderful that an earthly fear transforms into a joyful part of his time in Heaven," Josephine said. "The other evening, I saw a vision of Franklin and Jiff skipping across a suspension bridge, high over water."

Lea giggled. "I saw that too. The way Franklin leaned over the bridge and shouted into the sunset with joy, Jiff barking and running in circles around him."

"One day, Clara will cross to join her husband. But for the time being, it's lovely to see him occupied with his wonderful dog."

The pair sat in silence for a few moments until a squirrel appeared in front of them, shaking its bushy tail back and forth. Josephine pulled a large peanut out of thin air and presented it to the small creature's outstretched paws. "You know, I try to give more attention to these rascals since our conversations with Jiff. He once asked me if dog heaven is squirrel hell."

Lea laughed, putting her hand out to the squirrel who sniffed its emptiness and ran away with the nut Josephine had bequeathed it. "Jiff was such a character."

Josephine's face lit up with amusement. "He and Bear both." She looked to Earth again. "I enjoy tuning into Bear's adventures. Almost like a bit of heavenly television." She tilted her head. "But what I'm seeing doesn't feel like lighthearted entertainment."

Lea closed her eyes. "I don't sense anything. Though your vision on Earth has always been better than mine."

"Katie Hatch. Mary's cousin," Josephine said, closing her eyes. A thunderstorm brewed where the angels had been gazing. Dark clouds swirled over the area. "She's soon going to find out that the thing she needs next in her journey collides with what's caused the town, and everyone in it, great struggle."

Can Sleep in the Barn

Mary Bailey jumped at a sudden gust of wind. Startled, she put down the book she was reading and waited for a moment. A bigger burst of air soon followed, shaking the entire house. A random tumbleweed hit one of the back living room windows as sandy dirt pelted the glass with great force. Although she knew the weather was too cold for a tornado, the wind gusts matched what caused great concern to Kansans during warm summer months.

The Great Pyrenees laying at her feet rose up and growled.

"Sit down, Bear. There's nothing to worry about. Just wind that might blow in some rain for spring flowers." Mary was careful to keep her tone upbeat, her dog exhibited uncanny knowing where she was concerned and reflected her emotions in almost every situation.

Not convinced of his owner's words, the Pyrenees pawed at the door, careful not to scratch the glass. He whined, giving Mary a pleading look that usually worked wonders when he wanted to go outside.

As the wind continued to gust, she patted the sofa. "I'll let you on the couch if you come and rest before we head into the store."

The gesture of welcome was usually music to the dog's ears. This particular time, he groaned and began to howl, nodding to the outside area where he'd heard a sound, not perceptible to Mary.

"Theodore's still sleeping. Shush!"

He trotted back to Mary and then jumped on the couch and dropped his enormous head onto her lap. He punctuated his actions with a long sigh.

"Relax, good boy. All is well."

Mary's husband, Theodore, leaned on the doorway between the kitchen and the living room. His hair was standing on end in places and mushed down in others. He yawned and rubbed his eyes. "What *was* that?"

"Some crazy wind going on today. Even by western Kansas standards."

Theodore went to the patio door and searched the landscape. His shoulders dropped as he stopped mid-yawn.

"What is it?"

"Your oak tree," Theodore murmured. "It's down."

"What?" Mary jumped from the couch with Bear following. She joined her husband, gazing out at the wooded elevated hill in the distance. She'd known the old tree had needed cut down for years—one after another, brittle branches had broken away from the dried-up trunk. Memories of the tree and her mother when she was alive intertwined in her mind, causing Mary to leave it in place, praying for an arboriculture miracle. The wind had finally done what she couldn't bring herself to do.

Her husband put an arm around her and pulled her close as Bear leaned in from the other direction.

"I've never looked out and not seen that oak tree," Mary said, her focus on the horizon. The wind had lessened in intensity, though it still blew tumbleweeds across the backyard as she spoke. She let out a deep breath. "My mother is not in the tree."

"What?"

"It's what I say to myself when I come across things like Mom's paperwork or furniture that can't be repaired. I have to remind myself my mother is not in the item. She's in my heart and memories. And then I'm able to let it go," she said, looking up at her husband. "Though the tree seems so much more than old papers."

Theodore kissed Mary's cheek. "I'm sorry, honey. This is a big one for your heart to process."

Bear pushed his face to the glass, fogging up the patio door, giving his snout a comical look as he breathed.

"Apparently, Bear is letting us know he wants out." Mary chuckled. "In his usual, covert way." Since rescuing him as a puppy, the Great Pyrenees had been the antidote to the sadness in processing her mother's sudden passing, intuitively knowing what would bring Mary back to a happy state.

"He's always going to try and get to the bottom of whatever upsets you."

"That's why I always watch my emotions around him." She stroked the dog's large, white mane, one of the hallmark features of the breed.

Bear tapped the glass again with his paw.

"Don't go chasing the goats, Bear. I'm leaving for the co-op in an hour."

"Did that dog just nod his head at you?"

"You always seem surprised we communicate the way we do," Mary said, sliding the patio door open as she scratched Bear's head in affection.

Smelling the air, Bear stepped out onto the deck. The dark morning had carried the promise of rain. However, the wind pushed the clouds through the area before a single drop fell.

Mary studied the sky. "We needed that moisture."

"Look at you. Talking farmer on me. You said moisture, not rain."

"Yep, and I'm going to take my *vehicle*, not truck, to get *fuel*, instead of gas," Mary answered, gamely trying to joke, though she was still heartsick.

Sauntering between the house and barn, Bear began to pant in happiness as Lupe Posada emerged from the larger structure with her children, Pablito and Reyna.

"Did you hear that wind a few minutes ago?" Pablito shouted with wild gestures. "It shook the whole barn. I thought I was finally going to be in the middle of a tornado!"

The Posada family had lived with the Baileys for years. Initially, as Theodore worked on Lupe's citizenship paperwork, both families searched for housing in town. But everyone involved found myriads of reasons why it was best for the Posadas to stay close to Sagebrush Farms. Theodore and Mary hired a local contractor to expand the barn's single bedroom apartment into a barndominium so the Posadas could live in comfort and privacy. It was an arrangement that worked so well, Mary sometimes forgot they hadn't lived in the same proximity when she was growing up.

Lupe focused out in the distance to the fallen tree. "What a lugubrious morning."

Theodore raised his eyebrows in question to Mary and mouthed, *What?*

"Lugubrious is an adjective meaning something is especially gloomy or dismal," Reyna said, pulling a backpack over her shoulder.

"Did you know that, Mary?" Theodore asked.

"Yes, I did. Word of the Day, honey."

Reyna punched Theodore in the arm. "Tio Theo, get with the program. Mamá has everyone learning a new word every day. You and Pablito will also find yourselves in a benighted state if you can't keep up with the *mujeres inteligentes* around here."

"*Intelligent women.*" Pablito snorted. "We're smart too. Tell her what benighted is, Tio."

Lupe turned her attention from the half-fallen tree back to the conversation.

"I'll let you enlighten me on the word," Theodore said.

"You know this, *hermanito*. Don't act dumb to make him laugh," Reyna said.

"It means a lot of darkness."

"*Tú también*, Pablito?" Theodore asked, throwing his hands in the air in playful exaggeration.

"Shall we tell our darling Theodore how benighted can also mean a state of pitiful, intellectual ignorance?" Mary bit her lip to keep from laughing as Pablito giggled.

"You're the only one who didn't know, Tio Theo. You and the goats," Pablito said, pointing to the pathway beyond the barn. Loud bleating heralded the arrival of Sagebrush Farm's three goats—Billy, Skittles and Pandora. Theodore snarled in aggravation, narrowing his eyes at the interlopers who regularly awakened him early from his morning slumber.

"Pablito and Reyna," Lupe warned. "Be respectful."

Mary had been amused as she listened to Theodore being teased, but her eyes kept looking to the hill where the oak tree had stood during the entirety of her childhood. "I need a few moments before I go into the co-op."

"Yes, of course, Mary." Lupe put her arm around her friend's shoulders. "Go to your mother's tree."

This is the Place

The ground crunched under Mary's boots as she walked through the field of bare sagebrush with Bear in close pursuit. Though it was near Easter, there was not yet enough warmth from the sun to coax the light green leaves of the native brush to appear for the season. Taking great care not to break off the dormant branches, she looked for patches of ground to step on. Had someone been watching from the house, she and Bear would have appeared joyful in a child-like game of hopscotch rather than a somber walk to survey a fallen tree.

Arriving at the small grove of trees, also barren of leaves, Mary searched the area. "I should have spent more time here, Bear. My mother always made it a tradition that we picnicked under the trees when I was visiting. They were such happy memories."

Gazing at Mary with large and solemn eyes, Bear nodded to the ground. The wind-struck tree laid on its side. Large roots had been pulled up from the sandy soil.

"This has only ever happened one other time in my life, Bear." She put her hands on her hips. "I remember it because I was getting ready for Katie's twelfth birthday."

Bear groaned. The sound he made whenever he heard the

name *Katie*. It had made everyone around him laugh the first half dozen times he'd done it. Moving forward, it was his Pavlovian response whenever her name enter into a conversation.

"We need to be as kind as possible to her, Bear. Katie's had an incredibly tough time of it in her life. I wish I could have seen that when I was growing up."

Sighing, the Great Pyrenees dropped his weight to the ground in an exasperated manner, his eyebrows shifting from side to side as he listened to Mary speak.

"She started out this spoiled, petulant princess with the whole world at her feet. Her parents adored her. Gave her anything she wanted. Her room was a cotton candy-looking wonderland of sparkles. I was quite jealous of how everything bounced Katie's way. If she didn't have something, she whined and one of her parents made sure some ridiculous trivial and expensive item appeared on her bedspread to greet her at the end of a school day."

The sun was beginning to fight the morning cloud cover for space in the sky, and a random raindrop or two fell as Mary spoke. Distant thunder rumbled as the wind continued blowing in bursts and lulls.

"I remember Katie's birthday that year had such heavy rain, it was hard to see outside. Lightning struck so close, we thought it had hit our house." She searched the horizon, lost in thought. "But it was a tree in this same grove, split right down the middle. My mom was so upset with the loss of it. I didn't get why a tree was so important to her. Until now."

Behind where Mary stood, a rabbit lifted his head and then froze when it saw the giant dog. The two animal's gazes met, and at the pause, the rabbit bolted in the opposite direction. Bear's heart rate elevated but Mary was speaking, and he knew to stay in place rather than follow his natural instinct to chase.

"Later that day, every child in sixth grade arrived at Katie's house. She had a crown on her head. I can't remember the theme because somehow all of Katie's birthdays mushed together and she always found a way to wear one."

Bear put a paw on her foot, nudging her shin with his snout. He felt great love from Mary as she spoke of her cousin. A softness he generally associated with when she told him, *'Gentle, Bear, gentle. Never hurt any creature.'*

"Everyone was attending to Katie like she was royalty when the doorbell rang. None of us thought anything of it, just a latecomer to the party. Then the sheriff walked in with two deputies."

Bear raised his head in question. Mary's heart rate accelerated, and her cheeks turned pink as she spoke. He nuzzled into her closer as she continued.

"Her dad was arrested. I'm mortified when I think of it now as an adult." Her eyes moved back and forth as if the scene was playing out in front her. "I can't imagine what it was like to go to school after your parent is taken away in handcuffs."

Bear whined and pushed into Mary. The last of her words she'd spoke in a whisper as she turned her attention back to the oak tree.

"We drifted apart the whole time we were growing up. And then I moved away. Had it not been for you, Bear, we might never had been friends. And what a treasure I would have missed out on." Mary rose from her seated position and dusted off the back of her pants.

Theodore opened the patio door and yelled out to his wife. "Want to ride into town together?"

"He's worried about us and wants be our chauffer for the morning." She cleared her throat. "Be right there!" She waved her arm at her husband with Lupe at his side. "C'mon, Bear. Let's see how we can help Katie."

The Great Pyrenees looked up and groaned. He couldn't help himself.

Go!

Katie opened her eyes. The other women in her yoga class were speaking in hushed voices to one another as they remained on their mats in friendly, Zen-like solidarity. She took a breath and tried to calm the panic rising in her chest. A pulsing, whooshing sound began in her eardrums as the room seemed to tilt. She jumped to her feet to regain her equilibrium as someone touched her sweaty back, causing her to jump in surprise.

"How was class for you?"

"Wonderful. It was really wonderful." Though it was clear from her jittery hands Katie was feeling anything but.

"You're shaking like a leaf." Alicia, a tall, lithe woman who appeared like she was born for the activity, nodded at Katie supportively. "Deep breaths."

Katie grimaced with a fake smile on her face and widened her eyes as she tried to keep herself together. The instructor's two-word remedy for her out of control anxiety was beyond irritating. Like someone offering an adhesive bandage for a gashing wound pouring blood.

Alicia put her hand on the small of Katie's back. "Soften

your gaze and notice what you observe." She lifted her eyebrows and smiled with a kind warmth. "It'll work wonders, I promise."

"I'm fine. Really," she answered, taking a step backward.

Alicia was not fooled. She began to speak before another student came up from behind and interrupted. "Can you show me how to steady my crow pose? I feel a bit wobbly."

"Help the birds. I'm fine," Katie said, fluttering her hands as she spoke.

"Please come back. The prana that moves during someone's first class can be unnerving, but if you're feeling that much energy, there's that much force to work with. It's a marvelous thing, I promise," Alicia said over her shoulder as she moved with ease among the yoga attendees.

Rolling up her mat, Katie tried to steady her shaking hands and legs before making her way out into the chilly morning; the blast of air shocking and calming her all at once. She looked down the street. A dog was running toward her as a city patrol car slowly kept pace with it. The window of the cruiser rolled down as it got closer to her.

"Are you now the town dogcatcher too, Donkey?"

The sheriff—Justin Johnston—was rarely called by his given name. Decades before, jittery at the end of a school day in first grade, Justin brayed out loud when a teacher was reading a story about a donkey. The laughs it elicited from his fellow classmates made the random vocal misbehavior a lifelong nickname.

"On my way home from an overnight shift and saw this old guy roaming the streets. Does he belong to anyone you know?"

"No idea." Katie glanced at the plain brown dog of unidentifiable breed. "He's a wanderful…" She shook her head, still discombobulated from her anxiety and closed her eyes to gather her thoughts. "I mean, he's an old, wandering dog. It doesn't look as if he's ever had a home. Like the wind blew him into town."

Staring at her, the dog turned his head from side to side as if he were trying to understand her words.

"Someone must have dumped him as they were passing through town."

Fumbling for the keys in her purse, Katie stopped. "People still do that? Why aren't a ton of dogs running around town then?"

"Don't make me say it."

Nausea hit her stomach as she realized what he was insinuating. She let the keys fall from her hand and onto the ground as she glared at the sheriff.

"Farmers can only take in so many stray dogs. I have three formerly abandoned dogs at my house already. Carlotta and the kids would have a dozen if we could afford the food and vet bills."

Katie set her yoga mat down. It unfurled on the sidewalk as she knelt to pick up her dropped keys. "Wandering dogs deserve love too. Not…" She shuttered as she thought of the alternative. "I can't even bring myself to say it."

Taking two steps toward her, the dog looked up and whined.

"Should I do something here?"

"No, do not do something." Donkey put his transmission in park and opened the door. "You don't know if an animal is sick or will attack." As he walked to the pair, the dog remained still and unbothered.

Katie put her purse and keys on the hood of her car. "This dog is not dangerous, Donkey. Please don't take him in."

"He'll have a warm place to sleep tonight and some food."

"A warm place and food before he's put down?"

The old dog stepped on the mat then placed his head and front paws down as if he were bowing to her.

The door to the yoga studio opened and Alicia walked out. A look of bemusement crossed her face as she surveyed the trio gathered on the sidewalk. She studied the dog, before turning to lock the door. "Downward Dog. A pose signifying loyalty, courage and devotion."

"I could use those qualities in a man," Katie quipped, meaning the words to be lighthearted. She dropped her shoulders when she failed to convincingly convey the thought. In all likelihood, both Donkey and Alicia knew of her latest romantic relationship—a man who had moved to the area several counties over and failed to mention his marital status over the course of their three months of dating. She'd paraded him around town, sure the big-talking, handsome man who had lavished her with expensive gifts was nearly ready to propose. The night he'd asked to speak to her about something important, he ducked out after delivering the news he was married, leaving Katie sitting alone in her candlelit home.

Donkey approached the dog. "No collar. I keep treats in my car. Let me see if I can coax him into my backseat."

"This is a very unique dog. You can feel it." Alicia reached down and scratched the dog's head.

The previous Christmas, Alicia had ordered a dozen gift baskets from Bear Bailey's. In gratitude for the woman's patronage, Katie promised to take her yoga class. Though it had taken her a couple of months to keep her word. That morning, she'd listened as Alicia talked about prana moving through their bodies, loving intentions of hearts opening in gratitude, the energy of the attendees coming together and uplifting one another as they finally gave way to the resting savasana, or corpse pose.

"Be open to signs from the Universe."

Katie rolled her eyes at the recollection of the quote. She'd felt none of the energy Alicia spoke of earlier in class and was not swayed by her feelings about the dog.

"Do you have a pet?" Alicia asked.

"She's always had cats." Donkey waved a biscuit in front of the dog.

"No, Donkey. I do not and have never had a cat. Or a dog for that matter."

"I could have sworn you loved cats when we were in school."

"I'm clear about who I was growing up, Donkey."

The old dog groaned in a questioning manner.

"What?"

Shaking his head at her, the old dog stood, whining his intent to keep moving down Main Street.

"Maybe you could take in this noble dog?"

"Alicia, I think I've taken enough things home as of late. This dog will have to make someone else's dreams come true." She stopped. Her sarcasm felt disrespectful to the aged and humble dog. "Nothing personal, whatever-your-name-is. I think I've finally learned being alone is exactly what's supposed to happen for me."

"Be careful what you say with such strong feeling."

Katie stifled a groan as the rest of the group who had attended yoga entered The Hen's Nest for morning coffee, two doors down from the studio.

"The Universe only wants to help and support you. You just have to be clear with your desires."

Katie turned her attention from the restaurant, trying to keep her words civil when she really wanted to scream. "If the Universe is listening like some cosmic waiter anxious to fulfill my breakfast order, then here it is—"

The wind accelerated, blowing around debris and interrupting her words. Donkey and Alicia covered their eyes as Katie stood resolute, letting the element swirl around her. "I'd like a male who would just sit quietly in my house and let me be myself. No heartbreaking revelations to cause me embarrassment in front of the whole town and then leaving me to put the pieces back together all alone. No drama. No stories. No words. Someone for loyal companionship who doesn't hog the covers. Is that too much to ask?"

With another gust of wind, the front door of The Hen's Nest blew open, ringing the entrance bell before it slammed closed again. Donkey, Alicia and the stray dog stood in front of Katie as she gestured wildly. Her eyes filled with tears for a brief second. She shook her head to stop their flow.

Taking a step toward Katie, Alicia extended her arms as if she were going to calm a frightened child.

"Don't," Katie whispered, holding up a hand. "Don't you dare pity me."

One of the retired women from yoga class exited The Hen's Nest, jogging to the trio with an item in her hands. Her eyes lit with joy as she had no clue to Katie's outburst.

"We all got to talking as we left class and forgot to give you this." The woman held out a lavender water bottle with a sticker on the side and shook it with glee.

Katie stared at the outstretched item and took a few steps back.

"It is yours, isn't it, dear?" the woman asked, pointing to the words *Sparkle On*.

Katie gripped the handle that was pressed into her hand and then held it loosely.

"Exhilarating class, Alicia. One of your best!" The woman jogged back to the restaurant, moving her limbered arms and legs in a joyful and exaggerated dance.

Once the woman had entered the restaurant, Katie threw the water bottle down the street like a javelin and began shaking.

Alicia nodded at Donkey as they both circled around Katie in a protective way. The streets were not yet populated with traffic, and as Donkey kept an eye out for any other cars, Alicia put her arm around Katie and grabbed the keys off the hood while unlocking the car and gently guiding her into the driver's seat.

"I'm all right." Katie held the steering wheel, her knuckles turning white with her grip. "I don't know where that came from."

"It happens sometimes."

Katie's head snapped. "What are you talking about?"

"Someone's first yoga class. When it happens just remember what I said earlier this morning. *Let the emotions crest and allow—*"

"You didn't think to mention that when you invited me to class at Christmas?"

"When your nervous system begins to relax like a—"

"Let me guess, Alicia. My nervous system can unwind like a clock turning back time until the Universe can birth new opportunities for me."

"That's one way of saying it." Alicia's face lit in happiness.

Donkey put his head down and winced.

"I was being ridiculous. Absolutely, totally and insanely ridiculous, Alicia." Katie glanced in the rearview mirror. "What a stupid idea on my part to think that I could start my day in a new way and transform into someone I'm clearly not."

"You're very special, Katie. People with a lot of energy can oftentimes—"

"Stop with your canned yoga quotes! No more words!" Katie sat up taller. Her voice elevating as she spoke. She pulled her hair from a ponytail and shook the strands down on her shoulders.

"Do you want me to—" Donkey began.

Katie held her hand up. "Uh-huh. No words. I'm not even kidding."

Donkey backed away, standing on the curb with Alicia as they exchanged worried looks.

"I need out of here." Katie put her car in reverse before hitting the brakes when she glanced in the rearview mirror again. She rolled her window down, groaning. "Now what?"

Forgotten for a few minutes by the humans focused on Katie,

the old dog walked to the driver's door and then jumped onto his back legs with the *Sparkle On* water bottle in his mouth. He let it fall on Katie's lap, whining in encouragement. A train's horn blew in the distance as the dog stopped and turned his head to listen for a moment. He began to run toward the sound.

"*You are the Universe in ecstatic motion,*" Alicia said quietly, goosebumps appearing on her arms.

Donkey raised his eyebrows in question.

"Rumi. A 13th century mystic," Katie answered, her gaze on the canine's path as she spoke.

The dog stopped and looked back at Katie, eyes almost pleading. With a single nod toward her, he barked and continued on.

Katie opened her car door and followed the dog, leaving the *Sparkle On* water bottle sitting alone on the front seat like an abandoned child.

I Went This Way

"An old dog for Katie?"

A butterfly flew near Josephine. She held out a finger, letting the fluttering creature rest upon it. "There's nothing we should do. Dogs and humans are like two magnets meeting."

"I know that's generally true, but in this particular instance, Katie's already heartbroken, and he's a very senior dog near the end of his life. Is that the best pairing?" Lea asked, her voice heavy with emotion. Though she was an angel, any time a dog or human was distressed, Lea's emotions still tended to tilt toward the earthly side. At the sound of the beloved angel's concerned voice, all the dogs in the vicinity ran forward to comfort her.

Josephine raised her hands up and in a matter of moments filled the Golden Meadow with rows and rows of cornstalks. She then directed the sun's rays upon the crop. Hot kernels burst and filled the ground like accumulating snow, sending every dog present into ecstatic leaps and somersaults of joy. Big droplets of melted butter rained down from the sky but did not dishevel one dog hair.

Lea's face lit in happiness. The change in her demeanor instantly calmed the dogs. "Popcorn. The Jiff Special."

"Why did we never think of dogs and popcorn before Jiff and Franklin?" Josephine asked, laughing at the dogs' glee as they ate to their heart's content. She turned her attention back to Lea. "Why aren't you enjoying this the way I imagined you would?"

"I still don't understand why we can't send another dog that won't break Katie's heart into a million pieces when they cross in a short amount of time. We're us. We can do whatever we need to do up here over the Rainbow Bridge."

Josephine's face softened as pink clouds swirled above her head before a gentle breeze moved them onward. "The dogs know the best time to arrive and when to depart. Their intuition lets them know when a human learns the lesson that they've come to teach."

A piece of popcorn blew with the wind current. Lea caught it and then held it in front of a dark brown Golden Retriever whose black nose resembled the shape of a heart. "What a very sweet girl you are, Macy," she said. The beautiful dog cleverly sat and waited with the best manners before the angel lovingly tossed the morsel to her. Catching the popcorn with ease, she spun in a circle giving her thanks and sauntered away to all of her waiting friends. Lea watched her go, all-knowing that Macy had chosen her own special humans on Earth when she was just a puppy. "I guess it is one of the nicest things up here to see, isn't it? Which dogs gravitate to their beloved humans."

Josephine nodded, re-directing her attention to Earth. "After thousands of years on the Rainbow Bridge, I'm confident of one thing in any situation where canines and humans are involved."

Lea raised her eyebrows. "What's that?"

"Always trust the dogs."

Work Available Here

Three hours after the early morning yoga class had ended, Katie entered Bear Bailey's Co-op and Grocery, hair a mess, with no makeup or sparkle to be found on her person. People stocking their individual stalls watched her taking the most direct route from the front door to her office at the back of the store without uttering a word to anyone. Evident through the glass windows that made up the front half of her and Mary's shared offices, Katie dropped her bags on her desk, and then closed the blinds with her sunglasses still on.

Vendors in various stages of disbelief stared at the back of the building as Mary and Bear walked into the building. A woman at the large showpiece stall near the front door was unloading merchandise. The Great Pyrenees wagged his tail in affectionate greeting.

"Good morning, Cybil," Mary said, balancing a coffee mug in one hand and Bear's leash as well as papers in the other. Years earlier, when Mary had first moved back to town, she'd struggled with calling her former teacher by her first name until Cybil chose *Ms. Barnes* as a business name for her stall at the co-op.

And then, it seemed silly for Mary to be so rigid with her desire to be respectful.

"You need to check on your cousin."

Mary kept walking, Bear at her side, before turning back. "Everything all right?"

A customer knocked on the front glass. They mimed through the window, putting their thumbs under their armpits as they flapped their arms like a chicken. ""Can I grab some eggs?"

"I'll handle the breakfast emergency. You take care of our Katie," Cybil said.

※

"She wouldn't tell you what was wrong?" Cybil sat at the round table in front of the co-op's fireplace with Mary later that morning. The table had taken up its own identity as a place in the store to meet to discuss important matters. And, as if it was enveloped by a magic bubble, no one would bother anyone talking at it unless invited to do so.

"I walked into our office and her forehead was plastered to the desk. She held up one finger, mumbling to be left alone."

"Is she hungover?"

"You know she doesn't drink."

"A hard-to-shake, old teacher habit of keeping tabs on high school students," Cybil replied. "What do *you* think could be wrong?"

"I think she's burnt herself out trying to get all the grant paperwork together for our upcoming meeting. She's worked morning, noon and night turning herself inside out to get the project done."

"I don't think it's that. The grant submission was her idea, and she went about it with great joy. What about her last relationship?"

"She didn't say much but she bounced back." Bear leaned into Mary as she spoke. "Took a long weekend and came back saying she was fine."

Cybil took a slow drink of her coffee and was silent for a few moments. "Katie's personality is such that you may think she's bounced back." The older woman reached out to pat Mary's hand. "But your cousin is much deeper than she appears, even though she goes to great lengths to make sure we all think she can bounce and sparkle her way out of anything."

Leaving Mary's side, Bear went to sit beside Cybil.

"He does that when he strongly agrees with someone's sentiments."

Cybil put her hand on Bear's head and began to stroke down his back. "Do you think you would have stayed in Merivelle without this wonderful dog?"

"Probably not." Mary thought for a moment before shivering. "I mean, no. I would not have lived in western Kansas without Bear."

"I think it's funny you never call our town by name," Cybil said. She took another drink of coffee and raised her eyebrows.

"I don't?"

"You do not, my dear. Never have. Even in school. I distinctly remember you saying, 'I can't wait to leave this place' or 'I'm going to live anywhere else but Kansas.'"

"You know why that is."

Bear looked up at Mary and then to Cybil as he crinkled his eyes and groaned in question.

Mary arranged her face in a goofy expression, waving her hand. "Hello, my name is Mary from Merivelle. And I'm a yoka-doodle from Yokeytown."

"Is that how you introduced yourself to Theodore?"

"Absolutely not. He'd have run in the opposite direction."

The older woman rolled her eyes. "Your mother loved this

town. I'd think it was a happy homage to you, knowing the two things she loved the most were similar in name."

"My dear and kind mother," Mary said, staring out the front glass windows as a lone car passed by. "When you say it like that, I know I should be more open to the connection."

Cybil studied her friend for a moment before continuing. "Merivelle has a light and flowing pronunciation." The front door of the store opened, and a pleasant breeze reached the women. "Mare-uh-vell. Rhymes with bell. From a French word, Merivelle actually means a miracle, or an event which causes astonishment. It can also mean a wonderful story. It's quite lovely when you think about it."

"How do you remember all that you know, Cybil?" Mary asked her old teacher with great affection.

"It's easy to recall words that are near to my heart." Her wrinkled hands gripped her coffee mug.

"I'll do better." Mary's face assumed a sophisticated look and she said in a breathless voice, "Hello, I'm Mare-hee from Mare-uh-velle."

Cybil threw her crumpled napkin at Mary. "You're helpless. Anyway, what led us down this conversation loop is we're supposed to be thinking about how we can best help Katie. What do you think from your own heroine's journey of hating this place to owning a connecting, social hub in the community?"

"As we've discussed—Bear." Her eyes met her dog's with a sappy, yet sincere expression on her face. "Bear changed everything."

"Not Theodore being agreeable to live here?"

"That helped, of course. But Bear had a way of instinctively being present at the right moment where he was most needed."

"Like when you first moved back to Merivelle and the pair of you stumbled upon me in Cottonwood Cemetery that afternoon," Cybil added, scratching behind the dog's ears. "From the first time I met him, I appreciate that he listens deeply."

She brushed her lap collecting the ever-present white fur that emanated from the dog. "I remember us talking about the cottonwood puffs blowing in the air and the old legend about a woman bringing together a community."

Mary grabbed a tissue from the box on the table and captured the wad of fur in Cybil's hand. "Bear takes great joy in almost everyone he meets, which made me see the town differently. Merivelle is beautiful when I view it like I imagine Bear does."

The Great Pyrenees glanced between the two women, smiling his usual grin, clearly delighted at hearing his name spoken with affection.

"A wonderful dog changed our whole town," Cybil said.

The pair of women were silent for a few moments. They both put their hands on Bear.

"Are you thinking what I'm thinking?" Mary's face lit up with excitement.

"Maybe Katie needs her own wonderful dog?" Cybil asked, eyebrows raised.

Ruffling Bear's fur, Mary nodded. "She wouldn't feel so alone and—"

The door to the back offices opened, and Katie walked out into the co-op space. Her inside-out sweatshirt was worn over jeans that were several sizes too big. Still wearing her sunglasses, though they were askew on her face from laying on the office desk, she approached the table. "I need some time off."

Mary sat up in her chair, her eyes wide in concern. "Yes, of course."

"As soon as possible."

"You can take the day or whatever you need. You've helped me and the store so much."

"I just need the afternoon." Katie paused for a moment as she set her sunglasses straight. "To go fishing."

Though neither of their heads moved, Mary and Cybil's bodies jolted in surprise. Bear sniffed the air in question.

"I think it'll help me."

Mary cleared her throat. "Do you know how to fish?"

"Take a pole. Tie a hook. Bait a worm and drop it in some water."

"Are you sure you're all right?" Cybil stood up and then held Katie's hands, putting her cheek to the younger woman's forehead. "You're not running a fever."

"I used to fish when I was younger." Katie pulled away from Cybil's hold.

"When?" Mary asked with more surprise in her voice than she had intended. "I mean, I don't recall that activity in your history. Cheerleading, gymnastics, volleyball and dance—yes. But fishing?"

Katie shrugged. "I didn't tell everyone everything about me growing up."

"Well then, fishing's a fun thing to know about you, Katie." Cybil took a few steps from the table as a woman came through the front door, making a beeline for *Ms. Barnes*. "I'll let the two of you talk."

Bear began following Cybil and then stopped in place, turning around, and going back to sit by Katie. He put a paw to her thigh and whined.

Mary was puzzled. While Bear did not treat Katie like a coyote on the land he patrolled at night, he rarely went near her, always preferring Mary's company in the office. When Katie remained as still as a statue at his gesture, Bear stood up on his hind legs and embraced her waist, coming nearly eye to eye with her.

"What, Bear?" Katie asked, exasperated. "What do you want?"

The Great Pyrenees put his head on her shoulder and whimpered, gently nudging her jawline with his nose.

"Now I feel even worse," she choked, wiping behind her sunglasses.

"He knows you didn't mean anything," Mary responded. "He's made of tough stuff."

"Sorry, boy." Katie patted Bear in an awkward manner. He gave her a final sniff and then dropped to the floor, standing guard at her feet.

Mary stood up from her chair and put a gentle hand on her cousin's arm. "I'd do anything to help you, Katie."

"I said I want to go fishing."

"Do you want me to come with you?" Mary pushed in her chair.

"I just want to be by myself."

"What about taking Bear? He was the best companion when I needed one. Why don't you take him for the afternoon?"

Bear began to groan, and then stopped when Mary put her hand on his head.

After taking her sunglasses off, Katie folded them calmly. Her eyes were red and swollen. "I don't need *Bear* to help me." The emphasis she put on the dog's name caused the Pyr to wrinkle his eyes in confusion.

"We all love you so much, Katie. We only—"

"I don't want to hear that right now. I just need to be alone. Like I was always meant to be." She turned without another word and headed out the door.

Bear exchanged a knowing look with a nodding Mary. Obediently, he followed her cousin out the door.

Katie turned to face him on the front sidewalk. "Let's not make this awkward, Bear. I know Mary sent you out here."

Taking a couple of steps toward her, Bear put his head down in submission.

"Aw, don't do that."

Bear leaned forward, nudging her hand with his nose conveying hopefulness that she'd accept his company.

"Stay!" Katie commanded, her hand out in signal, though her voice was not unkind. She took a few steps back. "The last thing I need is a dog to further complicate my life."

Good Water, Good Camp

After leaving Bear Bailey's with the strong declaration of needing to fish, Katie sat outside the co-op with her head on her steering wheel before she remembered a fishing pole that had sat in the back of her garage since she was child. It's lack of use over the years had caused it to become nearly invisible behind rakes and shovels sharing the same corner. After she drove home, she shuffled through the old items, coughing from the dust and swatting sticky cobwebs off herself. A vintage tacklebox was tucked behind all the garden items and poles, like a loyal squire waiting to be in service again to the pole.

❦

"I have no idea what I'm doing here," Katie said to herself, pulling the fishing pole and tackle box out of the trunk of her car. She kicked her car door shut and then made her way to the edge of a large pond with a Styrofoam cup of nightcrawlers she'd purchased at the gas station on her way. Merivelle could be seen from where she was standing, but if she didn't focus on the town, she appeared to be miles away from anyone. Close, but far away.

She thought about the morning's events as she walked, kicking a rock off the dirt path in frustration. The yoga class had been a disaster. She wanted to choke Alicia for hounding her to attend. Being inside the co-op, sequestered at her desk, felt stifling, like she might lose her mind if she sat still. Even working her way through a simple pile of paperwork was hopeless. After reading the same lines of an order form over and over again, without comprehension, she decided to leave. But not to her empty house. And then the random and illogical idea of fishing popped into her head.

"I don't know why I told everyone where I was going," she mumbled. Her love of fishing had been a childhood secret of hers. She'd made her mother swear she'd never tell anyone where she'd disappeared to on summer afternoons with her dad. When he was gone, she'd stopped the activity.

Despite it being early springtime, and with the sun at its highest peak for the day, the air was still cold, though the shimmering surface of the lake bore no ice. She set the nightcrawler container down and began situating her fishing pole—a simple wooden rod worn from age with illegible carvings on the handle. The line was old but still malleable as she pulled it through the eyelets of the pole and attached a lead sinker, bobber and hook to the end of the line. Working deftly, tying knots with expertise, she felt her nervous system calm with the tasks. Even quickly loading the worm on her hook, a task she'd always made her dad do, eased her anxiety. They'd had a routine between them when it came to the worms. He would place the squirming bait on her hook while she turned her head making comical noises and dancing in place, knowing he found his only child's silly antics entertaining.

Standing on the edge of the lake, she cast her line into the water and waited, mesmerized by the light of the day shimmering off the surface. Dormant sagebrush peppered the bank, the natural sand and soil blend of it was almost beach-like at the water's edge. Over the years, people had dragged old logs to sit on, which had become petrified in the extreme, seasonal change of western Kansas weather. As a teenager, she and her friends used to park up the road, walk down and jump the gate the county locked at sunset. They would start bonfires and drink, though she never partook of the latter.

Not more than a quarter of an hour had passed when her bobber disappeared under water, and she felt the thrill of something on her line. *You're my lucky charm, Katie*, her father used to say to her when the first catch of the day was reeled in. She felt no joy at the remembrance of the words, in contrast to how she felt as a child when he'd uttered the praise. Back then, she'd felt special, unique and charmed in every way. She merely thought of what she wanted and it seemed the whole world jumped to fulfill any wish she had. Even fish.

As she was throwing her small catch back into the pond, Katie noticed a slow-moving car. Ignoring the vehicle, she loaded another worm onto the hook and cast her line into the water. Irritated at the interloper's snail-like pace, she turned her back, waiting for the car to pass. The sound of rocks crunching under tires, and then a pause as a vehicle door opened and closed, caused Katie to finally turn.

"Hello?"

At the greeting, wind blew into the area, causing her to take a few steps forward to steady herself.

"Are you okay?"

Katie groaned. Words. She nodded her head in the man's direction.

Squinting to ascertain Katie's response, the man adjusted his glasses and smiled. His demeanor had an eagerness about it, almost puppy-like. "Excuse me?" he called out, cupping his hands to carry the sound of his voice over the wind. "Are you missing a dog?"

She shook her head, keeping her eyes on her line in the water.

"Could you have a look at the dog to see if you might recognize him?" The man took off his glasses and wiped them on his dress shirt before putting them back on. "I don't want him taken to the pound."

A dog, she sighed to herself. She'd never paid attention to them before Bear arrived in Merivelle. The Great Pyrenees made her feel indebted to the entire canine species. "You'll have to bring him to me. I'm not going to your vehicle to look at a dog I can't see or hear from here."

Shivering as the wind blew his hair, the man stepped back and held his hands up. "Of course. I hadn't thought of how my request might be perceived." He paused at the passenger door of his car. "You don't even know my name."

Katie shrugged.

"It's Percy." He pulled out his wallet and held his driver's license in the air. "I'm happy to show you."

Surely, criminals don't show their ID before kidnapping someone, Katie thought.

Patting the front of his dress shirt and then his back pant pockets, he shouted politely. "I usually carry my business cards but can't seem to locate them at the present moment."

Not that I really care this morning. Maybe someone kidnapping and carrying me away from this town is the best thing anyway. She shook her head, begrudgingly remembering Alicia's words at yoga class—to be mindful of thoughts and words.

From inside Percy's car, a dog began barking and pawing at the windows, leaving a residue of slobber and pawprints on the glass.

"Would you like to see the dog, or should I keep on going

into town?" he asked, jumping to the side of the car with his hand on the door handle. The dog calmed and sat expectantly.

Taking solace in the dog's demeanor, Katie relaxed. She reeled in the fishing line, securing the hook to the handle, and rested the rod on a log. "Be right there," she mumbled.

With the respect of a chauffeur in service to an important dignitary, Percy opened the back door, speaking in a kind way as he waited. The dog that had fetched her *Sparkle On* water bottle earlier in the day emerged from the car. Katie's face dropped in surprise.

The old dog ran to her, panting as he wove through the sagebrush to get to her side.

"He wasn't that excited to see me when I picked him up off the highway trotting away from town."

Katie knelt to the dog. "I've only seen him one other time." She'd chased the dog down to the train station at the edge of town before losing him when a truck backing up from a parking spot blocked her.

"Well then, old friends." Percy smiled as Katie rose.

"Donkey's been looking for him."

"The dog has a friend who's a donkey?"

"No, the sheriff's name is Donkey."

Percy raised his eyebrows.

"Childhood nickname."

"I see," he said, smiling. "Makes much more sense." He studied Katie with great thought. "So might you know who the dog belongs to?"

"*Might I know?*" Katie repeated. "Who talks like that?" Her words had come out sharper than she intended. She sighed, disappointed with herself. Her dad had always cautioned her that bluntly pointing out things was her greatest and most challenging quality. The gift of inherent openness and transparency was one she needed to use with the caution of tact and kindness. With age, she'd learned to caramelize the gift with humor so as not to offend. Exhausted with the day, she felt no confectioner's urge to sweeten her observations. But she did feel moved to apologize. "I'm sorry. I shouldn't have said that."

"No, it's quite all right. I was listening to poetry as I drove into town, and it must have been leftover word residue." He cocked his head. "Funny you were just fishing beside the water."

"Where one usually finds fish," Katie answered, raising her eyebrows.

"Yes, of course," Percy said, flustered. "I only meant the poetry I was listening to was nearly perfect."

"I'll bite. What poetry might that be?"

Looking pleased, Percy recited, "*I know a bank where the wild thyme blows, Where oxlips and the nodding violet grows.*"

A burst of wind hit the area, causing the pair to bow their heads as sand blew around them. As quickly as it arrived, the gale disappeared as clouds moved away from the sun.

"In the absence of thyme, oxlips and violets, my guess is you're making that connection because I was fishing on the bank over there?"

His face dropped.

Slightly chagrinned from his downcast look, Katie tried again. "I get it. *A Midsummer Night's Dream.* One of Oberon's quotes in Act 2."

The sun rose again on Percy's countenance. "Do you know Shakespeare?"

"My cousin almost named her dog Oberon."

"King Oberon for a dog?"

"She was going to add an 'a' to the name and change it to O*bear*on. She ended up just calling him Bear."

"How very clever of your cousin," he answered, nodding his admiration and smiling. He paused for a moment. "We still have the issue at hand what to do with this *piepoudre*."

"Excuse me? What did you say?"

"*Piepoudre*. A French word meaning a traveler or wayfarer."

Katie bit her lip and knelt back down to the dog, not trusting any words that might come out of her mouth. "Actually, the only time I've seen this *piepoudre* was this morning," she said, responding with an impressive French accent, "After yoga."

Percy exclaimed, "I love yoga! Do they have a good studio here? Nothing like a good series of sun salutations to start one's day." He paused. "I mean, to start my day."

Katie cleared her throat. "There is a studio. And I've been once. This morning."

"Everyone has to begin somewhere. Did you like it?" His face was expectant with excitement.

"I hated it. With a burning passion." She stroked the dog's coat. The movement of her hands loosened short bits of brown hair onto her pants. She was softened by Percy's contrite look like he'd done something wrong by liking what she didn't. "Don't mind me. Apparently, an excess of prana has made me cranky today." She stopped petting the dog. "Where did you say you found him again?"

"It was the strangest thing," Percy said. "He came right onto the highway and stopped in the middle of the road as I was coming into town. He must be a bit of a hobo."

"Why did you say that?" Katie put her hands on her hips. Her heart felt protective of the old dog in the presence of the sharply dressed stranger.

Percy took a few steps back. "I've done it again, haven't I?"

"It's a curious thing to say about an old dog. It seems almost disrespectful."

"Quite the contrary. I imagined him as a traveling dog in want of a kingdom."

"But you called him a hobo not a king," Katie countered.

"Oh, dear…"

"Did you just call me '*dear?*'" Katie knew she was being ridiculous when she asked it but the look on the man's face as he backpedaled gave her a sense of satisfaction.

Growling gently, the dog pawed at her again, shaking his head.

"I can assure you that hobos were hard working, noble souls. Knights of the Road," Percy began explaining.

"Hobos didn't have jobs."

"That's a misconception. Hobos made an indelible contribution to the building of our country. They traveled with a purpose—to provide for their families back home and in turn helped build up communities all over the United States."

"I thought they were bums."

The man's face lit up, the expression of a person who thrived on sharing random information out of sincere love and interest in a subject. "Hobos traveled with the express purpose of seeking employment. It was tramps who traveled but had no interest in procuring work for themselves or bettering a community. And bums, they were an entirely different kettle of fish," he said, shaking his head sadly.

Katie winced. "Please enlighten me," she said, her voice tinged with sarcasm seeing the man's eager face. "What makes a bum different from a hobo or a tramp?"

"A bum neither worked nor traveled," the man said, his face as triumphant as if he were on a gameshow.

"How riveting." Katie chewed her bottom lip and scanned the road behind the man.

The man's face showed that he could tell he was losing his audience quickly. "Hobos had their own convention where they chose Kings and Queens each year."

"Hobo royalty?" Katie rolled her eyes. "With crowns and sashes?" she asked, defensively.

"Oh, no," he answered.

"Because that seems a bit ridiculous."

"They have royal robes. They don't cut corners at the Hobo Convention. It's a real honor to be elected."

"Of course." Katie turned toward the sun and squinted for a moment as she tried to maintain a straight face.

"You should read about it sometime, it's quite fascinating. Google '*The Hobo Ethical Code of 1889*' and find out about the fifteen rules hobos adopted so they helped the communities they visited, always leaving them a better place than they found them. You'll find their motives noble and kind. What a world we would live in if everyone lived by hobo ethics. Really make a note to read up on the subject."

"It'll be first on my to-do list, Percy."

"Hobos even had their own way of communicating. Clever marks they left to guide and help one another on the road. Much like Egyptian hieroglyphics."

"Really? Hoboglyphics?" Katie raised an eyebrow. "What a treasure of information I had no idea existed."

The man wilted. "I get carried away with random things I find interesting," he said, taking a few steps back. "I apologize for taking your time."

Katie took a breath to take the edge of her words. "I'm sorry, Percy. I'm out of sorts and it has nothing to do with you."

"Think nothing of it." He glanced at his watch. "The dog though. What do you think I should do with him?"

"Are you staying in town?"

"For a bit. I'm here on business. I'm not sure of the pet policy where I'm staying. I didn't procure my own lodging."

"Again, with the weird way you talk."

Percy shivered and reached into driver's door. He pulled a suit jacket off the back of his headrest. "And pray tell, what weird way is that?"

"That!" Katie exclaimed, pointing a finger. "*Pray tell, we are in want of a noble king. Might you know the nearest yoga studio so we can partake of poses that fill our hearts with joy and light as we ponder our humble existence in the stream of time through written code only a hobo would know."*

The dog pulled away from Katie's petting which had become heavy and overly enthusiastic as she spoke. He took a few steps toward Percy and stared at her, nearly the same curious look on his furry face as the human who listened to Katie with a blank stare.

"Nope."

Katie crossed her arms. "What does that mean?"

"Nope. Nothing. Non."

"See? You can't even help yourself. Sneaking in a little one syllable French word like I won't notice."

"I don't enjoy arguments." The man took a deep breath and bowed his head before speaking again. "I'm just trying to get into town and meet the good people of Bear Bailey's Co-op and Grocery. And while I'm at it, help this wandering and well-mannered dog to find his proper owner." He nodded with respect and backed away from her, the old dog following him back to the vehicle.

The instant she heard *Bear Bailey's*, a lightbulb of recognition hit. Watching the dust cloud of Percy's vehicle as he made his way into Merivelle, Katie held her head in her hand. She groaned. "Maybe next I could just set myself on fire."

Gentleman

The following morning, Mary was clutching a large pile of paperwork to her chest with Bear at her side. She'd put a backpack on him, the canvas emblazoned with a patch of his face and the words *Bear Bailey's Co-op and Grocery* under it. Other Great Pyrenees owners had taught her the breed thrived on performing meaningful tasks if they weren't herding livestock. A natural ambassador for the store, Bear walked around so customers could take flyers or wrapped goodies from his pack as they were shopping. "I can't tell you what a bright spot on my calendar this meeting has been for me," Mary said.

Cybil was arranging legal pads and pencils in front of each chair around the co-op's table. She looked up. "No nerves at all?"

"Substantial grant money to revitalize our downtown and then the rest of Merivelle benefitting is exciting." She shivered, smiling. "I wish my mom was here. This would have thrilled her. I'm just nervous to pull it all off."

"Don't worry, Mary," Lupe said, coming to the table and setting a coffee cup down with her own paperwork. "We're behind you. No need for any collywobbles."

"Word of the Day!" Mary and Cybil said in unison, a phrase

they'd come up with when one of them used a word from the daily email blast Lupe had insisted they all sign up for.

"Just be yourself," Lupe said. "And everything will work out. We're all behind Bear Bailey's success."

"*Our* success," Mary said. "Both of you speak up and share your ideas. Percival will get an idea of the cooperation of our community."

"Percival Bourne," Cybil said, her voice thoughtful. "That's quite a name. Very proper sounding."

Lupe repeated the name, rolling the R's. "Yes, very suave and dignified. But I also think, kind too."

"I think he just pulled up," Mary said, looking through the front windows. "Everyone look natural." On cue, Bear began to bark and the three of them danced dramatically in place around the table for a few moments before abruptly stopping. Mary shook her arms and stretched neck from side to side. "Much better."

"I wish Katie could have made it," Lupe said. "Mr. Percival Bourne would love her, I feel."

"It is a shame," Cybil agreed. "It was her idea to apply for the grant and sort through mountains of paperwork to get us to today's meeting."

The front bell jingled, and the door opened as Percival Bourne entered, staring around the co-op as if he'd entered a cathedral of historical note. He shook his head in awe and met the women half-way in the middle of the store, hand outstretched to Mary with a beaming smile on his face.

"Percival Bourne." She took his extended hand. "I'm Mary Bailey. It's a pleasure to finally meet you."

"Please, just call me Percy," he replied. "I use Percival in emails and correspondence to lend a bit of gravitas."

Lupe practically swooned with his use of the word. "You are very dignified. With much authority. Much gravitas."

"That's very kind of you…?" Percy lifted his eyebrows in a polite manner.

"Lupe Posada. *Mucho gusto.*"

"*Mucho gusto, Doña Lupe,*" Percy said, addressing her with the title bestowing great respect. "Gravitas is not for the people I meet, rather for the agencies we work with. I think it brings more weight to our requests for your community." He smiled warmly at Lupe.

"Of all the days for Katie for to miss," Cybil whispered to Mary. "Good grief is he handsome in a nerdy sort of way."

"Ms. Barnes," Mary whispered back, trying to keep from smiling. "Behave."

Percy smiled at the two women who looked as chastened as if they'd been caught passing notes in study hall. "And I haven't had the pleasure of meeting all of you."

"Cybil Barnes. And please don't mind my whispering. I was effusively complimenting you. It's the only talking behind each other's backs we do here at Bear Bailey's."

"Cybil was one of our high school teachers growing up," Mary explained. "And is now one of the co-op's best vendors." She pointed to the showcase stall at the front of the co-op, in full view of the windows. *Ms. Barnes* had become so successful, Cybil had enough inventory and online purchases she could operate her own store independent of the co-op. A fact not lost on Mary, who always breathed silent thanks for the anchor of the woman's presence and goods for the store. Thanks to her robust social media following, almost daily, tourists drove more than an hour from the Interstate to take a picture with Cybil and load up with cutting boards and metal art creations from her booth.

Percy took her hand, smiling. "How charming. You and Lupe were Cybil's students?"

"Lupe would have been a dream student. Sadly, she didn't grow up in Merivelle. But I did teach Mary and her cousin, Katie, who you'll absolutely love meeting. She keeps us all going with the behind-the-scenes mechanics of Bear Bailey's," Cybil said, slightly lifting her eyebrows.

"I'll look forward to meeting her. She sounds marvelous."

Bear placed a paw on Mary's thigh and questioned her with large eyes. Mary giggled. "And before we go any further, this is Bear Bailey. Without him none of this would have been possible."

At the sound of his own name, Bear turned to the new person, panting in delight to meet him.

Percy took Bear's extended paw, giving him a solemn nod of approval. "It's a pleasure to meet you, Bear Bailey. I've read all about how you've united this community from Katie's notes. You come by your business honestly." He shook Bear's paw again with a swift, but respectful tug before releasing it.

Bear took a few steps to Mary's side and sat down, his back to Percy.

"Was it something I said?" Percy glanced around in confusion.

"He's offering you a treat from his backpack," Cybil replied.

Percy eyes widened in joy. "Of course, let me have a look at this cornucopia," he replied, bending down to look through Bear's backpack.

With Percy's attention diverted, Lupe tapped her temple and mouthed the word, *cornucopia* as she gave a thumbs-up sign to Cybil and Mary.

Percy picked a button pin with Bear's logo on it, holding it up as he patted the dog's head. "Thank you, Bear. I'm going to put this on my backpack right now." He lowered the bag off his shoulder and attached the button to one of the straps.

Bear gave a small "woof" and grinned.

"Now that we're all acquainted, shall we get to it?"

The women nodded, motioning for Percy to take the place they'd prepared for him. Coffee, orange juice and water—both sparkling and still—were in the middle of the table.

"This is all very kind of you," Percy said, surveying the spread of pastries placed directly in front of him. "The croissants look like there's a European bakery nearby."

"As much as we'd love to have a bakery within our co-op and grocery, the age of the building wasn't conducive to it being here. The wonderful thing about the co-op is our sense of community. We still look for ways to support businesses like the *Prairtisserie* any way we can," Mary said.

"How clever," Percy said. "A *portmanteau*, I imagine. Prairie and patisserie married together?"

"Exactly." Cybil was incredulous. "You must have been a real joy to teach."

Lupe opened the notebook she carried around everywhere. "How did you say port… man…?"

"*Portmanteau*," Percy said, the word flowing off his tongue in a melodious French accent.

"Can you spell it?" Lupe waited like an expectant student at a lecture.

With kindness, Percy spelled the word out for Lupe, an encouraging look on his face as he waited for her to transcribe.

Lupe wrote the word and then underlined it for emphasis. "Thank you, Percy. I love this word."

"Three cheers to Prairtisserie. Nothing like a good portmanteau," Percy said, reaching out for a croissant.

"Funny enough, my cousin was the one who helped them develop their name and logo."

"And when will I meet this clever cousin?" Percy asked. "She sounds remarkable."

Mary smiled as she stroked Bear's fur. "She would have been here today but had unforeseen circumstances arise yesterday."

"Which reminds me," Percy said. "A gentleman in town has requested to join us later this week. You probably already know his interest in attending. He says you're old business associates."

Cybil had a curious expression on her face. "Who might that be?"

The door to the co-op opened. Mary turned and shielded her eyes from the morning sun coming through the windows. "Katie?" she asked, incredulously.

Everyone turned to the entrance as Mary's cousin emerged from the blinding light, an old, brown dog following her.

Doubtful

Mary's jaw was practically on the table. It took several moments of her brain scanning the woman in front of her to realize it was her cousin. Former homecoming, prom and rodeo queen, and winner of whatever county or state affair offered a crown and sash was standing in front of everyone with no makeup applied, hair in a ponytail and wearing overalls. She held her head high with the dog at her side as if she were Cleopatra entering the meeting with her pet leopard. She sat down beside Mary, pulling a legal pad and pencil to herself.

Lupe and Cybil's faces mirrored Mary's. Even Bear cocked his head from side to side, going to sniff Katie and then her dog.

"Good morning, Percy." Katie selected a croissant from the basket in front of her and poured a glass of orange juice. She slurped noisily, finishing with a loud exhalation. She wiped her mouth with the back of her hand.

"You're Katie Hatch."

"I am."

"Have you two met before?" Lupe asked, looking curiously between the pair.

Katie opened her mouth to speak, a flicker of hesitation pausing her.

"We've corresponded for a very long time," Percy interjected. "Practically old friends."

Cybil tilted her head towards Katie and widened her eyes to Mary in question. Lupe was frozen in movement, holding a pen above her notebook, as if the scene were from one of the *telenovela* episodes she'd introduced to Mary and Theodore.

"Why don't we take a quick break to gather a few more documents I've neglected to bring everyone," Mary said. "Now that my couldn't-do-without-her right hand has arrived, she can show me where they are." She rose from her chair.

"I want to gift you a cutting board, Percy. Let me show you my booth and you can pick one," Cybil said.

"I can't accept any gifts when we're working on grants, but I'd love to see your booth, nonetheless." Percy stood up and waited for Cybil to show the way as he extended his arm for Lupe to join.

"*Nonetheless,*" Katie repeated aloud, rolling her eyes.

"Katie!" Mary whispered in horror. Bear gave a small, exasperated groan. Percy continued speaking with Cybil and Lupe as if he'd never heard a thing. Nails tapping the concrete floor, the old dog followed the group.

"You're a man with real integrity, aren't you?" Cybil noted, leading Percy away while looking over her shoulder in wide-eyed concern of Katie. "Let's have a look at some of the other vendors here."

"I think I smell the copy machine on fire."

"I don't smell anything," Katie said petulantly, though she rose from her seat and followed Mary to the back offices.

"I don't trust your senses right now. You're wearing overalls, Katie."

"So?"

"Farmwear to a business meeting?"

"I thought we were a non-discriminating, inclusive company headquartered in a rural town." She shoved her hands in her pockets. "Side note—when's the last time you wore a pair of these? I never knew how comfortable overalls were."

As she rifled through papers on her desk, Mary glanced to her cousin. "Fine. Wear them if you must. But what is going on? Our family used to say you were born in a pair of high heels with a tube of mascara in one hand. You're dressed like Mrs. Green Jeans."

"Do you know how that makes me feel, Mary?"

Mary looked up, papers in both hands. "The Mrs. Green Jeans comment?"

"That you expect me to be shallow and vapid."

"Vapid?"

"Offering nothing stimulating or challenging."

"I know what vapid means!" Mary was close to exploding but was mindful that everything going on could be seen through the windows of the office. "What are you talking about?"

"What you said about heels and mascara."

"Wait a second." Mary stopped. "Are you telling me you never liked shoes and makeup?"

Katie shrugged. "I did. I still do."

"Then what's the problem?"

"I don't know. Nothing. But everything." Her shoulders slumped. "But nothing."

"As much as I'd love to condense it down with you right now. And I truly would," Mary said, eyeing Cybil giving her the wrap it up sign behind Percy's back as she and Lupe followed him back to the table. "We have a visitor here today because of your very non-vapid, incredibly intelligent and genius ideas in securing the co-op possible grants that would keep us going for years as we try and get our Main Street back to its former glory. Our hometown wouldn't be a blowing tumbleweed statistic. All because of *you*. So, get in there, finish what you brilliantly started and knock this guy's socks off!"

"*Knock this guy's socks off.*" Katie snapped. "I can't stand him."

Mary's face fell in shock. "Percy? You can't stand Percy? For the love of God, how does one not like Percy?"

Through the window, the women could see the old dog sitting on Percy's lap despite being much too large to fit. He licked the man's face whose only response was to laugh and pull a white handkerchief out of his inner jacket pocket and calmly wipe away dog slobber.

"*That?*" Mary asked, incredulously.

"Absolutely that!"

"Katie! He's letting a geriatric dog from parts unknown lick his face. He's practically a saint."

"He's carrying a hanky. He's fussy."

"The irony of that comment, Katie! You still won't let food touch on your plate."

"Would we necessarily call that fussy?"

Mary raised her eyebrows. "You once made our elderly grandmother dust off her couch before you'd sit on it."

"It was my best Easter dress up to that point." Katie put her head down in regret at the memory. "Perhaps you're right. I can be particular."

"Are you all right?"

Katie rubbed her upper arms several times. "About to come out of my skin. I feel beyond irritable since yoga yesterday. I don't understand what's going on. I can't tell if I want to jog ten miles or sleep for a week."

"Do you need to go home? We can all try our best with Percy."

"I promise you. I am not that kind of upset." Katie held her hand up like she was taking an oath. "Let's just get on with this."

The meeting proceeded without any issues. Katie stayed quiet unless someone addressed her. Though she spoke often, as she'd prepared all the paperwork for over a year, outlining their shared vision for Bear Bailey's and beyond.

"I'm impressed, Katie," Percy said at the end of the afternoon. "The co-op's paperwork is impeccable. Your knowledge of grant work is unmatched."

Katie was sheepish. "Thank you."

Mary let out a sigh of relief as quietly as she could, looking up as Cybil was doing the same. Lupe smiled and closed her notebook, placing her pen in the spiral binding.

"Well, she's calmed down. That's something. It was breaking my old heart to see her so worked up."

At the sound of the words, not heard by any human at the table, Bear's eyes opened wide. His tail wagged. He barked with great glee at the first dog's voice he'd heard since his friend Jiff had traveled back over the Rainbow Bridge several years before.

BREAD

Bear searched the co-op, not entirely sure if his active imagination was at work again. The four women were on a quick break from the meeting, attending to customers. Percy was arranging paperwork into his backpack in preparation of following the co-op's operations for the day, in an effort to see for himself if the grant paperwork matched the need outlined in within it.

"Do you mind pointing me the fastest way out of town, friend?" The voice came again, slow and thoughtful.

Bear whimpered.

The old dog put his paw on the much bigger Great Pyrenees. "I need to get back on the road."

Bear took a step back and whimpered in an expectant way. "Jiff?"

The dog began panting. "I have no idea what you're talking about."

"You're a Labrador on the Rainbow Bridge, but last time you visited Earth at Christmas, you were a corgi."

"Never been on a Rainbow, can't remember the last time I celebrated Christmas and my legs aren't short," he said.

"The only talking dog I've ever known was a corgi," Bear said.

"You're the only talking animal I've ever met," the dog said, scrunching his eyebrows together. "And how are you hearing the talking in my head?"

"Josephine, Josephine, Josephine!" Bear barked. He remembered when he'd said the name three times in front of his old friend. It had straightened the corgi out right away.

"I have no name," the dog said, his eyes drooping in confusion. "And just so you know, I'm not a she."

The Great Pyr took a few steps forward in amiable concern. A senior canine, his face was a mask of grey, his body brown, with elbows and the end of his tail worn away of any fur. Most worrying to Bear, the dog's ribs showed under skin that hung drooping on his frame. "Are you hungry?"

"I feel I'm always starving these days, friend."

"Come with me then." The Great Pyrenees's ears went up and his tail began to wag as he walked. "We always have plenty of food at Bear Bailey's."

The co-op's front door opened. Pablito entered after finishing early morning soccer practice. He walked to school each day from Bear Bailey's. His head snapped up in surprise at the sight of two dogs. "What is going on here?" he asked with a big grin on his face.

"You'll love this kid," Bear said. "An athlete and an artist. He's really going to accomplish a lot in his life." He stood up on his back legs. Mary was still busy, so he licked the boy's face in greeting.

"Showing him the ropes around here, Bear?" Pablito laughed, wiping slobber off his face with the back of his arm. He knelt to look at the old dog. "*Mucho gusto, viejo.*" His fingers traced the dog's face and neck before stepping back and appraising the elderly canine's build. "You'd be a good subject to paint. There looks to be many stories in your eyes." He patted the dog and stood up. "I'm starving," he announced, his voice echoing throughout the co-op.

From somewhere in the kitchen, Lupe's voice was playfully exasperated. "Ay, Pablito. Always so hungry."

Panting in happiness at the easy nature between Lupe and her son, Bear nodded his head. "She loves that kid. Would feed him non-stop if she could." He turned his attention back to the old dog. "I told you we had plenty of food. Let's go find you some."

Grimacing in a way that made all the humans in the area turn with concern, the old dog pulled himself up from a seated position and followed Bear into the office. "Please have all the kibble you want," Bear said. He nodded to his food and water bowls.

"I can do some work before I eat."

Bear shook his head in confusion. "Work? For *food*?"

"I could fetch something? Herd a few things," the dog answered, coughing. "Whatever you need." His ears went down submissively as he paused. "I'm not looking for a handout."

Bear tried to arrange his expression from shock to encouragement. "We always feed our friends. And they don't have to do anything," he replied. "Go on and eat." He took a few bits of kibble out of his bowl with his mouth, dropping them on the floor as he used his nose to nudge the food closer to the old dog before stepping back.

"If you take me to the alley, I'm happy eating out of the trashcans. I can scavenge and be on my way."

Bear's eyes fairly bulged from his head. "That's the saddest thing I've ever heard a dog say in my entire life." He whined. "Please share my food. In fact, eat it all."

"It's not my aim to wear out my welcome. I don't ever want to be a bother."

"I don't know why, but I feel like crying," Bear whispered, putting his head down. He tried to pant in a friendly manner. "Please, eat. You're my guest. We can figure out the rest later."

Shyly at first, and then with the slow acceleration of a machine warming up, the dog ate voraciously until every last morsel disappeared. He stood back from the bowls, letting out a loud belch and bowing his head. "Sorry, friend. I got carried away."

"Don't ever apologize for eating. Mary will bring us more food. She loves to share."

The dog's stomach hung heavy with the weight of the food he'd just devoured. "That should hold me for several days."

"Hold you for *days*?" Bear repeated, incredulous. "You can eat again in a few hours. With treats in between." He put a gentle paw on the dog's shoulder.

"What's a treat?" The old dog looked perplexed.

"An out of the ordinary item that gives one great joy and happiness," Bear said, before stopping. "I don't know how I know that."

The door to the office opened and both canines looked up. The old dog backed up from the empty food bowl like he'd done something wrong.

"You're not in trouble for eating. Look how nice humans can be." Bear went to Percy and put his head down. His back leg tapped the floor rapidly as Percy scratched behind his ears.

"I appreciate you didn't mention that we'd already met yesterday," Katie said as she entered with Percy.

"It wasn't my place to say anything," Percy replied, smiling at Bear and roughing up his mane. He turned his attention to the older dog, taking a few steps across the office to scratch the dog's back.

Katie set her paperwork on the desk. She kindly motioned an invitation for Percy to sit down in front of her. "Yesterday was an odd day. I was trying to engage in an activity I hadn't done since I was a girl. You caught me off guard. I was embarrassed."

"Fishing is a noble sport. Why would you feel that way?"

"It's not just the fishing. It's today too. My overalls are an old Halloween costume. I also have more than a toothbrush for grooming tools."

"Good to know," he said with a bemused look.

"I think I was trying to be the country bumpkin counterpart to your polished, big city suit. In my terrible mood this morning, it made perfect sense to me."

He chuckled. "Even in dungarees, I think you look perfectly lovely."

Katie studied him. She was no stranger to forward advances from men. Percy's behavior though, was one that could be used with a grandmother. Very sincere and safe. "Friends?"

"Of course." The relief on Percy's face was clear.

"How did you know where I live?" The question slipped out of Katie's mouth before she realized the thought had formed in her brain.

Percy's expression re-ignited in worry. "What do you mean?"

"To drop the dog off," Katie finished. "At my house."

"I have no idea what you're talking about," Percy stammered.

"You and I meet outside of town. You take the dog and leave. Later the same evening, he's scratching at my front door."

Percy's was as stunned as if he were being accused of first-degree murder. "I promise you, I have no idea how the dog arrived at your house."

Bear listened to the two humans talk. "I can tell he's not lying."

The old dog nodded his agreement.

"How did you get to Katie's house?" Bear asked.

"A weird feeling comes over me and I start wandering to my next spot," the old dog replied. "I left Percy and just walked until the feeling left me. Then I was looking for water and scratched at the first door I saw. Which happened to be Katie's house. You must know the feeling and want to roam."

Stepping close to Percy, Bear hooked his front paw on the

man's arm to calm him. "I only ever want to be with Mary. To protect her so she can always be safe and live forever."

"No one lives forever, friend," the old dog said. "We all die sometime. One last breath and then we board our last train." He stopped and thought for a moment. "I think the best we might hope for is *Eight and Sand*."

"What's an *Eight and Sand*?"

"Train crews say it at a journey departure for an uneventful, speedy trip. I hope that's heaven."

"I don't like that story." Bear eyes were wide with fright, but he still spoke in a polite way. "I need to go find Mary." He panted, exiting the office in a hurry.

"My whole career could be jeopardized for that kind of behavior," Percy continued. "Let's get Mary back in here and sort this out. She can't think such a dishonest man is working with you."

Katie held her hand up. "Stop, I can tell you're telling the truth. I didn't mean to upset you."

The co-op was beginning to fill with people. Percy nodded out to Mary and Cybil, who were talking with customers. "Do they think I dropped the dog off at your house?"

Katie shook her head.

Percy's face relaxed. "Oh, good," he breathed out. "I brought the dog to the rental house. I let him in, and he was the perfect companion, sitting on a throw rug. Until early evening, and then he was insistent he leave. I tried everything to coax him back."

"I was the one who booked your rental house for you," Katie replied. "It's clear across town."

"I promise I didn't…"

"I'm not saying that. Honestly. But I find it interesting that out of the whole town this hobo dog came directly to my home. From where you were staying."

"You didn't like the term hobo yesterday."

"I Googled." Her expression was meek. "You were right—hobo fits him perfectly. They were noble in their ideals and way of living."

Percy was pleased at her words, a smile on his face as he leaned in to hear more.

"And the markings they left for one another were more interesting than I imagined. I found myself reading up on hobo codes all evening."

"I believe you coined the term—*hoboglyphics*. How clever," he said. "I can't wait to share that with someone. All from a wandering dog."

"Poor old man—the way his skin looks like wrinkled pants ready to fall off." Katie went over and kissed the top of the dog's head. "He was a perfect gentleman in the house last night. I feel he needs his own regal name to reflect his true nature."

"*For though I speak it to you, I think the King is but a man as I am: the violet smells to him as it doth to me.*"

"Violets and Shakespeare? Again?"

"I thought it might work."

"You mean a disguised King Henry dropping in as a regular chap to discuss things before a battle commences with France?" Katie spoke with sincere warmth. "Henry may be the perfect name." She reached for her phone and began typing into a search engine. She looked up and smiled. "Henry means 'Ruler of the Home.'"

The old dog barked and began to pant.

"Do you think he understands what I just said?" she asked, looking at Percy.

Bear re-entered the room, looking around. "Of course, we know what they're saying. Why do humans always act like it's a coincidence?"

Looking between the dog and Katie, Percy was truly overjoyed. "You know *Henry V*," he said.

"I know a *little* Shakespeare," she replied. "Don't get too excited." She knelt down. "Shall we try out the name Henry for the day, old man?"

The bell on the door of the co-op opened. A man stood in the doorway, standing with the presence of a male half his age.

"Mr. Chapowits." Katie groaned. "The opposite of regal."

"Oh, yes! We love his name in Vermont," Percy replied. "*Good old, Chap*, we like to say."

"You call him *what*?" Katie asked, her tone the same one she'd used the previous day at the fishing pond. She grabbed Bear by the collar and held him steady as he began to growl at Mr. Chapowits' presence.

"Riven—the man I tried to tell Mary about. He's anxious to join forces with you women," Percy said, his smile bright. "He's charmed everyone at the Rural Initiative with his vision for Merivelle."

Gathering That Allows Hobos

"Mr. Chapowits showed up and acted like no big deal—we're all the best of friends and he was just dropping in to see if we could use any help with our Main Street grant proposal. Acted like Bear Bailey's Co-op and Grocery was his favorite place in the whole world," Katie fumed. "He was passing around croissants and beverages at the table like he was our personal waiter."

"Of all the nerve!" Theodore hit the counter, rattling his silverware.

"Be serious." Mary shot her husband a withering look.

"It's been so quiet the past couple of years, he's been off my radar. I almost forgot what a coyote he'd been to everyone."

At the word *coyote* Bear began to growl like one of the animals was right outside the door ready to hurt Mary.

"You almost forgot?" Katie was aghast. "He'd have taken the co-op away from your wife if the town hadn't stepped in and rallied around her. At Christmas!"

Holding his hands up in surrender, Theodore said, "I'm an original Bear Bailey's fan. All that love and cheer can sometimes make me forget that Riven almost railroaded our lives."

"That's a lot to overlook. Do not forget how he treated Mary."

Bear began to howl, startling all three humans before Mary shushed him with a kiss on top of his head. She reached into his treat canister on the counter to slip him a morsel. In turn, the Great Pyr took the treat in his mouth and dropped it in front of Katie's dog, wagging his tail in encouragement.

"Wait a second. Quick change of subject. Are we going to talk about the new, rather senior-looking dog?" Theodore asked.

"This handsome boy was wandering down Main Street," Katie replied, kneeling down to the dog, her face affectionate and soft. "I'm going to take him in."

"Katie! That's wonderful!" Mary said. "He'll change your life in the best way possible."

The old dog lifted his eyebrows. "I'll stay as long as I can, but to travel on in spring is my idea of heaven."

"I've always imagined that autumn is the perfect time for important journeys," Bear said, turning his head as he thought for a few moments. "Why is it that you like this time of year for traveling?"

"The temperature is moderate. There's usually rain for baths. And with spring flowers blooming, it still feels like a new beginning for an old and wandering dog like me."

Bear's face was puzzled. "But with so much travel, you would have to leave the people you love." His ears turned down and he began to whine in a mournful way. "It sounds like a Dark Den to me."

"What's a Dark Den?"

"Where coyotes lead you away from your family and they trick you into believing no one loves you or ever will." Bear began quivering in place. "It's the worst feeling in the whole world."

The other dog was incredulous. "You've actually been kidnapped by a pack of coyotes?"

Eyes wide, his body paralyzed in fear, Bear whimpered. "I can't exactly tell when it's happening. A Dark Den is the worst thing," he said. "My friend Jiff had to help get me out of one when I didn't believe in myself. He showed me how my life had meaning to the people around me, even when I hadn't realized it." He sighed heavily. "I don't know if that even makes sense to you. But I promise you if it isn't real, a Dark Den sure feels that way—all your worst fears come to life."

The old dog nodded. "I think we all have our own versions of a Dark Den. I used to think I was adventurous. The older I get I realize that I move along before someone abandons me first."

"You've been abandoned?"

"A few times when I was young."

"This happened to you more than once?" Bear whimpered as he leaned in.

"My own fault." The dog sighed, shaking his head. "Left at home alone—I'd get anxious and chew shoes or bark too loud. Kids were my favorite thing. But then I'd get too excited and knock them over on accident because I loved playing. I never meant any harm. I was just a young dog."

"Playing is no crime." Bear gulped to keep from crying in front of the dog. He remembered plenty of times he almost toppled people because he loved them so much.

"I'd be taken away. Once to a pound. A couple of times, they'd feed me a big meal, put me in a car and then let me out in the country before they drove away." The old dog huffed at the memory and closed his eyes. "I used to chase them. My heart felt like it would break. I wanted to show them I'd try harder if they'd give me another chance." He hung his head. "It was really hard for me to understand what humans wanted in each home."

"I don't know what to say here." Bear had tears in his eyes. He looked up at the humans talking, unaware of the old dog's distress and wished they could hear him.

"So, I decided my place wasn't in any home. On the road is, and has always been, the best route for me. If I chewed something or got too excited, I didn't hurt anyone. Who needs a family when you have the freedom of the open road?"

"If you have a home and kind people who love you, you have everything in the whole world. My friend Jiff taught me that when I was just a pup."

"Maybe. But if you can't find people who love you, adventures by yourself are nice too." The old dog's eyebrows closed together as he thought for a moment. "There were times though, when the coyotes howled or I hadn't eaten in days, I felt very lonely."

Bear dropped to the floor, right beside the old dog. "If I could pass on anything to you, please remember—you are never alone." He reached out to one of the old dog's graying front paws. "You gotta remember that."

"And what's this fine dog's name?" Theodore asked as he scratched behind the dog's ears. "Hobo?"

"Hey! Why does everyone keep calling him that?" Katie asked.

"I don't know why she gets so protective," the old dog replied, shaking his head. "Perfectly reasonable observation about my appearance. I recently startled myself in a window reflection. I can't believe how old and wrinkly I've gotten."

The human's conversation continued as Theodore winced. "Putting it politely, he looks like he needs a good tailor."

"Your tail looks great to me." Bear nodded in an encouraging manner. "I'm sure that's what he means too."

Katie lifted her chin, looking unruffled. "There's nothing wrong with being a hobo. Did you know that hobos had a whole set of standards, like coming to a community and leaving it better than they found it? Never wearing out their welcome or taking excessive help from townspeople, in case other hobos might need help in the future? There was a network understanding of how important it was to encourage runaway children to go home. It's quite impressive if you take the time to educate yourself about hobos and all they've done to better our communities across this country. And don't get me started on their extensive code of symbols. Their communication system that spanned the entire country was remarkable."

Theodore's mouth fell open. "Our Katie is fascinated with hobo culture? Am I hearing this right?"

Mary lifted her eyebrows, giving a quick shake of her head to silence her husband.

"You two forget how lonely it can be without each other." The light in Katie's eyes dimmed for a moment before she continued. "Right now, this noble, well-behaved dog might be the answer to a lot of my issues. He's quiet, lets me have my own space, and doesn't have a wandering eye. Best yet, he won't get up and leave when I need him most."

"Is it just me or is it hot in here, friend?" The dog went to the patio door and looked out, steaming the glass with his heavy breathing.

"Get back over here. You can't leave town because you have a phobia of being abandoned. Katie's already had her heart broken plenty of times—the tears I've seen flowing from her at this house." Moved by the memories, Bear went over and licked Katie's hand, nuzzling it with affection until she scratched his ears in recognition. "Maybe it's time for you to get used to being taken care of instead of running. Katie would be the perfect home for you"

"I wouldn't even know how to live in a house at this point."

"I can show you. For starters, take my place with Katie."

The old dog meandered to where Bear was standing. "Then what?"

"You lean into your human," Bear's said, his tone heartfelt. "With great love. It's almost always the answer."

"Lean in with love? I'll give it a try." The old dog dutifully pushed into Katie's legs. As if by magic, her face lit in joy as she knelt to look at him. She kissed his nose before standing up again.

Bear was triumphant. "You did great. No pressure to stay. Just give it a little time. You two might be the perfect match."

"I don't want to disappoint any more humans." He gazed outside the patio door. "It makes it easier to leave when the feeling comes over me if someone doesn't name me."

"Too late." Bear tilted his head toward Katie. "I'm pretty sure she's getting ready to—"

"I've named him Henry. It sounds regal. It might be one of my favorite boy names."

"*Henry*," Mary said thoughtfully, repeating the name aloud several times. "I love it. Are you sure you don't want to keep in the queue for a baby sometime in the future?"

"I've never let myself dream about that subject." She then snorted. "I think with my history with men, I'll be safe. Hopefully, my dog luck is better than my man luck."

"King Henry it is!" Mary exclaimed. "What a wonderful name."

Bear gave Henry a side-eyed look. "She named you a really cool thing. You've gotta stick around."

"I can't make any promises. Most of the time, I don't even understand why I go." He yawned in a loud and vocal way.

"Is it my imagination or are you even more tired than you seemed yesterday?" Bear laid down beside Henry. "I couldn't even hear your heart beating when you were under the table at the co-op."

"It's faint. But it's still ticking, friend."

"It's none of my business, Katie and as much as I'm a massive fan of you getting a dog, darling Henry won't fix all of your problems." Mary reached over to massage the dog's back. "Not all men are jerks. Look at this one." She gestured a thumb over her shoulder to Theodore who froze with a French fry hanging out of his mouth. "Maybe it's time to talk to someone about your dad."

Theodore chewed his food as slowly as possible to seem empathetic to the gravity of the situation.

"You resemble a lizard," Katie said. "Just eat, Theodore. I'm not going to freak out because Mary said the very obvious. My dad left."

"I thought your dad was incarcerated."

"Theodore!"

"It's fine, Mary. It's true. He was. He served his time for something minor, I think," Katie explained. "And when his sentence was over in ninety days, I never saw him again."

"See why you can't get up and leave?" Bear nudged Henry with his snout. "Look how Katie's getting blotchy around her neck, even though she's trying to act like it's no big deal. Try it again—lean in with love."

Henry went over to Katie and backed into her legs. Bear nodded, his face solemn with the energy of the room.

"I'm so sorry. I was just a goofy kid and didn't know how to help you."

An involuntary shiver went through her body. "I don't want to talk about it anymore. Maybe just with Henry." She sat down on the floor and pulled the dog close to her. "Isn't he the most handsome boy you've ever seen?" Katie put her cheek to the old dog's face. As he smiled, gaps of space in his mouth revealed the poor dog had mostly broken and missing teeth.

"I would have thought her a poodle sort of woman," Theodore said, his arm around Mary, with a big grin on his face. "Then she goes and gets the dog I least expect."

"My eyes may be closed, but I can still hear you, Theodore."

"You know I'm just kidding you. Love the new dog," Theodore said. "And to bring the conversation full circle here, people change and do unexpected things all the time. Like you taking in this dog, Katie. Maybe Mr. Chapowits wants to play nice. Join in all the Merivelle fun. You two have certainly made

Bear Bailey's a joyful place to meet friends and conduct business. Perhaps he sees this as his opportunity to jump into the fray in a better way."

Bear groaned as Katie shook her head in disagreement but was soon lost in snuggling the newly named Henry.

Mary's eyes were serious with concern. "I can't put my finger on it, but I have a feeling Mr. Chapowits has an agenda. I'm afraid he's just getting started."

Prepare to Defend Yourself

The next morning, Katie arrived at Bear Bailey's bright and early, dressed in her usual impeccable and polished style. She was determined to show Percy a different side of herself. Upon entering the co-op, Bear ran forward barking in excitement, greeting the pair. "You didn't leave, Henry! Well done!"

"That doesn't mean it won't happen. I told you that I can't tell when it's going to hit me. But it'll be soon."

Looking up from the paperwork he was arranging at the table, Percy's mouth fell open in admiration.

"Back to normal," Lupe exclaimed. She fairly danced a jig at the sight of Katie's resurrected wardrobe before she turned to her left. "She always looks this beautiful, Mr. Bourne."

Percy blinked several times before clearing his throat. "You aren't wearing overalls today," he stammered.

"No, I'm not." Katie placed her laptop bag on the table. "You saw the first and only day in my career." She began to unload the contents of her bag with a pleased expression. "Though I do reserve the right to wear overalls when fishing. I'm still amazed at their comfort."

"She does look very nice today," Bear said, barking in Katie's direction, reflecting the excitement he felt from everyone at the table. "It's nice to see her sparkling again, Henry. Good work!"

"Did you really put a necktie on your new dog?" Mary asked, beaming.

"Bear has his own backpack when he's at work." Katie sorted her paperwork into different stacks on the table. "I thought Henry could look like he was part of our team too."

"So, you've dressed him like a canine CEO," Cybil said, laughing. "Please tell me those glasses have no prescription in them."

"Of course not, I have half a dozen cosmetic pairs for different occasions when I want to seem smart."

"But you *are* smart, Katie," Mary said. "Very smart."

"One might even say perspicacious," Lupe said, looking directly to Percy. "We couldn't do without her. With or without her ridiculous glasses."

"Lupe!" Mary laughed as she reached for orange juice.

"We're all friends here. Just giving each other a hard time," Cybil said.

Katie pulled out a chair and patted for Henry to sit at the table. He jumped to his place, looking around with an unbothered expression. Katie announced, "Everyone, please welcome, Henry Hughes Hatch."

Everyone around the table began to laugh and clap, welcoming the new dog to the meeting and the Bear Bailey team.

Percy cleared his throat. "Henry Hugh? Like Henry Hugh Armstead, the English Pre-Raphaelite sculptor?"

"Knowing how you value honesty, Percy, I did not use whoever you're talking about as my inspiration. The name is in honor of a dear friend of Cybil's who always found beauty in all things. Especially where most people overlooked."

The older woman held her hands to her heart and nodded in gratitude. "She would have loved humble and good-hearted

Henry." Her face was radiant as she spoke. "I'm always thankful when Honey's students remember her impact in their lives."

Her face joyful at Cybil's response, Katie pulled out another bag with dog supplies and then placed a mat in front of Henry and continued. "But how clever that you know all the things you know, Percy. I'll Google Henry Hugh Armstead later this evening." She placed an accordion-style water bowl on the table. After popping it open, she began to fill it with water from her lavender *Sparkle On* water bottle.

"I can't tell you how uncomfortable all this attention makes me," Henry said to Bear on the floor. "Maybe I'll just disappear while they're talking." He jumped down and headed to the door with Bear in quick pursuit.

"I'm a guarding dog, Henry. You won't ever get by a Great Pyrenees who understands their purpose." Bear positioned himself to stop Henry as the western Kansas wind blew the door open momentarily. He pushed his body against the older dog's frame with the strength he would attend to a young lamb with wobbly legs. *Gentle, gentle* as Mary always told him around anyone not as big or strong as himself.

"How am I *your* purpose?" Henry was already breathless with his failed exit from the co-op. He allowed Bear to guide him back to his chair.

"Mary's my purpose."

"But I'm not Mary's dog."

"Katie is Mary's right hand—she says it all the time. Therefore, we've got to keep you here to make Katie happy so Mary's happy which makes me happier than you can possibly know." Bear grinned as he laid down on the ground.

Groaning with exertion, the old dog struggled to get back on the chair. "This noose around my neck, Bear. If I stay, the tie has to go."

"You gotta wear it."

The old dog's face dropped in disappointment. "Why?"

"I still haven't figured that out. But it makes women indescribably happy when they dress their dogs up."

"It's so scratchy." Henry stretched his neck from side to side. Ignoring Bear's explanation, he began to scratch at his collar with one of his hind feet.

"Mary says we can't ever have fleas in the co-op." Bear nervously scanned the table. All the humans were in conversation or looking down at paperwork. "Any chance you have fleas?"

"Friend, not after that bath she gave me last night. She scrubbed me like there was no tomorrow in suds that smell like—"

"Peppermint and cedarwood. Natural flea deterrents," Bear answered, sniffing the air. He turned his head in question. "I don't know how I know that."

"I'd trade the fancy smell to lose the tie. I don't like collars, leashes and certainly not neckwear. Makes me feel claustrophobic." He looked to the door again, scanning the storefront windows.

Sensing Henry's growing panic, Bear advised, "Start biting at the end of it like it's a big ribeye steak. A few gentle growls. Katie will think you're going to ruin it."

"That easy?"

Mary had once tried to attach brightly colored felt turkey feathers on a headband for him to wear at co-op for Thanksgiving. Even knowing it was his beloved owner's favorite holiday, he shook his head and chewed the feathers until a disappointed Mary gave up and took the item away. He felt a little guilty about letting Henry in on the tip.

"Why is she wanting to dress me?" Henry asked. "I've had three wardrobe changes this morning."

"If I know Katie, this is only the beginning. You're going to be the best dressed hobo dog ever."

"Maybe the visiting man can take some attention off me."

Henry shook the glasses off his face and onto the floor. "He looks like he wouldn't mind being fussed over."

Both dogs looked over. Percy was watching Katie speaking to the other women in good-natured morning chatter. She was so put together and collected in her thoughts; it would have been hard to believe she was the same woman who had previously stumbled into the co-op in chaotic disarray. He smiled in a mesmerized way.

"Everything all right, Percy?" Cybil asked, barely above a whisper. Katie was discussing paperwork with Mary before the meeting started.

He blinked several times and shook his head. "Yes, I'm fine. You caught me daydreaming a bit."

"She's a peach. Don't let her try to convince you otherwise." Cybil laughed quietly. "Smart as a whip and even more kind and heartfelt, if she lets you see her softer side." She winked in a conspiratorial way.

Percy nodded, "We better get started." He cleared his throat before addressing the rest of the group. "I'm eager to let you know some good news for Bear Bailey's."

Excited by his tone, all conversation around the table came to an abrupt and silent halt.

"I talked to the Rural Initiative office today. As I've already mentioned, they're pleased with the proposal sent in by—" His face grew red as he involuntarily glanced at Katie. He cleared his throat again. "—the staff of Bear Bailey's."

Katie was listening but busy placing dog food in another pop-up dish to place in front of Henry. He had no interest in food and was looking for a way to join Bear on the floor.

Sighing, Lupe leaned over and whispered into Katie's ear. "Listen to what this poor man is trying to say and quit fiddling with your dog."

Katie stopped, smiling as she met Percy's gaze.

"One concern, however. There seems to be a bit of a disconnect with the need of the community and the funds available to it from a local source."

Mary's face flushed pink. "What funds might be available to us that we aren't aware of?"

"Yesterday, after I'd already arrived in Merivelle, Riven Chapowits called our headquarters. He said he'd heard some local chatter about applying for grants. He let us know his offer to generously contribute, if not entirely fund, your downtown refurbishment proposal. He says it's been a dream of his for years to see Merivelle flourish."

"Mr. Chapowits?" Mary's energy dropped in shock. Bear began howling. Henry joined in, lending his own mournful howl to the outcry, though he was unclear of exactly why.

"What did I say?" Percy asked, looking around the table. "I thought you'd be thrilled with his very open-handed offer. Riven said he's funded many businesses through the years. It would give him great pleasure to see them united in a common goal of growth for the community."

Mary and Cybil glanced at one another. Lupe folded her arms as Katie scowled. Both dogs drew quiet with the women's silence.

"What Mr. Chapowits says and what he'll actually do are two different things." Katie sat on the edge of her chair. "I can't believe after all our research and work, one phone call from an unknown man could unravel it all. If we thought there was even a minute chance to get assistance from Mr. Chapowits, we wouldn't have reached out to your initiative. We were floored to see him yesterday. We haven't seen him for years."

Percy pulled at his tie, looking pained as he spoke. "We have hundreds, if not thousands, of requests from people in small towns like Merivelle. The majority lack a local citizen willing to share their wealth to help their community. We were thinking that if there's any way you could work with Riven, our funds might be better served in a town without a generous benefactor."

"Generous benefactor?" Mary almost choked as she said the words. She reached for a glass of water, her hand shaking in emotion.

"Before Mary came to town and used her *own* inheritance, Riven was charging our beloved Lupe an arm and leg for rent. Her living conditions were criminal," Cybil said, hitting the table with her fist.

Lupe nodded at Cybil, clearly touched by the woman's protective manner toward her family.

Katie rose from her chair and locked eyes with Percy. "Surely, this is not the first time in your travels that you've found yourself dealing with a local bully trying to separate the townspeople from help."

"Actually, it is," Percy said. "Are you sure—"

"*Yes!*" All four women shouted before he could finish. Bear barked enthusiastically. Henry pawed his dog dish on the table sending dry kibble all over the floor.

"I don't know what to say. He's headed here right now to join us," Percy said, searching around the table for any fragment of anticipation. "I apologize for upsetting you, but I thought yesterday you were open to him joining us."

"We were caught off guard," Mary replied. "And weren't sure what to say without involving you in decades worth of small-town drama."

"A real coyote move when he showed up unexpected," Bear said, raising his eyebrows and looking over at Henry.

"He must have called with one whale of a fish story," Katie said.

"I don't know what he said," Percy replied. "I only received the quick update."

"There's no doubt in my mind, the phone call was nothing

more than an attempt to stop our funding," Mary interjected. "He's smart enough to offer help—"

"Then you drive three hours to the nearest airport to fly home." Katie was fuming. "And before you land, Mr. Chapowits's offer evaporates. Trust us, Percy. We've lived here with the man since we were children."

The co-op's front door opened. Riven Chapowits entered Bear Bailey's with a smile on his face. "I see Percy has let you know of my offer to help Merivelle."

Good Road to Follow

"Remember, we aren't the only people with good perception. Give Percy a few minutes. He'll see right through him," Mary said. Her cousin and Cybil had expressions of doubtful glares.

Riven ignored the women entirely. He spoke only to Percy, his handshake overly lingering, listening to every word that came out of the visitor's mouth as if it were the most profound and intellectual comment he'd ever heard. Slowly, taking small steps back by merely leaning into Percy, Riven moved him out of earshot of the group and near the door.

Katie nodded at the pair with one raised eyebrow. "Well, how long do we wait for Percy's perception to kick in?"

Mary rolled her eyes. "Give him longer than ten minutes."

"Where's Lupe? Some of our best ideas come from that clever woman," Cybil asked, turning around and searching for her.

A short time after the old man arrived, Lupe disappeared without a word, only poking her head out from the co-op kitchen, to mouth an apology to Mary as she crossed herself and then shook a fist in Mr. Chapowits's direction.

"She's terrified," Mary replied. "She doesn't want to ruin getting her nationalization certificate."

"Surely, Theodore is close to getting Lupe's papers. She shouldn't have to run in the opposite direction when Chapowits is near," Katie said.

"Immigration can take years to sort through," Mary answered. "It breaks my heart as she and the kids wait." She watched the kitchen where Lupe was hard at work, preparing box lunches to stock the co-op's Grab-and-Go cooler. "You know that old coyote would like nothing more than to cause a little chaos for the Posadas."

"Let's keep ourselves focused on the good we can accomplish for Merivelle. Or else I'll strangle Riven. And then lose our funding, for sure." Cybil said, slightly grinning. "I was *mostly* kidding." She reached down and petted Bear. The older dog positioned himself under Cybil's other hand. "We'll handle the old coyote most effectively by doing the right thing, not the easy thing."

"That man has been hurt." Henry sighed. "Perhaps be as kind to him as you were with my own history."

Bear stopped and whimpered, his eyes moving back and forth between Riven and Mary. He tried to remember Mary's words to never to intercede on her behalf, lest she lose him. He shivered recalling his own vision with Jiff at Christmas when Mr. Chapowits was intent on Bear being separated from Mary.

"He may act like a coyote," Henry said. "But I sense he's in pain."

Bear narrowed his eyes and growled at a low decibel level. "You don't know him like we do."

The old dog was not dissuaded. "You've only known great love, Bear. And thus, you're open to friendships with everyone."

Bear tilted his head. "What does that have to do with anything?"

"Dogs on chains don't know how to be social," Henry said.

"They've often spent their lives alone. You have to be patient and show them a better way."

Bear jumped back. Henry's vocabulary surprised him. Not that he'd had any talking dog to compare him to except Jiff. "You're a very smart animal. How can you tell that about him?"

"Life on the road. You have to be fast reading humans. It was the difference between someone feeding me or throwing rocks to get rid of me. I'm pretty good at sizing people up. Not many wandering dogs make it to old age."

"You always make me very sad, Henry. I wish we could have met you years ago to help take care of you."

"Thanks, friend," the old dog replied. "You would have been a real pal on the road." He nodded at Bear in an admiring way. "Not to mention your size and ferocious, yet gentle manner."

Mr. Chapowits held his hand out in invitation for Percy to join the table while he searched for a place sit, seeming baffled at the round table's arrangement.

"Odd for you, isn't it, Mr. Chapowits?" Katie stood in front of Mary in a protective stance. "No head of the table here." She smiled as she maintained eye contact with him. "You're simply one of us."

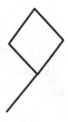

Hold Your Tongue

Riven introduced himself as if everyone in attendance had never met him before. Mary, Cybil and Katie had trouble keeping their jaws off the floor as he spoke in glowing terms of his decades of personal service bringing aid to Merivelle through catastrophe after catastrophe. Natural disasters, labor shortages for harvest, as well as banking failures—both local and national, were droned on and on by the old man.

Katie passed a piece of paper to Mary.

Mary opened the note on her lap. *Never let the truth get in the way of a good story, huh?* She nodded in agreement, tucking it under her pile of paperwork.

Katie drummed her fingers on the table and Cybil sighed as they listened to the man's soliloquy espousing his love of all things Merivelle. Before starting the meeting, they'd agreed as a group not to deluge Percy with stories of Mr. Chapowits's past misconduct, lest they undermine their effusive grant proposal based on peaceful communities working together for the good of every member in them.

"… the very building we're sitting in today is testament to my faith in Merivelle."

Mary cleared her throat.

"Had I not bought the bank holding the note of this building, the co-op would have ceased to exist," he concluded.

The three women glanced at each other.

"How interesting and informing, Mr. Chapowits," Percy began.

The old man seemed comfortable that no one was going to challenge his narrative. "Percy, please. All my friends call me Riven."

"Mr. Chapowits." Katie sat up in her seat.

Under the table, Mary reached for her cousin's hand and squeezed it in warning. "Remember our agreement before the meeting started," she whispered.

"Yes, dear?" Mr. Chapowits's tone was awkward speaking the endearment, the smile on his face appearing unnatural and forced.

"I'm not your dear and you certainly haven't ever used that term in Merivelle, so let's cut out all the nonsense you've been espousing and get to helping Merivelle. You've had every opportunity to do good throughout the years, and all you've done was try to destroy and divide."

Percy listened to Katie, looking between her and Riven, trying to piece together the puzzle of the situation.

Avoiding eye contact with either man, Katie continued. "A little over three years ago, you almost lost this co-op, Mary. *At Christmastime.* You used your entire inheritance Aunt Margaret left you. And what did Mr. Chapowits do instead of helping Bear Bailey's and all the vendors? He bought the small bank that held the mortgage on the property and tried to force you out.

The people of Merivelle saved this beautiful place—repaying debts they owed your mother who never charged them interest or demanded payment for loans over the years. Others gifted the difference. And now Bear Bailey's has become a cornerstone reminder of our hard work, our beloved friendships and where we all want to celebrate our triumphs." Katie rose from her chair, her cheeks fired in color. "Mr. Chapowits had nothing to do with it."

"Is this true?" Percy asked.

Cybil nodded. "We didn't want you to think we were a bunch of small-town gossips, so we hoped we wouldn't have to say anything."

"It's a matter of perception," Mr. Chapowits responded. "Non-business people don't always understand what we do, Percy."

"I can assure you that Ms. Hatch's paperwork is impeccable. What the women put together for a vision is inspiring. In fact, Merivelle has become somewhat of a beacon for us back at the Rural Initiative. I find it hard to believe they lack the business acumen you're speaking of."

"I want to fight for my place on this committee. I challenge you to find anyone still active in the community who has lived here as long as I have. I belong here."

Katie leaned into the table. "It's probably safer you're here and we know your thoughts on things. However, once we're approved for grant funds, we're going to fill all the places at this table with individuals who represent the fabric of Merivelle. The true reflection of our town as it changes with time, while we still hold our traditions near to our heart."

"Wasted time," Mr. Chapowits began. "We don't need to slow our progress down trying to select members for a committee."

"We can add one right now with ease," Katie said. "Lupe," she called out, her voice elevated but controlled. "Would you please come out here?"

Mr. Chapowits looked slightly confused and then a look of worry passed over his face.

"This man has terrorized our beloved friend, who is the first person in and last person out of the co-op every day. Right ahead of Mary and me," Katie explained. "No offense, Cybil."

"None taken." Cybil's eyes were bright as she watched her former student. "Tired old bones or I'd be here with you younger folks at the crack of dawn."

"Mary's husband, Theodore, is helping the Posada family finish their paperwork to be legal residents of the country, and community, they cherish so much." She eyed Mr. Chapowits. "And while I'm on the subject, they seem to be missing personal correspondence of any kind. Theodore is concerned someone interfered with their mail when they lived in your rental property."

"Theodore doesn't know what he's talking about."

"Mr. Chapowits, you could only hope to be half the man Theodore is—kind, loving and a friend to everyone in Merivelle, even though he's a relatively new transplant. A crash course in all things Theodore Bailey would move you light years ahead in personal development." Katie's eyes flashed with protection for her cousin's husband. "I can't imagine a man I respect more."

Mr. Chapowits's gaze was curious and steady as he let Katie continue without interrupting. Lupe approached the table, holding a silver coffeepot in her shaking hands, avoiding eye contact with the man.

"Put the coffee down, Lupe. You're here as a full-fledged member of our committee," Katie said. "The new Merivelle. We welcome everyone who contributes to our community in a meaningful way. And no one exemplifies that more than you, Lupe Posada."

Standing up to take the coffeepot from Lupe's hands while her cousin continued talking, Mary nodded to an empty chair and smiled for her to take a seat.

"You are not to scare this woman or her children. They want nothing more than to be accepted as a family within our community. It's time you stop bullying them."

"Lupe?" Percy took his glasses off and rubbed his eyes before putting them back on. "Riven? You've hurt *Word of the Day* Lupe?"

"Yes, our darling Lupe," Katie said. "Now she'll have a place at our table and our protection and friendship. And if you want to join her, Mr. Chapowits, you'll sit here with Lupe as an equal and listen to her thoughts without prejudice."

Everyone's attention went to the man.

"I don't think you understand—"

"Think carefully before you finish that thought. Or we'll happily open your spot up to someone else."

"Will I have any say with the other members when the time comes?" Mr. Chapowits asked.

"You can have input like all the rest of us. We'll decide together," Katie said. "Can you agree to those terms?"

"I'm not disagreeing."

"That's as agreeable as he gets," Cybil said. "Let's take it as a yes and get on with the business of growing Merivelle."

~

During the meeting, the small group agreed to meet daily during Percy's visit. Upon grant approval by the Rural Initiative, other members would then be added for a Bear's Bailey's Round Table to decide how funds would be disbursed in the best interests of the community. After the meeting was adjourned, Mr. Chapowits left in a hurry. All four women went about their tasks with an elevated sense of hope. Percy shadowed their activities in the office and with the co-op's customers, showing sincere admiration for their work. At the end of the busy day, Bear and Henry stood with the women at the front door. Henry yawned with a dramatic and drawn-out groan as Bear pawed the glass door.

"I've been meaning to apologize to you all day," Katie said, taking a deep breath in. "I jumped in without thinking. Like I always do."

"You were our heroine today. You saw an opening to speak for us all and took it," Mary said, smiling.

Katie shook her head. "This is *your* co-op. Yours and Bear's. I should have let you speak when you saw the best opportunity."

Years of memories with Katie swirled in Mary's mind. Small toddlers in each other's paddling pools, teenage sleepovers and drama, separation by life choices—both good and bad, and then the adventures bringing Bear Bailey's into a thriving center of Merivelle. Mary was near tears with the love she felt toward her one remaining relative still living in Merivelle. "I may have started Bear Bailey's, but you're our protector and champion. We're all behind you on this next stage of our journey together."

Good Place to Sleep

"What a difference a day makes, Henry."

The dog sat in the darkness of the entry of Katie's home, waiting for her to turn on the lights so he could see his way forward. His eyes, a milky hue from cataracts, allowed him only to see a few feet in front of where he stood. With nothing to illuminate his steps entering the house, he was nearly night blind and relied on his sense of smell and touch to guide him forward.

Katie put her keys in the bowl on the front entrance table and flipped on the lights, sighing as she dropped her bags to the floor. The house was empty and after the triumphant day handling Mr. Chapowits, her nervous system hadn't settled down.

"You've been wonderful company, Henry. Just what I've needed." Katie gave a tired smile to the dog. She took a few steps and grabbed for the television remote, turning the TV on to an old re-run and then hitting the mute button. "No words but it makes me feel less alone in my house."

The old dog watched a few moments of the TV show before quietly howling at the screen and trotting to the front door.

"You've done your business, good boy. Aren't you tired?"

The dog pawed at the door and whined.

She knelt to the dog's height and scratched the front of his chest. "Please don't want to go. It's so nice to have you here."

Whimpering, Henry's attention remained steadfast, his eyes darting back and forth between the world outside her house and Katie speaking to him encouragingly.

"How about a nice hamburger with a little bacon? It would do wonders getting rid of those ribs showing on you."

Henry grinned, his tongue pouring out from in between his missing teeth. He may never have had a long-term home but like all dogs, he understood the word *bacon*.

Charmed by the dog's reaction to her words, Katie searched over his body. "You've had a rough life, no doubt about it," she said, stroking his fur. "But you're impeccably clean. And you don't bark or whine to complain even when I can tell you might be in pain from old joints. Dignified, despite your circumstances, Henry. True nobility."

At her words, Henry held a paw out to Katie and sighed. His desire to leave had evaporated with the woman's gentle touch and kind words.

She took his paw. "You rest, and I'll get you some food. We'll both have the same dinner. How about that, handsome Henry?" She rose to go to the kitchen.

Henry jumped onto Katie's sofa—the one piece of furniture geared more to comfort than the style of the rest of the room. The blanket Katie had tucked him into earlier that morning as she readied for work was still on the cushions. He circled over it several times before groaning in contentment and lowering into the nest of fabric.

The scent of cooking meat soon filled the small home as Henry lifted his nose and sniffed, his stomach rumbling with anticipation. Katie opened the window over her sink, letting an evening breeze move through the house. It was still too chilly to reasonably do so, but it felt cozy to her, so she ignited the gas fireplace to add to the ambiance of evening.

"We need a little music."

Henry lifted his head in question.

"I like to listen the same way Mary and I did when we were kids. There's nothing better than music with a little crackle, Henry." She went to her record player, a birthday gift from the Bailey's, and pulled out an album she'd rummaged at the local antique store when she was alone one afternoon.

The dog lifted his head, unfailingly polite in his attention to Katie. Years of traveling alone had made Henry conscious of the yearning, no matter how faint, to connect outside of one's self once the comfort of solitary time had run its purpose. A need for a soul to come in from the cold of reclusive thoughts and join strangers in stories and food while traveling. *Campfire time*, he'd called it over the years. One of his favorite things in life.

"All right, it's cheesy but I love it, so bear with me as I present to you—*Camelot*! My mom played this when I was a girl." Holding out the album cover, she said, "I challenge you to find a better overture." Her eyes were weary, though her voice strained in excitement.

Henry began to scratch at his blanket as he tried to settle in again. But the lights, television, flickering fireplace flames, noise from dinner preparations and added loud music was an overload to his senses used to vast night skies and silence. He sighed heavily and whimpered.

"Do you not like all this fuss, Henry?" Katie came around the bar counter.

The dog looked up, panting as though he'd run several miles.

Katie's shoulders dropped. "I overdo it and get theatrical when I'm feeling alone. It's just when I was little, sometimes my mom would be especially happy and then she'd sing this soundtrack as loud as she could while she danced around the house." She thought for a moment and grimaced, shaking her head of the memories. "How about I just stop that nonsense right now, Henry? Someone with a lot of energy when you just want to be cared for can be—" She blew out a long breath. "—exhausting."

Not taking his gaze off of her as she spoke, Henry seemed to nod in agreement.

She shut off the muted television and lifted the needle off the record. "Can we still leave the fire on though? I still think it's nice for the two of us here in the quiet springtime, don't you?"

Henry gave a little bark.

"The quiet springtime," Katie said, repeating her words as she went to the front door and leaned her head against the doorjamb. Her cell phone rang from the kitchen counter.

The gentle breeze that had moved through the house since she opened a window morphed into a gust of strong wind, fanning the gas flames of the fireplace. Henry burrowed deeper into the sofa.

Answering her phone, Katie was mostly silent on the call, a look of puzzlement on her face as she listened to the voice on the other line. After a minute, she answered, "You can come over. We'd love some company." There was a pause as she smiled to herself before continuing. "We as in 'Henry.'" She listened again. "You aren't bothering me at all. I can even add a hamburger to be ready by the time you get here. Unless, Henry eats it first," she said, smiling in the direction of the sleeping dog.

OK, All Right

Walking up the sidewalk to Katie's house, a freshly showered Percy looked around the manicured yard. Observing him through the open door as he was lost in thought, Katie noticed Percy's eyes taking in everything around him, like he was joyfully learning in the classroom of a favorite and beloved teacher. He began to ring the bell and then stopped with his finger mid-air to turn to the sound of birds in the tree beside the entrance.

Katie went to the front door and opened it.

"Do you hear them?"

"Mourning Doves?" Katie asked, confused by his enthusiasm for the ever-present birds.

"Yes! A pair are nesting!"

"I try not to pay attention in the evenings. They always sound like they're grieving to me."

"Do you think so?"

Startled by the conversation below, one of the doves flew away leaving a trail of sound in its departure as it found a new perch higher in the branches of the old elm.

"*That* dove didn't sound sad," Katie conceded, her eyes following the bird's short flight path.

Percy's face lit with happiness at her observation. "It's because the dove didn't actually make that sound."

"I just heard it with my own ears."

As his expression grew in further bliss at the conversation, Percy said, "That's called a wing whistle. When the doves fly away, air rushes through the feathers on their wings causing a vibration that sounds almost like a kazoo."

The second bird followed a few moments after, leaving an empty nest of sticks and twigs blowing in the wind. With both birds gone, Percy shook his head. "You've graciously invited me into your home and I'm standing on the doorstep blurting out mindless bird information. Please forgive my blabbering."

"Think nothing of it. This house has seen worse than a someone sincerely marveling at ornithological information."

◈

"Dinner's ready."

Henry jumped off the sofa and trotted to the kitchen where Percy watched Katie preparing food.

Katie took two burger patties and cut them into bite-size pieces, placing them in a bowl. "He's missing so many teeth. A meat milkshake might have been a better option." She pulled a chair out as Henry approached the table, sniffing in curiosity.

"You feed him at the table?"

"I've never had a dog. Is that not how you do it?"

"Does Mary feed Bear at her table?"

"I thought she didn't because of his enormous size. Do all dogs eat from the floor? I wonder what else I don't know about dogs."

"Have you always had cats?"

"Why does everyone assume I had cats?"

Percy shrugged his shoulders. "Just a strong hunch, but apparently a wrong one."

Henry jumped onto the chair. Katie tied a tea towel around his neck. He carefully ate one piece at a time, before licking the dish clean. He belched in appreciation, directing a gaze toward the kitchen.

"Dessert?" Katie asked, removing an aerosol can of whipped cream from the refrigerator door. She shook it several times, popped the lid off and sprayed three swirls into the empty bowl.

With great appreciation, the dog licked the treat clean. The end of his nose was covered in white dairy fluff, which made Katie laugh like a delighted child. She put the nozzle right into Henry's mouth and gave him a few more zips of whipped cream.

Percy had a bemused look on his face.

"Was that wrong too? I remember that being fun when my dad did it for me when I was little."

"I think if you want to feed your new dog whipped cream at the table, then you absolutely should. As long as you're kind, there's no rules to how you handle Henry." He paused as the dog continue to lick the tip of the aerosol can like an anteater's tongue seeking tiny insects from a mound. "Although, I think I'll skip dessert," he said, laughing.

Katie wiped the top of the whipped cream canister with a paper towel, raising her eyebrows at Percy. "What about now?"

"Nope. Not even after you've wiped the nozzle clean."

"You sure are fussy."

"Yes, very much so. It's a definite calling card of mine."

"Truth be told," Katie said, raising her hand, "me too."

"No!" Percy said, acting aghast.

"It's been said a time or two." She shrugged. "Let me get some plates, and I'll make sure the edges of our food don't touch."

"You don't drink at all? Or just don't care for wine?"

"I hate the smell of any alcohol. It's a long story," Katie answered. "Mary knows and that's enough for me."

"Of course. No need to say anything else. I was just curious."

Henry sat between the pair on the sofa after dinner, enjoying alternating back rubs and scratches from each of them as they chatted away in easy conversation. His eyes were as heavy with sleep as his stomach was with food.

"You didn't have to cook for me," Percy said. "I only wanted to come by to let you know how bad I felt about today's events, but you took everything in stride."

"Small town living. I'm used to crazier things than Riven Chapowits strolling in trying to take control of things. The man's been at it since I was a child."

Percy's head turned in question.

"Why are you looking at me like that?"

"You're very forward and to the point in how you address things."

"Yes. Always. My best and worst quality." Katie absentmindedly stroked the back of Henry's back. The dog's sharp, bristled hair tickled her fingers as she moved her hands back and forth over his body, the texture of his fur comforting to her fingers.

"My parents were always strict with how I addressed them."

"And that has to do with me how?" She reached for a glass of water with her free hand and took a sip.

"Addressing your dad by his first name. You say his name more like he's a character in a book or movie." He made long two dashes in the air as he said in a theatrical way, "*Riven Chapowits.*"

Choking on her drink, Katie's eyes were wide. "I'm sorry—what?" she sputtered.

"Your dad. Riven."

"No. I can't tell you how very mistaken you are on that front." Katie shook as she began laughing. A full-on giggle-fest.

She slapped the sofa and wiped her eyes. "I can't wait to tell Mary you thought my name was really Katie Chapowits." She busted out laughing again.

Still serious, Percy said, "I know you're Katie Hatch."

"Then why do you think Mr. Chapowits is my father? Starting with the fact we have very different last names?"

"My parents are divorced. I have a different last name than my remarried mother," Percy said.

"But if he was my father, I'd always have his last name. Not my mother's." She turned her head to the side. "Is that right? I'm so confused on the subject." She wiped away tears of laughter before stopping. "Percy? I'm sorry. I missed a beat. Your parents aren't together?"

"Recently separated and divorced."

Noting the sadness in his eyes, Katie's face softened in expression. "I don't think I've met anyone whose parents split late in life."

He shrugged. "No childhood trauma but it definitely takes a while to get used to. They're finally cordial with one another. Which is one nice thing from the whole situation, I expect."

"What do you mean?"

"I hadn't realized how snippy they'd grown with one another over the years. I thought it was a family trait. The fussy and snippy Bournes." A sorrowful look shadowed his face for a brief moment. "The *fuppy* Bournes."

"You have a thing for portmanteaus, don't you?"

He was sheepish. "I know. I'm weird."

"I like marrying random words too. Things that shouldn't go together but somehow they work. A good portmanteau is sometimes better than the two words separately." She paused, before smiling. "Somehow being invited to brunch feels more fun than being invited simply for breakfast or lunch."

Percy's eyes again lit with interest. "You know, the original meaning of portmanteau had to do with—" He stopped and shook his head. "Wait. There I go again with ridiculous, nonsense facts."

Katie reached out to touch his arm in a gesture of solidarity. His sleeves were still rolled up at the cuffs from doing the dinner dishes for her. "Jabberwocky. Absolute jabberwocky, Percy Bourne."

At the sound of the word synonymous for *nonsense*, Percy was a wilted flower given warm spring rain. "You know Lewis Carrol's poem?"

"Portmanteaus—the blending of sounds and meanings of two different words. From the poem '*Jabberwocky*' in *Through the Looking Glass*." Her face was amused as she began to stroke Henry's back again.

Sitting up straight with the electricity of shared random knowledge, Percy added, "Portmanteau—from two French words meaning *to carry* and *to cloak*."

"I researched portmanteaus for the *Prairtisserie* trying to come up with a concept that would blend the Kansas prairie with a more sophisticated French patisserie bakery concept. Who else but the author of Alice in Wonderland could have used the term in literature to combine two words—"

"—when the original meaning of portmanteau was two traveling trunks combined into one luggage bag?" Percy interjected, slapping the sofa in triumph. He smiled broadly. "Do you generally sit and discuss things likes this with men?"

"I can assure you that you are the first and only. I can't think when I've spent any amount of time discussing word etymology."

"I get carried away with the smallest of encouragement." Percy sat at the edge of the sofa. "We did have fun tonight, didn't we?"

Henry opened his eyes and raised his head, as he waited for Katie's answer.

"We did." She smiled in sincerity, before sighing. "I look forward to a time when I only think of baggage as only a travel consideration."

No Use Going This Way

"Why did you tell Percy if you didn't want him or anyone else to know? I find that bit to be particularly of interest." Alicia was sitting on her yoga mat and stretching her legs as she spoke. "On some level, you must want it known. He's a complete stranger, and you told him something of a very personal and private nature."

"*I do not want it known!*"

The yoga studio was a large, unfurnished space which echoed with noise when it was filled with people during class. When Alicia gave private lessons, she dropped the decibel level of her voice, so it was more calming and serene to her students. The vibration of the singularly loud voice caused a bell suspended on a stand in front of her to ring slightly. She reached out to steady and quiet the object.

"I was out of line. I'm sorry."

Alicia observed her pupil who had been coming to after-hours classes several times a week, entering through the back-alley door so no one would see him.

"Now what? Have I ruined everything by yelling?"

"Remember the power of your breathing. Riven. Exhale—let it all go. Then inhale for four seconds. Hold four," she said, pausing before beginning again. "Exhale four. Take yourself through a few rounds while you get to a space of calm." Alicia's voice was barely above a whisper, but firm and strong.

Nodding, Riven closed his eyes and breathed as Alicia had instructed. "I'm ready," he said, opening his eyes. "Now tell me what the hell is going on with me. Now I'm shaking too."

"I suspect your heart is trying to help you better connect with the people important to you."

"I already have a plan," Riven said, tapping his right temple. "I found a way to be around her more at the co-op."

"The mind is smart, but the heart is wise."

"Must you always speak in such a confusing way?"

Alicia uncrossed her legs, switching out sides before returning to a lotus position. "And what way do I speak?" she asked, biting the inside of her lip to keep from smiling.

"With endless riddles. Just tell me why I blurted out my words? I've always had a handle on my life. Lately, I feel like a pig on ice."

"Sometimes the heart…"

"No yoga talk. Just tell me."

"Your body is tight and weak. You say you have no friends. And the heaviness of an old secret is your own to bear."

"Of course, it's mine to bear!" Riven snapped. "Who else is supposed to swoop in to help?"

Alicia appeared unaffected by the outburst. "We carry our own loads of personal responsibility. But we help each other with burdens—the unexpected or the stubbornly unresolved issues we face in life. You need friendship to help show you a path forward. Another perspective. Which may hold the very key you're seeking."

"What does that even mean?" Riven sat up and stretched his hips side to side.

Thinking for a moment while studying the man, Alicia said,

"There's a saying that's helpful when one begins a healing journey: *You're only as sick as the secrets you keep.*"

He pondered the floor, turning the phrase over in his mind a few times. "You can't go around always blabbering about your private life. People will think you're a looney toon."

"When you share information with an open heart and a sincere desire to be a better human, it's never *blabbering*. You've been alone for so long. Coming together with others might seem unsettling at first."

Riven clenched his fists at his sides. "Just tell me what I should do."

Alicia glanced at the clock behind her. Daylight hours were becoming longer each day but even so, the veil of evening was settling into Merivelle. The streetlights flickered on over the top of the partition that provided the lesson privacy.

"*Well?*"

Reaching for Riven's hands, Alicia pulled him forward in a stretch. "Speak from your heart. Without any victimhood." She began to gently extend each of Riven's fingers back from their clenched position. "And show who you are through your actions. I think you'll be pleasantly surprised how people respond."

The serene woman's touch, almost like a kind mother with a stubborn child, calmed Riven. He was quiet for a moment. "Do you really think people would still listen to what I have to say?" His face was soft and expectant as he waited for her answer.

Alicia patted his feet. The old man insisted on wearing socks every lesson even though she assured him each time, his balance might be better served without them. "How you are right now in this moment is an excellent way to behave with others in Merivelle."

He blinked a few times and shook his head. "I only care about fixing the one situation. Everything else is water under the bridge." He reached behind to push himself up before falling backward onto the yoga mat.

"I was merely trying to advise you on the wisdom of engaging other people with an open heart. Transparency will open many closed doors for you Riven." She extended her hand to help him off the ground.

He ignored the gesture and then paused. Taking a deep breath, he reached out for Alicia's hand, his head down as he rose to meet her.

"Better?" Her face was etched in slight amusement.

"I'd appreciate if you'd stop all the heart talk and just help my muscles feel better," he said, turning away and then looking back at her. "I'm only halfway kidding."

"I think you're not kidding at all. And that's fine. Honesty is the important thing."

"Again, with all the words," he said, shaking his head and reaching for his cowboy boots. He sat down on the bench at the back of the studio, looking almost remorseful. "I shouldn't give you such a hard time. Especially when you stay late on my account."

"Thank you, Riven. An empathetic step forward."

He stood and reached for his jacket hanging on the hook over the cubicles, draping it over his arm. "I overhear all the women in town going on about how much they love your classes."

They walked to the back door as Alicia turned off the lights, nodding in gratitude as Riven pushed the back door open for her to pass.

"Anyone fighting yoga as bad as I am?"

"I can't say who but there is one—" Her attention was interrupted by the sound of garbage cans toppling.

Riven's eyes searched the area behind The Hen's Nest. An old dog was standing on his back legs, his nose searching through the day's remnants of the restaurant as his front paws dug through the trash.

"The same dog again," Alicia whispered, closing the door and locking it.

Startled at the appearance of the pair, Henry dropped on all four feet, his head down as if he'd been caught in a crime. He lifted his eyes giving a mournful expression.

"Get out of the trash! I can smell you from here," Riven snapped, stomping his foot on the ground. "Shoo! Go home or I'll call the pound." A gust of wind blew down the quiet alley. Riven shivered as he put on his jacket.

Jumping in fear, the old dog began to run down in the opposite direction but stopped, hacking the food up he'd just managed to choke down.

"Probably full of worms and who knows what—"

"Riven! Stop! He's Katie's dog. He's been at Bear Bailey's."

"He's who?"

"Katie's dog—Henry. I wonder what he's doing downtown this evening," Alicia said. "He must be so used to searching for his food, he's doing it even though we both know Katie has probably fed him his own steak tonight." She took a few steps forward. "Don't be scared, Henry. We want to help you."

The dog bowed his head and tucked his tail between his back legs. A look of profound regret was on his face as he whimpered. He began trying to tidy up the debris he'd pulled from the trash can by pushing it back on the ground with his nose, then picking up a piece of trash with his mouth and dropping it back into the receptacle.

"Oh, my goodness," Alicia said, clutching her keys to her heart. "That poor dog."

Riven pulled his glasses out of his front jacket pocket and put them on so he could gaze at the dog. "Good evening, Henry. I didn't recognize you. I won't take you to the pound after all."

Alicia cleared her throat.

"What?" Riven asked, clearly perplexed. "I'm being nice to Katie's dog."

"Should it matter it's your daughter's dog before you're nice to a creature?"

A flicker of remorse shadowed the man's face before disappearing. "One thing at a time, Alicia." Approaching the dog in a gentle manner, Riven picked up all the remnants of trash, covering the can with the lid Henry had knocked to the ground. He pulled a bandana out from his back pant pocket and wiped his hands as he knelt to examine him, grimacing at the smell of trash on the dog. "Let's get you a nice bath, some warm food and a safe resting place tonight. What every wandering man—" He stopped before correcting himself. "What every wandering dog is looking for as they make their way home."

Nothing to be Gained

The following morning, Katie pushed through the co-op's front door as if she was missing a plane about ready to take off. Her eyes were swollen, and her cheeks flushed in patches. Mary jumped up from the table so fast her chair fell onto the concrete floor, sending a loud echo throughout the store. At the sound, Bear startled from his laying position and got straight up onto his feet, running after Mary. Percy was at the co-op center table and followed.

"Henry! I can't find Henry. I let him out when we got home last night, and he disappeared. I can't find him."

Bear began to whimper, taking a paw and gently tapping at Katie's knee.

"Thanks, Bear," she whispered as she patted his head. "Do you know where Henry's at?"

Upon her words, Bear went to the front of the co-op windows and stared in each direction before his tail began to wag. He barked, turning his head back and forth between Mary, Katie, Percy and outside the window as he jumped up and down in excitement.

"We'll find him, Katie," Percy said, his voice low and kind.

"Don't worry. I'll walk the streets of Merivelle to bring him back to you."

Frustrated at the humans for not taking his cue, the Great Pyrenees stood on his hind legs and placed his front paws on the chrome push bar of the door. His tail wagged furiously as he licked the glass door. Riven met his gaze as he approached the door from the other side and tried to open it.

"Bear! No!" Mary rushed to intercede between her dog and his longtime foe. She placed herself in the middle of the threshold between the pair holding up one of her legs to keep Bear back and away from the old man.

"It's okay, Mary. I love all dogs," Riven replied, grabbing the door from her and smiling as he let himself and Henry in. "Your wonderful dog won't harm me."

Bear dropped to the ground as Mary seemed thunderstruck.

"I have a sparkling clean dog that I believe belongs to someone here." He handed the end of a makeshift leash to Katie.

"Henry!" She was crying and laughing in equal measure. "Where have you been all night? I searched everywhere!"

"I happened across him last night after an appointment. I thought I would bring him with me this morning."

Katie knelt to Henry and kissed every square inch of his head.

"I had to use an old tie for a leash." Riven turned with a hopeful look. "Have you ever thought about a stall in your co-op to stock dog supplies, Mary?"

Mary's eyes went to Bear as her face lit up for a moment considering Riven's words.

"I think there might be a real need in Merivelle for quality collars and leashes. And possibly a whole line of dog products for that matter. You could sell on the internet something of a Bear Bailey's brand—"

"Where exactly did you find Henry?" Katie interrupted, a storm brewing with her countenance.

"*Where?*" Riven practically croaked, withering under Katie's glare.

Standing up and placing her hands on her hips, the makeshift leash still in one of her hands, Katie said, "Yes. Where? Exactly how did you come to be in possession of Henry?"

"The old boy was walking downtown last night."

Katie took two steps toward Riven, eyeing him with suspicion. "Why do you seem all twitchy?"

Acting as if he hadn't heard Katie's question, Riven stammered, "So I… put him in my truck and thought I'd… just bring him to you. This morning."

Katie eyeballs practically bulged out of her head. "You did what?"

"I don't understand what you don't understand about me picking Henry up to keep until I saw you this morning. I thought it would please you."

"He's *my* dog." Katie pulled the tie from around Henry's neck and extended it to Riven.

Dumbstruck, Riven froze.

She dropped the tie on the ground. "Just leave Henry alone. He doesn't need your sudden interest in him."

◈

The two dogs met under the table in conversation.

"You spent the night at Mr. Chapowits's house last night?" Bear asked once Katie had gone to the bathroom to splash cold water on her face and collect herself.

"He's an interesting fellow," Henry replied, his eyes closed.

"I pictured winged monkeys—no wait make that winged coyotes—to do his dirty work." Bear shuddered and whimpered. Mary reached down to pat his head.

"You have a very active imagination for a dog."

"That's what I've been told," He yawned, letting out a tiny yelp as he did so. "I can't seem to help it sometimes."

"You nervous?"

"Yeah, I'm weird. I always yawn when I'm worried."

"All dogs yawn when they're nervous, Bear."

Katie came back to the table and scooted in, her ankles near Henry's face.

"Oh, I thought it was only me." Bear scrunched his eyes together in thought. He turned to Henry. "What were we talking about again?"

Henry opened one eye. "Riven."

"We call him Mr. Chapowits in Merivelle."

"I call you Bear, not the Bailey dog. You call Mary by her first name too."

"But we love one another. And take care of each other." Bear began to pant. "That man was going to have me killed at the pound."

Henry opened the other eye and stared. "When was this, Bear?"

The Pyr thought a moment. When Jiff had arrived from the Rainbow Bridge and showed him what everyone's life would have been like without Bear's presence, one of the scenes was of Mr. Chapowits taking Bear to the local pound and trying to bribe an employee for his immediate euthanasia. Bear began yawning again. This time a long and vocal sounding one. "I don't even want to say it out loud but my friend Jiff showed me. Mr. Chapowits is a very bad coyote. Trust me."

"Coyotes can be tamed. I have a little bit in me," Henry said, closing his eyes again.

"I don't have a speck of coyote in me," Bear said, stubbornly. He sat up in a resolutely, hitting his head on the table before lowering back down on the floor.

"Sure, you do. All dogs have a bit of wild dog in them. Down the line someone thought to bring us in from the cold to feed by the fire. We joined humans' tribes. And over time, our species stopped behaving only like scavenging coyotes or dangerous wolves and instead began to behave like beloved pets who guard and love the people who domesticated them."

"You don't talk much but when you do, I learn a lot." Bear thought for a few moments. "How do you know all of those words?"

"I don't know how I know. I just know."

"Jiff and I used to say that to one another all the time!" Bear said, wagging his tail joyfully as it thwapped the cement floor.

"To you, Mr. Chapowits is an old, wily coyote."

"He's bad news," Bear said, growling. "The worst thing is he made Mary cry. Very, very hard. She almost lost the co-op." The sound of the Great Pyrenees growling caused the humans at the table to pause in their discussion. "If he'd been a coyote, I'd have taken him out." He stifled a howl as Henry jumped.

"He's all right," Mary said, above at the table. "Bear dreams a lot. He's imagining taking care of coyotes, I'm sure." There was laughter at her words before the table returned to conversation.

Henry sighed. "You feel strongly about Riven. I don't have a history with him. Let me see what I can work out for him and Katie." The old dog licked his mouth several times, and then closed his eyes as he coughed and dry heaved loudly. "I think the rest might iron itself out easier once that's settled."

"What does Mr. Chapowits have to do with Katie?" Bear asked.

"More than you know."

Telephone Available

"When are you going to move away from Merivelle? I keep saying a bright and clever woman like you belongs in a big city. You wouldn't believe how wonderful your life would be, Katherine."

"Mom! That's not my name. It's not even on my birth certificate."

"It fits you more than Katie. I was a childish girl to pick that name out for you. But it doesn't matter—I can still call you the grander version of your name."

"Please don't. It's weird."

A long pause was followed by a sigh on the other end of the line.

"Mom? What is it?"

"Nothing. Just thinking."

"About what?"

"How I should have put you in the car with me the day after you graduated high school and driven you halfway across the country away from Merivelle. With your hard work ethic, business acumen and good looks, you could really be something away from that little town."

"Julia, calm down."

"Do not call me by my first name, Katherine."

"Then stop calling me Katherine, *Julia*." Katie leaned onto her kitchen counter, balancing her elbows on the granite as she stared out to the front yard, rolling her eyes to Henry.

"Why do we do this when we talk to each other?"

Katie watched Henry sunbathing in the early morning light. She'd begun leaving the front door open for him to get the most amount of warmth and light; the dog seemed perpetually cold and shaking. "Do what?"

"We bicker and fight over what? Nothing. We can show we love one another with better ways, Kath… Katie."

She and Henry sighed in unison. "You're right, *Mom*."

There was silence for a few moments. "We don't spend enough time together. We need some dedicated time polishing our relationship. Maybe I should come see you."

Katie walked to the front door. She was surprised how many people were out and about walking at the early hour. "Do *not* come to Merivelle."

"Why?"

"You get so weird here."

"What are you talking about?"

"You're so *odd* here." Katie waved to a woman pushing a stroller who had started to come into Bear Bailey's mid-afternoons to tire her toddler. "I prefer to visit you in Cincinnati. You're a better version of you there." She yawned. Just the thought of a visit from her mom exhausted her.

"I wish I could tell you more. But with a wedge already between us, I worry if I'm honest when I'm with you, it will get even worse."

Katie pulled the phone from her ear. *What is she talking about?* she mouthed to herself.

"I don't even see you for holidays as it is," Julia said.

"Here we go with the guilt."

Her mom either didn't hear her or chose to continue on anyway. "You're my only child, and I should get to see you at Christmas, at least."

"You know I've been helping Mary with Bear Bailey's, and the past few holiday seasons have been key in getting it on its feet."

"Mary's dog store should not trump seeing me at Christmas!"

"I've told you a hundred times, Bear Bailey's is a co-op that helps the community sell their goods so the evil and mean ogre, Mr. Chapowits lessens his grip on Merivelle, and the villagers can live in peace and prosperity." Katie's voice was dramatic, as if she were narrating a movie trailer.

Julia cleared her throat. "Are you done, Katie?"

"I think so."

"Good. I know what Bear Bailey's is. You tell me about it all the time. And I don't care. It anchors you in a place you should have left years ago."

Katie shook her head the entire time her mother was speaking. "I will not leave Merivelle."

"Is Mary behind this? Is she keeping you too busy?"

"Stop trying to put your issues with Aunt Margaret onto me and Mary. She's the sister I never had, and I won't let you come between us."

"You don't understand about Margaret."

"Let's give her a break."

"Why? Why does everyone always side with Margaret?"

"Mom! Aunt Margaret's dead!"

Julia sucked in air like she'd been plunged into cold water. "Really, Katie. There's no need for shocking speech. You don't have to say it like that."

"Apparently I do. You stayed away from her funeral and let Mary stand at the grave alone."

"Mary had you. And her husband."

"She needed her mother's sister to share the grief." Katie

gestured as if Julia was in the room. "Someone older than Theodore and me who could give her a sense of family continuity. You know it's really very nice when the people older than you act that way. It's exhausting trying to take care of a parent."

"We're just having a conversation, Katie."

"Yeah, well—"

"Back to the original subject." Julia cleared her throat again. "Why all the love for Mary? You barely call me, but your cousin who was your frenemy growing up—"

"Who could have been my friend if you hadn't stirred things up against her like you were trying to even the score somehow with Aunt Margaret."

"It just doesn't make any sense. What happened?"

Katie glanced at her watch. Her mom had no job and could talk all day, repeating the same point to infinity if Katie let her. "I keep telling you—Bear Bailey's."

"The dog? *Again*?"

"Mary and I worked together to bring our community together. And now, we even have the possibility of revitalizing Main Street with new shops that provide goods and services that could find their place anywhere in a big city, while giving a fresh facelift to the existing ones—both can work together for the good of all. Small towns have the most remarkable, ingenious people. They only need a forum to showcase their skills. So, there's no need for them to move away to find employment."

"Rural flight is a big concern to small towns."

"You know what that is?" Katie blinked in surprise.

"Of course, I know what rural flight is. I'm a bird who's done it myself. Urbanization wrapped up with a metaphor. Migration paths to bigger cities with more social, educational and financial opportunities. You have an enormous boulder to push uphill trying to solve that issue."

"We're starting small and trying a first step. We've assembled an initial Bear Bailey's Round Table Committee. We hope as we progress, other people are also excited with the possibilities for Merivelle and they'll want to join in. Mary and I are over the moon with all we can accomplish in the future."

Julia began making loud kissing noises.

Grimacing, Katie put her phone on speaker. "Are you talking to those birds while I'm pouring my heart out to you?"

"Sonny and Cher can feel when I'm upset. I'm trying to calm them down so I can listen to you in a more effective and supportive way." Julia clicked her tongue twice more and whispered, "Pretty birds. Pretty. Pretty."

Henry raised his head in question while Katie wound her forefinger around her ear. "So, if the ridiculous parakeets are settled, Julia, I can finish by telling you how Bear Bailey's has changed everyone. Even Mr. Chapowits. The co-op is more impactful than you can imagine."

The sound of sudden commotion on the other end disconnected the call. Katie shook her head as she held the phone in her hand and waited. After a few moments, the words, *The Mother* moved across her phone screen which was a picture of Julia with a parakeet on each shoulder while a ringtone clip played the beginning movements of *Dance of the Knights* from the ballet *Romeo and Juliet*.

"What do you mean by that, sweetheart?" Julia's voice was elevated.

"Where did we leave off?" Katie asked with a sly smile on her face. "I think I was telling you about how impactful Bear Bailey's is in the life of Merivellians."

"No, not that."

"You're exasperating. That's all I was talking about. You kept asking what brought Mary and I together."

"You said Mr.—" Julia stopped. "You were talking about *him*."

"What?" Katie forehead creased as she replayed her last words before her face relaxed in remembering. "Once again, you weren't listening. That wasn't the main point. I'm spending time with Riven at co-op meetings. No big deal."

"You call him Riven?" Her mom's voice was nearly a shriek.

Feeling a small thrill that, though she hadn't consciously tried to ruffle her mother's feathers, she had—in what felt like a big way. Katie smiled to herself. Anything to keep her mother's mind off the ridiculous birds. "Someone else also thought it was odd I called him by his first name."

"Where's Cybil? Is she on the doggie committee?"

Katie grimaced.

"And why doesn't she like you calling Chapowits *Riven*?"

"What? No. It wasn't her. It was Percy."

"Who's Percy?"

"Our Rural Initiative representative. He's here evaluating Bear Bailey's and our grant proposal." Her mom's questions were making her feel pecked. "I've got to go before I'm late," Katie said, rubbing Henry's fur, warm from laying in the sunlight.

"Wait, why would a random representative care if you call Riven by his first name?"

"It doesn't matter. Why are we on a wild conversation goose chase on this issue?" Katie muttered to herself.

"Why did he mention it?"

"Percy said it seemed disrespectful."

"Oh, a brownnoser. *Suck up to the jackass with all the money* sort of guy." Julia took a deep breath and resumed bird kissing noises.

"He said it seemed disrespectful to call my father by his first name."

On the other end of the line was the sound of parakeets screeching and flapping their wings. The noise of their cage toppling to the ground followed.

A smile returned to Katie's face before her mom's next words.

"I'll be in Merivelle for Easter."

Doctor Here

After daylight savings time, when the clocks jumped forward in the spring, the golden evening light extended itself by minutes each day. Which afforded everyone more time for outdoor activities. Across a great deal of the town, the giant field lights of Merivelle's softball complex could be seen in the distance as leagues began to practice for upcoming games. On a quiet evening, with a breeze blowing into town, the impact of aluminum bats hitting softballs could be heard by people sitting on their front porches. The metallic *ting* was a reassuring sign of the warmth of summer soon to come. And though dry from lack of rain, many Merivellians drove across the bridge at the edge of town, bringing blankets and food to sit in front of campfires on the Arkansas River's sandy banks, lingering well past sunset. Once Katie had revealed her love of fishing, Cybil asked to join her, and the pair were frequently found at the Round Pond to soak up the last light of the day.

"Your mom called me last night, Katie."

"Now what?"

"The same. How she wants you to move near her," Cybil answered. "Or really anywhere but Merivelle."

Ignoring the perpetual advice her mother hammered down on every phone call, Katie changed the subject. "Have you ever thought about why this pond is named what it is?"

Cybil focused on her bobber under the surface of the water. Her face lit in happiness before it sprang up again. "Damn turtles," she whispered under her breath.

"I mean, how much imagination was put into the name of this small body of water?"

Cybil nodded somewhat in agreement, reeling in her line to replace the worm the turtles had just taken.

"Round Pond. Seriously. Round Pond. You couldn't get away with anything like that with another point of interest," Katie said, her cadence and breathing rapid. Henry was lying beside her feet, head on the ground, moving his eyebrows back and forth as she spoke.

"Maybe long ago, someone from Merivelle had visited the Round Pond in London and came home with the name in their head and bequeathed it to this small but worthy body of water."

"There's a Round Pond in England?"

"In Kensington. A rather beautiful one," Cybil answered. "Honey and I visited it on a trip. She sketched and painted the area almost every day. Some of my happiest memories."

"What about other examples? Like Long River. You never hear of a Long River. Rivers have actual names. The Mississippi or Missouri Rivers, but never a Long River."

Cybil had a worm in one hand and the hook attached to her line in the other. "Actually, there is a Long River."

"Where?"

"In China." Cybil threw her line back out again. "The third largest river in the world, I believe."

"You're making that up," Katie said, before looking down at Henry. She'd wrapped a scarf around his neck to keep him comfortable when the sunset ushered away the warmth of the day's light. "Cybil has made the whole Long River thing up, Henry."

"Honey and I were in Hong Kong on a different summer vacation and didn't see it with our own eyes, but I can assure you—Yangtze River, translated as Long River, flows through China."

"Well, fine. But still, nothing like, like… *Big Glacier*. That would be silly. Like the name of our Round Pond."

Cybil bounced her line in the water, and then reeled in a bit of the slack. "There is a Big Glacier."

"Where? What far-off province has named a large chunk of ice named Big Glacier?"

"The country you're standing in right now."

"The United States has glaciers?" Katie asked, her face sincere.

"Yes, lots of glaciers. Malaspina Glacier or translated, Big Glacier, is in Alaska."

"How am I supposed to know the name of the *one* glacier in the *one*, far-flung state in America that has glaciers?"

Cybil cleared her throat. "There's also glaciers in Oregon, Washington, California, Nevada, Idaho, Montana, Wyoming and one of our neighboring states."

Katie lifted one eyebrow in question. "Where?"

"Colorado."

"Really?" Katie lowered her fishing pole. "There's glaciers that close to Kansas?"

"It's not surprising if you remember that near Leavenworth there's a Glacier Hills Scenic Byway where the landscapes were formed by ancient receding ice. A young adventurer named Amelia Earhart probably gallivanted through the same region's hills when she was growing up near Atchison."

"Round Pond, Long River and Big Glacier," Katie said,

repeating the words in a disheartened tone. Her eyes were unfocused on the water as she spoke.

"Sometimes the best way is just to call things what they are. Once you know the proper name of something or someone, you can begin to understand how it relates to you."

Katie lowered her chin. "How did I not know all of that, Ms. Barnes?"

"You're very smart on other subjects. You can't know everything about everything." Cybil's bobber went below the surface and her pole bowed to signal a fish on the end of the line. She began reeling it in as she spoke. "It's good to be curious about the world around you. But perhaps right now, you should focus on knowing everything about yourself. The rest will fill in when needed."

The women were silent as Cybil pulled in her fish, examined it for size, before throwing it back in the water. The sun began to set as the dust of the region combined with the evening's last light, firing up the vast expanse in vivid shades of orange, red and pink, and swirling deep violet hues giving a hint of the nighttime soon to envelop the sky.

The hair on Katie's arms stood up. "What do you mean I should *know everything about myself*?"

Cybil baited her hook again and threw her line into the water as the worm simultaneously departed from the hook in a flying acrobatic gesture. Reeling in her line and cursing the empty end of it under her breath, Cybil pulled a small pair of needle-nosed pliers out of her back pant pocket and clipped the hook off her line. "From my own experience and watching quite a few other young folks around here grow into adulthood, your age is around the time a person starts asking questions."

"About what?"

"The good ones. The questions that allow you to know yourself. What you truly love. How you've got where you are so far.

Where you're headed with your precious time here on this beautiful planet. Good, deep questions about what resides within." Cybil had attached another weight and a jig to the end of her line and cast it back into the water.

"Tell me again how we got on the subject of glaciers?"

"I believe I was telling you that your mother called me last night," Cybil said, her eyes dancing in amusement.

"Before or after she and I spoke on the phone, I wonder."

"She'll have to clue you in, my dear."

Katie watched Cybil in the twilight. *Better than family*, Franklin used to say when he was alive and she and Mary visited him. She smiled at the remembrance of his words she then connected to her old teacher at her side, like the silken string of a flying cobweb come to rest. Cybil was better than family. In the last light of the day, while Cybil was working with her skilled and aging hands, Katie felt great love wash over her. "Everyone goes to you with their troubles, don't they?"

"I don't know about everyone," Cybil said, "but since Bear Bailey's, I've felt more a part of this community. It makes me feel purposeful to be graciously included in so many people's lives. It's why I got into teaching in the first place, and I've missed this element in my life since I retired. Without the store, I'm afraid I'd have been a recluse, hoarding art until I could barely walk through my own house. The loss of Honey would have pulled me under completely." She shivered in the evening breeze. Shaking her head to shoo the images away, she said, "My third act could have been much different without the relationships from the co-op." A quick burst of light from the setting sun illuminated Cybil's face.

"I hope you know what a treasure you are to all of us. Merivelle wouldn't be the same without you." Katie paused for a moment, sensing Cybil's melancholy. "You're the wise mentor we all need and love. Yoda, Dumbledore and Glenda all wrapped in one. Our own *Yumbledora*."

Cybil laughed. "Thank you. I'll just stick with Ms. Barnes, if you're choosing nicknames."

Henry put his head up, giving a raspy bark, his tail wagging like a happy pendulum.

Holding onto her pole, Katie sat beside the dog and then cradled his head in her lap. "So, let's hear it. What did my mom say to you on the phone?"

"The usual I hear from Julia. How much she misses you. How she'd love it if you came to live with her."

Katie snorted. "I will *never* live with my mother."

"You know what I mean. The same town."

"There is no municipality big enough for me, my mother and Sonny and Cher."

"Sonny and Cher?" Cybil asked, before recognition registered on her face. "Ah. The parakeets."

"Yes, apparently, my younger brother and sister."

"Please don't say that," Cybil replied, laughing and swatting in Katie's direction. "It's crazy talk. Funny, but complete nonsense."

"Tell that to my mom so she'll stop. She'd listen to you."

"Julia actually says those birds are your siblings?"

"I mean, obviously not birthed siblings, but chosen siblings. By her."

"Good heavens." Cybil shook her head. The two of them laughed together for a moment while Henry panted, showing his gap-toothed smile. "I've known Julia for decades. Give her some space to speak to you from her heart. She'll come around after she feels seen and heard. I think you're at a point in your life, you need to hear what she wants to say to you. Give her awkward overtures some grace. Try and be open to what you can learn from her."

Katie turned away from the pond for a moment. The colors

of the setting sun shifted like the turn of a vast atmospheric kaleidoscope, the same hues then beginning to slowly drain from the sky, second by second. A soft breeze blew over the water, moving both women's fishing lines. "My mom makes everything messy."

"Perhaps it's why you put everything in order. You're meticulous in almost every aspect of your life."

"I'm no more orderly than anyone else," she said, holding a hand to shade her eyes so she could see Cybil as the sun set behind the older woman.

"Look at all the Bear Bailey's grant paperwork you plowed through for months. How many people would have had the patience to take something like that on? Even when I was teaching, you were meticulous."

"You were my industrial arts teacher. Not much paperwork included in the course." Katie scratched behind Henry's ears. "And besides, you think anything I do is inspired."

"I substituted enough hours in other classrooms to know the impeccable schoolwork you produced. Your cheerleading, prom queen sashes and crowns were not the best things about you. You have incredible talents in almost every area." She paused and winked. "Except glacier geography."

Katie bowed her head slightly and smiled. "You haven't been my teacher for years, and yet here you are out here in the early spring evening air, still trying to help me."

"What can I say? I love to fish." Her expression softened. "And I do love to spend time with all you crazy kids that Honey and I had the pleasure of teaching."

"And Henry Hughes and I love spending time with you." The dog barked at the sound of his name. "How else are we going to know about the Guanxi Province?"

Turning from the last light of the day, Cybil said, "You might check me out on that one. Just going by memory." She winced and tapped her left temple. "I'm starting to see little cracks in it. Nothing serious yet. It just seems I'm perpetually looking for my keys."

"I'm sure you're spot on. You know everything." Katie stopped. "Is an iceberg the same thing as a glacier?" She chewed on the inside of her lip for a moment. "I'm embarrassed that I can't quite remember."

Cybil eyes widened ever so slightly. "An iceberg is a piece of a glacier that has broken off and sets off on the ocean currents on its own. The process is called 'calving.'"

Henry had been laying at Katie's feet, listening to the women speak. The sound of human voices had lulled him in and out of sleep but suddenly he felt electricity fill his body and he sat up, sniffing the air. The earlier, gentle breeze gave way to a sharp burst of wind as both women ducked their heads. Katie held up the crook of her arm to cover her eyes from blowing sand. Henry was halfway around the pond, looking over his shoulder to see how far behind Katie was following.

"Funny how we're here in Merivelle on the sandbank of an old muddy fishing hole, talking about icebergs on the move in the ocean," Katie said, reeling in her line for the last time that evening.

Two Women

"Why do I have the sense on our walks that you're going to bolt from us any second?"

"An old habit," Henry said. "I never want to be a bother. Or ruin it for the next dog wandering into town needing help."

"Katie loves sharing her home with you. You'll break her heart if you leave." The pair of dogs were following Katie and Mary as they walked in the morning before heading into town to the co-op. The sun began pushing onto the horizon and Bear remembered his old friend, Franklin. The gentle man lived each day as if it were his last, searching for small miracles in which to give thanks. The sunrise was particularly one of Franklin's favorite times of day. Sometimes Bear couldn't believe how much he missed Jiff's owner.

"Are you okay?" Henry asked. "You smell like rain."

"Just remembering an old friend and the miracles he loved."

Henry didn't respond, instead he put his head down and walked forward, not unlike a donkey pulling a heavy plow.

Bear trotted beside Henry's slow pace with ease. "You should have known my friend, Franklin. He would have loved you."

The old dog was touched at Bear's words. "My life has had its perks too. Lots of freedom, doing whatever I wanted. Sometimes when the trash cans were dry, or the wind turned bitterly cold, a kindhearted human would offer me food and shelter at the perfect time."

"People helped you out?" Bear asked, his voice full of hope. His face was sincere with concern. "That's wonderful."

"Sometimes. Most people get a little scared around a homeless dog. But I had tricks to show I meant no harm. I'd chuck a dummy, so they weren't scared of me."

"Chuck a what?" Bear pulled his ears back in confusion.

"*Chuck a dummy,*" Henry repeated. "It means when you pretend to faint. The older I got sometimes it happened without me trying. But before that, I only wanted to show I wasn't dangerous—I only needed a little food to get me back on the road again."

"But look how good you have it now." Bear's tail wagged like a big, furry windshield wiper. "You couldn't be further from having to beg for food. Katie's spoiling you rotten."

"You mean dressing me up like a middle-aged man every day?" Henry asked, looking over at Bear with droopy eyes. "I had a vest on yesterday. *With* a pocket square."

Bear began laughing, his eyes lighting up. "I don't know what was funnier, the vest or the look on your face from wearing the vest."

"Katie tried to put a hat on me too. I used your tip and growled like I was going to chew it and she took it away." Henry paused and took a deep breath.

Bear stopped, careful not to rush the dog and further labor his breathing. Once they were walking again, he said, "You always seem so tired when you're at the co-op. Like you can barely get up. And you drink so much water."

"Old bones, Bear. Old bones," Henry said, shaking his head. "When I was younger, I was a much more muscled dog.

Sometimes, people thought I was a Boxer." He held his chin up with an expression of pride lighting his eyes. "But those days are long gone. I look like a shabby old specimen now."

"That's not true. We're out here on a walk with Mary and Katie, and you bounce up and down like you're a few years younger than when you're at the co-op."

"I already told you I feel most alive out on the open road." Henry stopped and began hacking, wheezing for several moments as he tried to catch his breath. "Mostly, I just feel I need to disappear before I start to be a problem."

A few feet ahead, Katie jogged back to the pair of dogs. "What's wrong, King Henry?" she asked, leaning down. "Are you hurt?" She searched him over and finding nothing, began to lift each of Henry's paws, kissing each one after examination. She brushed her hands over his coat, kissed the top of his head and then continued talking to Mary.

"The fussiest woman I've ever met just kissed your feet, Henry. You can't leave her. Mary would walk on fire for me, but she's never kissed the bottom of my paws." Bear stopped and thought for a moment. "Maybe when I was a pup. She was pretty silly about me when I first arrived." A rush of love for Mary swept over Bear. He wanted to run to her side and jump up to put his arms around her and lick her face, though she always laughed and told him it was bad manners. He could tell she never really meant the words. He began barking with great joy.

"What is wrong with these dogs today?" Mary said, turning around. "Are we going too fast?" The women stopped as the dogs caught up with them. She knelt to Bear and buried her face in his fur.

Bear closed his eyes, relishing the attention from his favorite person in the whole world. He nuzzled his snout into the side of Mary's face and smiled at the other dog. "You don't want to ever be far from this feeling, Henry. You could travel the whole world and not be happier than with a kindhearted woman."

"How old is Bear now?" Katie asked.

He was literally drooling in glee.

"Five and a half years old. This October he'll be six. I don't know the exact date, so we make Bear's birth date the day after our anniversary so he's part of our celebratory week."

Bear leaned into Mary as she spoke, loving the softness of her voice when she spoke his name.

"You know, before Henry, I thought you were a little over the top with Bear," Katie said. "Correction—I was sure you'd lost your mind."

Mary's face not at all surprised nor offended. "I remember quite clearly all the mocking comments."

"I thought naming a co-op after a dog was a bit mad. I wondered if because you didn't have children, you went a bit over the top. Or maybe you really missed your mom after she was gone."

Mary stood up, petting Bear's head as she did so. "And now?"

"I understand your love for Bear because that's how I feel about Henry." Katie's face was tender with affection. "He's nothing like a dog I imagined for myself. Truth be told, I always saw myself with a fluffy white cat if I ever got a pet."

Cat? Bear mouthed the word and shook his head at Henry.

"But now with Henry in my life, sitting with me in the evenings, sighing when I sigh, leaning into me when I need it most and a hundred other little things he does that makes me not feel alone, I'd pick him if given the choice of every dog in the entire world."

"Well, then. True love," Mary said, smiling. "What a treasure of a dog you have in Henry. And out of nowhere."

"You mean how he was trotting down the street nonchalant after the worst yoga session on record?"

"I can't believe I haven't told you something."

"About Henry?"

Mary shook her head. Her face was clearly delighted at what she was about to say.

"Why do you look like the cat that ate the canary?" Katie asked.

Bear moaned in an exaggerated way. "What's with all the cat references this morning?"

The women were standing in the middle of a rural road, the sun rising in the east, beginning to fully light the landscape for the day. "You know how we've taken an oath not to ever talk about anyone behind their back?"

"Wait, we have?"

Mary shook her head. "You know what I mean, not a hand-on-a-Bible-in-court kind of thing, but as our general co-op community value system."

"Yes. We only talk good things behind each other's back."

"Precisely," Mary replied. "But do you think out here in the middle of nowhere I could tell you a small snippet of information?"

"Let's call a cousin loophole of some sort," Katie said, playfully solemn.

"Only between us," Mary admonished. "I'm not even going to tell Theodore."

"You're not?"

"The breakfast crowd at The Hen's Nest sometimes gets my darling husband carried away."

"Theodore's a small-town gossip?" Katie laughed. "Big city attorney Theodore Bailey?"

"The one and only," Mary answered. "He good-naturedly loves all their stories, and I don't want him to forget and mention this."

"Stop stalling."

Reflecting Mary's excitement, Bear began panting with his

trademark Great Pyrenees grin. Henry was as blasé as if they were considering a bug on a twig.

"Mr. Chapowits takes yoga lessons!"

"*Our* Mr. Chapowits?"

"I wouldn't call him *our Mr. Chapowits*. But yes—the one and only Mr. Chapowits with whom we are both acquainted."

"There's something I would have lost a large amount of money betting against." Katie pulled a leaf off a tall wildflower growing next to the road.

"I saw him in the alley behind Alicia's studio."

"That's doesn't mean anything."

"He was carrying a yoga mat."

"Why do we care if Mr. Chapowits is taking yoga classes?" Katie said. The women began to walk again, the dogs at their sides instead of following them.

"I know it's silly after all he's done put us through, but somehow this man approaching his seventies and trying something new to better himself kind of softens my heart toward him," Mary said. "He actually seems to listen to other people at our meetings."

Bear growled. "She still needs to be on guard with Chapowits."

"You might change your mind one day," Henry said, turning his head and nodding knowingly. "People will often surprise you if given a chance."

"How can you say that when you told me some of the horrible things people did to you when you were a pup? You were abandoned more than once," Bear whined.

"I'm still here though, friend."

"This is for the people who weren't good to you." Bear said, growling in a menacing way. "*And* a little for Mr. Chapowits." He bared his teeth in a menacing way.

"Are you done, Bear?"

The Great Pyrenees dropped all signs of aggression and began panting as he grinned. "I just want you to know, I'll always have your back and protect you, friend."

"Do you ever get the impression these dogs understand what we're talking about?" Katie asked, looking between Bear and Henry.

"Oh, yes. Of course, they do. Bear comprehends almost everything. I'm very careful what I do and say when I'm around him," Mary said. "He reflects everything about my personality and what I'm saying."

"How's that?" Katie asked.

"She's going to tell Katie about Mr. Chapowits," Bear explained. "But first she'll start with something that's the complete opposite. Maybe something sweet and cuddly. Listen," he said, knowingly.

"I love little things. When Bear finds an abandoned rabbit's nest on our property, maybe coyotes got the mother, he brings me bunnies in the gentlest way. Conversely, when I wanted to strangle Mr. Chapowits, Bear wanted to attack him. Therefore, I am very, very careful with any anger. I'd rather be amused and somewhat admiring of him trying yoga poses as I sit across from him at the co-op. In no way will I ever jeopardize my beloved dog by being angry and provoking Bear to bite a man who might put him down."

"He would definitely put me down, Henry." Bear nodded solemnly. "Mr. Chapowits would flip a switch in an instant."

"I don't think it's true anymore," Henry said. "He gave me a bath. And put me in his robe to dry. Then he grilled me the biggest steak I've ever seen. Cut it up into pieces smaller than Katie does and told me I was a handsome dog. Even with my teeth missing."

"*He what?*" Bear asked, running into the back of Mary's legs.

"He's good at pep talks. Told me to keep my chin up. That

there was nothing wrong with being a wandering dog. Some of the best people he knew liked to keep moving."

"I truly have no words."

"And to top it off, he insisted I slept on the foot of his bed. It was like sleeping on a cloud."

Bear dropped his head forward and let his jaw dangle in shock.

"Can I tell you something?" Katie paused as a vehicle approached.

Mary noticed her cousin's face was much more serious than casual conversation. She nodded. "Hang on. Let's chat with Clint first."

A truck slowed down as it pulled up to the women. The driver lowered his window. "Morning, Bear Bailey and crew!" He touched the tip of his hat.

Hearing his name, the Pyrenees barked and took a few steps to the truck before he stood on his hind legs, careful not to scratch the side of the truck.

"I remember when you were just a little pup. And now, Bear, you're almost eye-to-eye with me." The man chuckled, ruffling the dog's mane. "And who's the other handsome fellow up ahead?"

While the group stood talking at the man's truck, the old dog had continued ahead on the dirt road at a slow trot, leaving little puffs of dust with each of his steps.

"That's Henry. He wandered into town, and I took him in," Katie answered.

"I'd say it looks like he's ready to move along again."

"Henry!" Katie shouted in a gentle way. "I don't understand. He's happiest wrapped in a blanket cocoon at home or trying to move along. There is no middle ground." She put her fingers in her mouth and whistled. Henry finally stopped and turned around, returning to the group. "He might be a little deaf too."

"He looks like a blowed-in-the-glass dog if I've ever seen one," Clint said.

"A what?" Katie asked.

"Blowed-in-the-glass. A genuine and trustworthy individual. Or in this case, a genuine and trustworthy *dog*." Noticing the women's confused expressions, he clarified, "It's a hobo phrase."

Bear barked his agreement and ran to Henry, running in circles in excitement before licking the dog's head. He stopped mid-lick. "Sorry. I get carried away, Henry. I'm just happy you're part of our group."

"Good work, you two. I hear you're really trying to get some things done at Bear Bailey's for the rest of Merivelle." He reached into his center console, fishing around for something as he spoke. "Don't let anyone keep you from your big dreams. It's been fun seeing you two growing things around here." After tossing Wishbone treats to the dogs like they were bird seed, he tipped his hat again and drove away slowly, careful not to leave the women in a dust cloud.

"Why is everyone such an expert on hobo life these days?" Katie asked.

"No idea. But what were you saying before he drove up?"

"I know this is weird, and I don't want you to hate me when it seems like we're getting along better than ever now that you've moved back to Merivelle."

"You and I are square no matter what. Like I always say to anyone who listens—I couldn't do without you."

Katie took off her jacket and tied it around her waist. "I've always had this weird fascination with Mr. Chapowits. Even when he was making our life hell with the co-op."

"That's the big revelation, Katie?" Mary said, puzzled. "Why would I care?"

"For one—he almost ruined you financially. You'd have lost everything."

"But I didn't. And in a weird twist, I learned a huge lesson from Mr. Chapowits's shenanigans. I saw how many people appreciated my mother's legacy and where I belonged."

"You really feel that way?"

"Without Riven Chapowits, I'd be in Chicago working myself into a female version of his worst self." She shivered as her eyes searched the ground.

"What's wrong?"

"It just gave me the chills even thinking about my old life. I wonder why?"

Bear began to howl, remembering how Jiff showed him Mary's life in Chicago without him. She was a cold and selfish woman without Theodore in her life. He knew it had been just a vision to teach him but sometimes at night he still had bad dreams about it. He would wake startled and shaking, not able to settle down until he saw Theodore and Mary sleeping in bed.

"See? I told you. I have to be careful what I say around Bear," Mary said, leaning down to reassure him.

"As noble as you're trying to be, some part of you must want to choke Riven for all he put you through."

"If I'm truthful—sometimes I feel my mind wander and I do want to strangle the man. What would that ever have to do with you?"

"Percy thought Riven was my father."

"Really?"

There was no trace of Katie spunk as she nodded.

Mary burst out laughing. "But that's hilarious."

"Is it? My mother flipped her lid when I told her."

"She'd naturally be protective of you associated with the town villain, for lack of a better word. That's all."

Shaking her head, Katie said, "My mother will talk about anything for days, but after I brought up Riven, she was weird and abrupt, saying she was on her way to Merivelle."

"She never comes to Merivelle—for *anything*," Mary said, pausing in thought for several moments. She shook her head and smiled. "How are Sonny and Cher doing these days?"

Katie's voice was petulant, bordering on anger. "They're ridiculous. I don't care how they are."

"Your mom means well but she's bored. So, she has stand-in parakeet children. Any story you bring her, she's going to make into a soap opera."

Bear licked his jowls. One Wishbone was left on the dirt road. But the old dog was spell-bound with his focus of it. He nudged the treat with his nose and pushed it to Henry's side.

"Thank you, friend. I haven't been this hungry since I was a young pup and looking for spare biscuits."

"Spare biscuits?"

"The hobo word for digging in the trash can for food."

"Sometimes you break my heart, Henry," Bear said, bowing his head. "You really do."

In a short time, Henry had finished the last biscuit and sniffed around for another.

Mary reached down and picked up a small bit of treat left on the ground. She put it under Henry's nose with an open palm, smiling at the dog before turning her attention back to her cousin. "It's really simple when you think about it. You're a little mesmerized by Riven. Who hasn't cheered for the bad guy sometimes? Percy, a new visitor to Merivelle, mixes up who's related to who. And Aunt Julia, bored and lonely with only your feathered siblings to mother, perks up with unusual news on a phone call from you. No big deal."

Katie sighed. "I guess you're right. It just feels so weird. Why do I feel so rebellious towards him when he makes a move in my direction?"

"You do?"

"Like the day he brought Henry back to me. I didn't need to

be bratty when he'd taken such good care of my lost dog. It just seemed like he was hiding something."

Mary shrugged. "I couldn't say what goes on in the mind of Riven to give you any good advice."

"Riven is Katie's father," Henry said, licking his whiskers of crumbs. "She's absolutely on the right track."

"What?" Bear began barking in surprise, not unlike if a pack of coyotes had suddenly appeared in the road.

Katie and Mary both jumped at the commotion.

"Why would you say such a thing, Henry?"

"The time Riven kept me overnight. He was practicing out loud how to talk to Katie's mom. He kept dialing the phone and hanging up before she answered. He just wants Katie to know the truth about him."

Bear swayed in place and whined. "I feel like I'm about to chuck a dummy, Henry."

Mary stroked his head to calm him down before the women began to walk again. "You know, I haven't ever asked you, but your dad who we grew up with—"

"The one arrested at my twelfth birthday party in front of all my friends?" Katie held her stomach. "I feel sick just thinking about it."

"*Lean in with love,*" Henry whispered to himself. He walked beside Katie as closely as he could.

Bear watched the other dog with great pride. "Like the man said, you're a blowed-in-the-glass dog."

A flush from Katie's face radiated down her neck and onto her arms. "Did you know, when I was sixteen and crying my eyes out after we'd fought over some teenage thing, my mom told me Lance wasn't even my real dad?"

"What?" Mary stopped and faced Katie. "Why didn't you ever tell me?"

"I thought if I tried to explain '*the man who was arrested in front of my whole class is not my real father'*, it would only make me seem more guilty."

Mary was aghast. "Katie! What are you talking about? Guilty of what?"

"I don't know. Having a ridiculous family. It felt like someone should take the blame for that birthday party debacle. No adults were stepping up or smoothing out the mess. So, tag—I'm it."

Mary gently touched Katie's arm. "That's a tremendous burden that you've been carrying."

Katie pulled the jacket around her waist tight as she spoke. "It was mortifying. I thought it must be a joke. Like a skit for my birthday," she said. "Remember when I started laughing? And nobody else did?"

Mary nodded, her face etched in empathy.

"It all jumbled in my head. Only when I saw my mother crying as he was led out the door did I realize something horrible had just happened. I've never felt so lonely in my life as I was in the middle of that party."

"I don't know if I'm doing this right," Henry said, as he leaned into Katie more. "She still seems very upset."

"You're doing great, Henry," Bear said. "She might still be sad but won't feel so alone with you beside her. Sometimes throw in a little whine. It's the closest thing we can do to talking with them."

The old dog whimpered his sympathy causing Katie to look down and pet him in gratitude.

"What does it say about me that I can't show emotion about that insane day? Not even the tiniest bit of crying." She blinked several times, almost like she was checking to see if tears were forthcoming.

"To think how young you were trying to sort it all out in the moment." Mary squeezed Katie's hand.

"I loved the man I thought was my dad. With all my heart. I poured things out to him while we were fishing that I never even thought of telling my mom. He was such a good listener." She wiped her eyes with the back of her arm; the gesture unnecessary as her eyes were dry, though the look on her face was one of deep and utter sadness. Like an oil rig pumping a dry well.

Mary nodded as she and the dogs fully focused on Katie.

"I felt so wanted and valued around him. He used to tell me I was his lucky charm—that I made everything better." Katie's gaze was on the horizon.

"You're still that way for everyone, Katie. All our lucky charms. I had no idea you didn't know that."

"My mom always made me feel like I was some sort of trouble. How she could have really been something had she not had a kid to weigh her down. She moved the day after I graduated high school."

Mary's eyes widened. "I never put that timing together, Katie."

"I was only ever a travel delay to my mother. Until she could be free to continue her journey far away from me."

"Underfoot and unwanted," Henry said. "It's the worst feeling. It breaks your heart."

Bear suppressed the crying howl he wanted to unleash. "We love you here, Henry. There's always a home in Merivelle for you. I promise."

"Katie's stories. I'd never guess how she grew up. And still, she makes me feel like a king. Despite my shabbiness and inconvenient arrival."

"You've arrived at the perfect time, Henry. When a human needed you most. Don't you ever forget that." Noticing the edge of Henry's ears and tail bare of hair from years of fly bites, Bear's eyes filled with tears. The dogs walked in silence listening to the women talk.

"You know I never realized that when we were growing up, after my dad died, and we were both dealing with losses, I ran away and you froze in place," Mary said. "I didn't have the emotional maturity to know that you were hurting in your own way. To me, you always seemed so happy in Merivelle."

"I burrowed in to show I wasn't embarrassed and hurting—just *sparkling*. If I just rose to the top of everything, no one would dare to make fun of me," Katie said. "But somehow all I ever do is get involved with romantic drama that shames me. I'm sure people make fun of me all the time."

"I promise you; no one makes fun. You always seem so confident," Mary answered. "No matter what you've been feeling inside over the years."

"She's like her father," Henry said.

Bear closed his eyes and shook his head, refusing to believe anything kind about Mr. Chapowits.

The old dog was not dissuaded. "They refuse to let people see their hurts."

"If I could go back and do everything over again, I'd have taken you with me," Mary said. "We would have had a ball in Chicago."

"But now you're home in Merivelle and it all worked out with Bear Bailey's." Katie leaned down and for the first time since he arrived when he was just a young pup, she kissed the top of the Great Pyrenees's head. "Thanks for listening, Mary. I just have one request."

"Anything."

"Can we not tell the Theodore? Just keep my bananas family history to myself for a bit?"

"Of course, Katie. I wouldn't dream of telling him without you. Only when you're ready."

Bad Tempered Owner

Riven Chapowits had lived alone in his enormous house sitting outside Merivelle's city limits for so long, he chose not to recall any events before he occupied the residence. Beginning to build before he had begun amassing the majority his wealth, he'd used every dime to buy the land first, and then began construction on the mammoth-sized house. *It looks like a giant fraternity house* or *It's Tara from "Gone with the Wind,"* he'd heard people from Merivelle murmur over the years. But he didn't care. Living in the biggest house in Merivelle had been his first big dream come true.

Strolling through the halls, hearing his footsteps echo in the expanse of the house that resembled a museum more than a home, Riven realized he still delighted in the size of it, even after decades. He glanced at the large grandfather clock ticking down time to an appointment held within his house, feeling his agitation level begin to climb.

A visitor mindlessly rang the doorbell several times in a row. Riven growled, cussing his idea to have someone come to his house. Making his way through the expansive entryway of his home, he opened the door.

"Good afternoon, Mr. Chapowits."

"Theodore Bailey." Riven held the door open, his body turned sideways. Not quite a welcome but an invite inside his home, nonetheless.

"Sorry about the bell. I got lost in thought standing there." The younger man entered the large foyer, scanning the grand nature of the home. A blast of wind gusted through the house. Theodore startled, nearly knocking over a vase on an entry table with his elbow.

"Would you quit messing around and come in?"

Theodore turned toward the door to leave.

Riven's shoulders dropped. "Wait. I shouldn't have said that."

"I'm half a step from walking out of this mausoleum, El Chapo."

"I'd appreciate if you stayed. And I've never been a fan of your nickname for me."

"Then act different and it won't slip out with ease."

Riven nodded and walked back out of the entryway. He made his way through a large living room into a den off the side of a massive kitchen with Theodore following. The room had a wood fireplace ablaze. "Please," he said, motioning to a tufted leather couch.

Theodore sat down. "Let's get right to the point. Why have you invited me to your home citing an emergency as the reason I should drop everything? I see no burning fires other than the one in your fireplace."

Silently, Riven studied the younger man who came easily to all things he found difficult—particularly friendships struck up with ease. His face was puzzled as he focused on Theodore for a few moments before speaking. "I've been watching you. Your habits, who you're friends with, your work patterns—"

"Whoa. You're freaking me out a bit there. I should let you know I've left a sealed envelope with my last known whereabouts in the unfortunate event I don't return home in a timely fashion."

"I'm guessing you're trying to be funny with me. Though I can't remember the last time someone tried that with me," Riven answered, lifting one eyebrow. "I have no intention of killing you. Yet."

Theodore laughed a bit uneasily. "A little overstretching with the murder angle, but an "*A*" for effort. Now what do you have in mind for our meeting today?"

"Someone in town advised me that you're the guy who sets the standard with male behavior."

"That's very generous of you to say." Theodore's face registered sincere surprise. "I don't understand the connection though."

"I've got myself in a bit of a situation."

"Obviously, with your past with my wife, I may not be able to represent you if it's a conflict of her interests, namely Bear Bailey's Co-op."

Mr. Chapowits's face tightened as his faded blue eyes fired in anger. "I don't need an attorney!"

"Then why am I here, Riven?" Theodore sat at the edge of his chair, eyeing the door.

"Because I need a…" Riven pulled his collar away from his throat and stretched his neck from side to side.

"You need a what?"

Riven mumbled an undecipherable word under his breath.

"I'm sorry, I didn't hear whatever it was you said. It sounded like you said 'forefend.'"

"What are you blabbering on about?" Riven got a handkerchief out of his pocket and blotted his face. "*Forefend* isn't even a word."

"Oh, yes it is. It means to defend or protect."

"How do you know that?"

"Lupe insists we all expand our vocabulary," Theodore said, nodding his head. "Back to you. What word did you just say?"

Riven grimaced. "Friend."

"*You have a friend?*" Theodore said encouragingly, sitting back in his chair, looking as if he were ready to hear a story.

A miniature Zen garden was sitting on the table. Riven picked up the accompanying small rake. "I need a friend," he clarified, tracing in the sand.

Theodore's eyes widened. "I don't know…I mean—"

"*Please close your mouth* is the closest thing I can think of to politely tell you that you look ridiculous." Riven laid the rake down. "I don't know why I keep blurting things out lately."

Theodore closed his eyes for a moment before continuing. "I'm sorry, I'm still stuck on the fact you phoned me citing an emergency and come to find out you just need a *friend*?"

"One who won't run their mouth with what I'm going to confide in them." Riven crossed his arms and stared at the younger man. "You'd be legally bound not to break my confidentiality. A man operating as my attorney *and* my friend. An ideal combination that ensures my conversation with you doesn't become town gossip."

"But that's not how it works, Riven."

"I wouldn't hire you?" Riven turned his head in thought as if he were solving a complex mathematical problem.

"No!" Theodore exclaimed. "That's not what friends do." He leaned forward. "Are you really telling me you think the only way to keep information private with another human is to pay them?"

"I don't think it's good manners to invite you to my home and threaten you with a local thug."

"I'm going to pretend I didn't hear you say that or you're testing out your newly acquired comedy skills," Theodore said, glancing at Riven's shaking hands. "Are you sick?"

"I don't know."

"How do you not know? It's an easy question. Are you ill?"

Riven gripped each of the armrests of his chair as his hands steadied but his feet began to tap. "My heart rate always seems to be elevated. I've had it checked but my doctor says everything's fine. Raging anxiety is keeping me up at night and I don't know what to do with what I know. I need to rectify a situation. I feel time is running out."

"I can't hear anything that might break the law. I'm not your attorney and because you talk to one does not mean you have client privilege with me. Do you understand?" His words were blunt, but true to his personality, he attempted to deliver the words in a kind way.

In frustration, Riven hit his fist on the table beside his chair. "Can you just try and work with me here? Not make everything so hard?"

"You can't wave a scepter and knight someone a friend when it's convenient to your life."

"Why not?"

Theodore physically jolted with the question. "Really?"

"Why is that so ridiculous?"

"Because a friend is someone you spend time with. You trust each other with the small pieces of your life and then when there's something bigger, which whatever you haven't told me seems to be, you have full confidence they can hear your words with the same trust as the smaller issues."

Theodore waited as Riven gazed into the fire. The room was heavy with heat and unspoken words.

"Why do you have a fire going inside your home today?" Theodore took off his lightweight jacket. "It's a warm spring day."

"Is it a problem that I like fires?"

"I think most men like time in front of a campfire."

"Really?"

"You ever been on a guys' trip before?"

"Men have slumber parties?"

Theodore laughed. "You really have no point of reference on this subject, do you?"

"If you're going to make fun of me every time I try—"

"Mary tells me all the time that I need to chill on the constant joking," Theodore said, holding a hand up in conciliation. "But at the same token, that's what a friend does. They rough you up. It shows they accept you as one of the tribe. You never joke around with people you don't care about."

"No one ever jokes around with me."

"Exactly!"

"That's rude."

"No, that's honest and another thing a good friend would do. They tell the truth. Even when it hurts," Theodore said. "And if you have a really great friend—one you really treasure, they'll combine humor with truth to help you on your journey."

The two men sat in silence for a few moments. "I hear you have quite the following down at The Hen's Nest every morning," Riven said. "Never miss a day."

"I love friends. Outside of Mary, they're my favorite thing in life. I'd do anything for a buddy. Wouldn't matter if I saw them yesterday or in first grade." Theodore paused. "But I think we're a bit off-track here."

Riven sighed. "I have a relative in Merivelle. They have no idea. And I don't know how best to enlighten them on the subject."

"Just tell the truth."

"It's not that easy."

"Do I know this person?"

"You do. Very well," Riven said, his gaze turning to Theodore.

Looking as if he'd been struck by lightning, Theodore asked, "Are you and Cybil Barnes siblings?"

"It's not Cybil, but she knows. I have to hand it to her, she never breathed a word over the years." Riven's voice was one of quiet appreciation.

Theodore forehead scrunched as he thought. "I'm stumped."

"She's a young woman. Well-regarded in Merivelle. She works at the co-op—"

Theodore wiped his face. "Is it hot in here? It feels suffocating." He stood up, looking about the room like a wild squirrel fallen down the chimney, trying to find an exit outdoors again. "*Are you Mary's father?*"

"Let me explain," Riven said, shaking his head.

Theodore tried to steady his breathing. "She will lose her mind when she hears this."

"You are not to say anything about this to Mary."

"I can't *not* tell my wife her nemesis is her *own* father."

"*I am not Mary Bailey's father!*" Riven said, standing to meet Theodore eye to eye. "Now would you please sit down?"

Unclenching his hands from his side, Theodore swayed like he'd been close to fainting.

"It's Katie."

"Katie?" Theodore's head snapped up. "*Our* Katie?"

"Yes, the very one," Riven said. His face softened, and he lifted his chin, not breaking eye contact with Theodore. "Katie is my daughter."

Theodore let out a low whistle. "That was a close one," he whispered. He ran his fingers through his hair. "Is this like a small-town secret everyone knows but pretends not to know?"

"I don't think so. It started with my anxiety, I was tired of my doctor giving me more pills. I went to a yoga class—"

Theodore put his head down, much like he was praying, though his body was shaking with suppressed laughter.

"Go ahead and laugh, you jackass."

Looking up, Theodore grinned. "I deserved that one. Please, go ahead with the yoga bit."

"Out of the blue, I told Alicia."

"Why?"

"She tricked me with all the *open your heart* nonsense, and I thought it would help me."

"Did it?"

"My anxiety is still through the ceiling, and I haven't been able to shut up about the secret."

"Who else knows?"

Riven rubbed his temples. "Bear Bailey's gives me a real opportunity to get to know Katie. I was so proud of how she conducts those meetings. I could tell Percy felt similar. I accidentally said, '*my daughter*' after one of our meetings when I was talking to him alone. I left my blunder uncorrected, hoping not to draw attention to it. Unwittingly, Percy mentioned it to Katie, who then called her mother.—"

Theodore grimaced.

"—Who *will not* quit calling me. She's threatening to come to Merivelle."

"Aunt Julia might visit?" Theodore asked. "I've only ever heard stories but still—" He shivered, shaking his head in exaggerated fear. "Let's get to the bottom of this problem as soon as possible."

"You think we can keep her from coming?"

"Not a chance from what I understand about her personality. Just a small joke. To help lighten the mood."

"Then it's a matter of time before she shows up here." Riven closed his eyes for a moment. "All because I confided in people. I should have kept my mouth shut like I have for decades!"

The clock struck the half hour. "And yet, you've summoned me to your home and told me the same thing you say you regret telling Alicia and then Percy. On some level, it's important to you for others to know Katie is your daughter."

Riven sighed. And though he appeared tired, there was also a sparkle in his eyes as he spoke. "I'm sitting at your wife's co-op and my daughter is leading the meeting with kindness and respect to everyone in attendance. And she's smart. She gets straight to the point. But the other people feel seen and heard too. I think all the time how she's able to balance being so driven yet likeable."

Theodore started to speak and then stopped, smiling for the man to continue uninterrupted.

"The level of pride I feel overwhelms me." Riven picked up a fireplace poker and nudged the embers as he spoke. "At the same time, I've never been lonelier. I could spend decades locked here in my house and I'd feel less of an outcast than I do at those meetings at the co-op."

"It's all by your own choice, Riven. You can't tell a sad story about how you're not invited to play ball. Not a long time ago, you tried to take the co-op from the community."

"It's Mary's co-op."

"That's not how she sees it. Bear Bailey's is for the community, so Donkey's children have braces, people can make ends meet selling eggs or honey, others can bring their hobbies to market to cover an extra high heating bill, for instance. Cybil's been swept back into things like when she taught at the high school. Lupe and her family are becoming known in town for the treasures they are. In Mary's mind, Bear Bailey's isn't her store at all. She's merely the steward of it for now. For the good of everyone in Merivelle."

"Mary sounds like Margaret."

"She'd take that as the highest compliment," Theodore said, before pausing. "Tell me what does feeling lonely at the co-op meetings have to do with anything though?"

"I need you to tell me how I can right my wrongs so when Katie finally finds out I'm her father, she's not ashamed of me. She might even feel proud." Riven stood expectantly. "Do you think that could be done?"

Theodore took a deep breath. "You know, you've caused an enormous amount of pain to a lot of people. And I'm just going off what I know in my own house. My wife was a nervous wreck for a long time due to your actions. Thinking about it, I want to reach over and punch you in the nose. Sorry, but I really do."

"You have every right to feel that way," Riven said, putting his head down.

"And as mad as I get at what you've done to the person I love most in the entire world, I know you've done worse with others. Don't even get me started on the Posadas. I'm still sorting through their Gordian knot of paperwork. Not to mention, they're sure Lupe's husband would have written by now. They haven't received one piece of mail from the man."

"One day that might make more sense. But for now—"

"You do know you could face prison time for messing with the postal service?"

"I mentioned I have an issue with anxiety these days, didn't I?" Riven's voice was meek.

"I'll give it go trying to help you. Remember, you have some big bridges to mend. You can't snap your fingers. It going to take time and building trust through meaningful actions. Things your money can't buy."

5

SOMEONE'S HOME

"I NEED A little extra jolt to finish some Bear Bailey paperwork," Mary said as she finished pouring herself after-dinner coffee later that evening. "Do you want a cup?"

"I think I'm too revved up for coffee." Theodore was fairly dancing in place.

"Where were you today?" Mary raised her eyebrows as she took a drink from her mug.

"Somewhere possibly good. I think it has the potential to be a nice surprise with some time passing." He chewed his lip in thought. "Or maybe not."

"Sounds mysterious. Very *telenovela*-like."

"I'd much rather hear all about your day and how Percy's finding Merivelle. Does he think our downtown will qualify for funding? I'm anxious to help with an ear or a hand," he said, a look of sincere affection on his face as Mary began explaining her day.

Bear used his nose to examine Theodore's shoes and pant legs, his breath coming in short and rapid bursts as he suddenly stopped in confusion.

"You okay, friend?" Henry asked from under the table. Before the sun had rose that morning, Katie dropped him at the Bailey's, kissing the dog profusely and promising to return the next day to pick him up again.

"He smells weird. It's making me anxious." The Great Pyrenees began panting and pacing around the kitchen island before sitting in front of Theodore, narrowing his eyes as he growled in question.

"What's got into Bear this evening?" Theodore asked. "You'd think he had no idea who I am."

"I feel I should know this scent. It's making me want to howl," Bear said.

"I haven't been able to smell for a couple of years now. Couldn't smell a gump if it was being battered and fried right under my nose."

Stopping mid-sniff, Bear asked, "What's a gump?"

"On the road, we call that chicken." He sighed heavily. "You sure it's not your big imagination at work again?"

"I know Theodore almost as well as I know Mary, and something's different with him tonight." Bear took a step back from Theodore, turning his head suspiciously.

"Buddy, it's me." Theodore's expression was puzzled as knelt to Bear. "You're acting like I'm a coyote or something."

"A coyote!" Bear exclaimed, backing up as his black pupils grew large with fear. "He smells like…" The dog sniffed the air and growled again. "A Dark Den!" He began barking in alarm.

Startled by the dog's sudden emotion, Theodore stumbled in surprise. "What is going on with your dog?"

Mary walked to the patio door and opened it as the western horizon was ablaze in color. "Bear, calm down. It's Theodore, you big goof. Get over here and enjoy the view. Get some fresh air to clear your head."

Obedient to Mary's words, Bear pointedly walked around Theodore in exaggerated avoidance, though not breaking eye contact with him. Henry followed behind, giving a polite sniff.

"Everything is under control, Bear. You don't always have to be on guard, good boy."

"Yeah, clock out, you big goof," Theodore said, joining his wife and the dogs on the deck.

Mary smiled at her husband. "I love springtime. So much hope in the air." She reached down and ruffled Bear's mane. At Mary's gentle touch, Bear melted into a heap next to Henry letting out one final, muffled growl.

"Calm down, friend. He means you no harm." Henry shifted in place, trying to find a comfortable position. "My bones can't take much ruckus." He closed his eyes and sighed.

"Do you think there's coyotes nearby?"

"I think he's clearly growling at you, honey," Mary said. "He's scared, not ready to attack though."

"You can tell a difference in his sounds?"

Mary's face was surprised. "Of course, I can tell the difference. You can't?"

"A hundred and twenty-pound dog who tears coyotes to shreds is growling at me. It's hard to focus on intent."

"If you really go after the coyotes the way everyone around here says you do, then why are you so worried about how Theodore smells?" Henry asked. "It seems to me you could handle things just fine."

"Everything I do is to protect Mary."

"Does she look like there's a problem, friend?"

Mary planted a quick kiss on Theodore's cheek as they both studied the land behind the house, their backs forming a silhouette against the evening light. The Bailey's goats bleated in the background as Theodore groaned and Mary giggled. Chickens scratched in the pathway between the house and the barn on their way to settle into their coop for the night.

"When can we think about a horse, Theodore?" She snuggled into the crook of her husband's neck. He groaned in the exasperated tone he reserved for when Mary asked for any living animals to add to the farm. She snickered in reply.

Bear loved the banter between Mary and Theodore and took a deep breath to release his previous anxiety. "You're right, Henry. Mary's fine. But it *is* my job to stand guard."

Henry nodded in agreement. "Of course, we protect the things we love the most. But stay calm, friend. We only ever have the present moment in any of our lives."

"I don't understand but you say it in such a wise way," Bear replied. The hair on his back smoothed down as he relaxed.

"If you focus too much on the past and can't focus on how good your life is, Bear, you'll start to drive yourself crazy. Seeing things that may or may not be there."

Lowering his head, Bear nodded. "I do that a lot."

"Don't let your worries wring out the love of a good home. The past already had its moment. And the future may never have the moment you imagine it will possess. I bet you'll find the years ahead are more wonderful than you can imagine."

Staring at the old dog for a few moments, Bear sighed. "The more I get to know you, the more I want to defend you too, Henry. I only want good things to happen for you from now on."

"Don't you worry about me. I can handle myself." Henry held his head up for a moment. "I've known some real bone polishers in my day—"

Bear's ears went up in alarm. "What's a bone polisher?" he cried, sounding like he'd stepped on a sharp object. Mary and Theodore stopped talking and turned to check on him.

"A real mean dog. Canine or human. I've met a lot of them in my day. And I still survived."

Bear eyes were wide as he gulped at Henry's explanation. "Be right back, Henry."

"Now where's Bear going?" Theodore asked.

"He's fine. Looks like he's on a mission of sorts." Mary

pointed to the beehives in the distance and began to outline her plan for a wildflower field around them.

Inside the house, Bear went to his basket of toys that Mary had taught him to keep tidy in the living room. He returned with an oversized stuffed Easter bunny, a recent addition to his collection. He dropped it on the ground in front of Henry, pushing it under the old dog's chin. "Here's a nice, soft pillow for you."

"Thanks, friend," Henry laid his head on the gift. "Don't be sad for me. I've also known great kindness. A nice meal when I least expect it, a dry place to sleep when I'm not covering with the moon."

"Covering with the moon?" Bear repeated. "Wait… don't tell me." He thought for a moment. "Does that mean sleeping outside?"

"Spoken like a hobo dog on the road." Henry closed his eyes and smiled.

"Covering with the moon. It seems less lonely when you say it that way." Bear sighed.

"Things are less lonely when you're square with your own thoughts," Henry replied, straining to rise.

Bear followed the old dog, patiently waiting for him to make his way across the patio. "I'm glad our paths crossed, Henry. You have a way of making everything better."

"Go make nice with Mary's sweetheart and then let's camp out tonight. Pretend we're two 'bos on the road." The prospect of a night outside gave Henry new energy. He jumped to his feet with a wagging tail.

Bear trotted to Theodore's side and nudged his hand in apology. He ran into the sagebrush with Henry as the sun set, looking high into the sky as he waited in excitement for the moon to cover the pair of them.

Two Dogs

HENRY REMAINED AT the Bailey's house overnight as he waited for Katie to pick him up again once she returned with her mom. Julia hated train transport with a burning passion, causing Katie to drive across nearly the entire state to retrieve her mother in Kansas City. A trip requiring overnight accommodations with her mom, punctuated with frequent dining and bathroom stops on the way back to Merivelle. The old dog positioned himself in the Bailey's living room, in full view of the front door, eager for Katie's return.

"Lupe will be here in an hour after Pablito's art lesson, and then you two can watch *Dos Caminos, Un Corazón* and get your weekly drama fix, Theodore," Mary said, laughing as she shook her head.

"What's so funny?"

"In our old Chicago life, you didn't even like television. You were a bit of a snob on the subject."

"Latino television! Where has it been my whole life?"

Henry lifted his head. "Why is he so excited?"

"He loves Latino soap operas," Bear said. "You know, *telenovelas*."

"We don't turn those on at Katie's house."

"Then you're both missing the best show in the whole world. *Dos Caminos, Un Corazón*."

Henry laid his head back down. "I understood half of what you've just said."

"It's the name of the *telenovela* we watch with the Posadas," Bear answered, his tail wagging and thumping the wood patio. "It's Spanish for *Two Roads, One Heart*."

"I like the theme. Very travel oriented," Henry said, his voice thoughtful. "Why is everyone so excited about it though?"

"Where do I even start?" Bear said, panting. "Our heroine, Esmerelda de Leon or Esme as she likes to be called because it's less grand, was raised by a couple without any children. The Del Bosques. Really good *gente*."

"*Gente?*" Henry scrunched his eyes together.

"The Spanish word for people."

"Got it," Henry replied.

"Anyway, we find out through a series of episodes that Esme's real mother is the wife of the owner of the estate where the elderly Del Bosques have worked and lived their whole lives."

"Then why doesn't Esme live with her parents?"

Bear shook his head. "It's never that easy with *telenovelas*. Rogelio, the owner of the estate, is not Esme's father."

Henry shook his head. "I don't understand."

"Esme's mother came from a poor family. She was very beautiful. The love of her life was working hard to get a home ready for them when her father paid a gambling debt promising her in marriage to Rogelio."

"This is not going to end well," Henry said, sitting up.

"Poor Margarita was pregnant. But she couldn't be honest because she needed to marry Rogelio to help her family."

"Wait, where did a margarita come from?"

"That's Esme's mother's name. *Margarita*. It means a pearl."

"Is this one of those things you don't know how you know but you know?" Henry asked.

"Nope, I know because of last season's opening flashback episode. Margarita tells her little baby, Esmeralda, before she sends her away with the caretakers, both their names mean fine jewels and it's their connection even when they're far apart, and one day they'll find each other again."

"Why is Katie's dog all of a sudden looking like Bear is a television?" Theodore asked. Henry had scooted up to nearly in front of Bear's face and was mirroring his facial expressions. "Look how he's following Bear's every movement."

"Maybe Bear is an excellent storyteller," Mary said, laughing.

"Your imagination with your dog has gone wild again."

"Don't listen to Theodore. Keep going, Bear," Henry said, pawing at the Pyrenees. "What happens after Margarita sends Esmerelda away?"

"For a few years, she sneaks to the small quarters of the Del Bosques to see her little girl. But then the pain of the family she can't have becomes unbearable and she pushes Esme from her mind." Bear stopped. "Or Margarita hit her head and had amnesia. Sometimes it's hard to keep track of all the things that happen on the show."

"Either way, go on," Henry said.

"On Esme's sixteenth birthday, Margarita's memory returns."

"How?"

"She drinks a potion from a mysterious vendor at an outdoor marketplace and achieves total clarity. She doesn't ever want to be apart from her daughter again."

"What about her dad and the gambling debt?"

"Good catch, Henry!" Bear said, excitedly. "Margarita's father recently died so there's no danger he'll be killed if she chooses a different path."

"The poor woman. She didn't have a marriage. She had a

prison sentence," Henry said in an empathetic tone. "But she's married to a man who threatened to kill her dad—what is he going to do when he hears the news?"

"Margarita is willing to die because the way she's been living has no meaning. She goes to Rogelio and tells him the truth. She has a daughter from her true love."

"Does Rogelio kick her out?" Henry asked, panting.

"He does not. Rogelio is excited to have an heir because his son with his first wife died in a plane crash, so he welcomes Esme with open arms."

"How do Margarita and Rogelio explain a sixteen-year-old daughter suddenly showing up?"

"Rogelio and Margarita decide to say to their friends Esme was in a coma in one of the back rooms of the mansion attended by a nurse and it made them sad to talk about it, so they kept it their secret," Bear said, smiling. "*Telenovelas* always find a way!"

Henry sighed in a contented way. "That's the perfect way to end the story," Henry said. "Margarita and Esme were reunited."

"Not a chance. This is a Mexican soap opera."

"The very next episode we find out the particular reason Margarita chose to send Esme with the old caretakers." Bear's face was as joyful as if he had a sizzling steak in front of him. "You're not going to believe this, Henry."

"Try me." Henry tilted his head toward Bear and whined.

"The Del Bosques are Esme's real grandparents! She was never alone! Man, that episode was a great night. We all danced around here for an hour with the Posadas."

"She was never without family?" Henry wiped a tear from his eye with his paw. "That's the best thing I've ever heard."

"Oh, we're just getting started," Bear said, sitting down. "We find out their son, Roberto, is a handsome boatbuilder living in the faraway Mexican port town of Yelapa meaning *Where Two Rivers Meet the Sea*." Bear got up and barked in excitement. "All this time, the two *caminos* were really two rivers leading to the sea where Roberto lives."

"Why doesn't he know about a daughter living with his parents?"

"He was too impetuous and left heartbroken after Margarita's wedding, vowing never to return. The pain was too great."

"No kidding?" Henry said, looking flabbergasted.

"Roberto is going to lose his mind with happiness when he meets Esme in this week's episode." The Great Pyrenees got up and began barking and jumping in joy, zooming off the porch and tearing around the yard off the patio, continuing on where he tore a path through the sagebrush, chasing a rabbit and then running back up the steps of the deck to Mary, Theodore and Henry.

"Your dog is crazy," Theodore said.

Mary reached out to Bear, a big smile of affection on her face. "He's ecstatically happy. I wonder one day, when we arrive in heaven and all life's questions are answered, if we'll know what makes dogs suddenly get the zoomies."

"*Fine Latino programming gives me the zoomies*," Bear said, returning from his water bowl on the patio. Water dripped down his mouth onto his mane. He was all out of breath. "Nothing better than a good narrative."

The doorbell rang, re-routing Bear's enthusiasm into a joyous front door greeting.

"Katie's here to get Henry."

"This is going to be one wild week—"

"Uh-huh. Don't start *telenovela*-ing. Katie needs all our support this week," Mary said, opening the front door.

Her cousin stood under the porch light as if she'd emerged from treading water for hours. "I need Henry. Now."

Henry wagged his tail enthusiastically.

"I need to hurry. My mom's waiting in the car with Sonny and Cher."

Theodore hit his forehead with his palm. "On top of everything else, she's making you listen to a 1970's singing duo sensation?"

Katie rubbed circles around her temple. "She brought two emotional support birds. On a plane." She knelt down to Henry and kissed the top of his head.

"Wait!" Bear said to Henry, putting a paw out to stop the old dog for a moment. "Katie still doesn't know Mr. Chapowits is her father." Bear sniffed the air again and howled.

Katie jumped in place. "Bear! My nerves are shot! What is going on with your dog, Mary?"

"Chapowits! Yesterday, Theodore smelled like Mr. Chapowits!" Bear said. "That's where he'd been all afternoon."

A woman in the passenger seat of the car rolled down her window. "Katie, that dog is an absolute mongrel! Where on earth did you find him?" she shouted, alarming the two birds in a pet carrier on her lap. She waved to the Bailey's as if she were a homecoming queen in a parade. "See you at a more convenient time, Mary! The birds aren't used to flying!"

Katie punched a laughing Theodore right in the stomach in warning. He disappeared behind the door in response to his wife's glare.

Opening her car door and sitting in the driver's seat, Katie put the transmission in gear before slamming on the gas. Gravel sprayed in the air as her mother continued yelling undecipherable dialogue out the window.

"Was that a real person?"

"You love *telenovelas*, Theodore. Congratulations. We have a character straight out of *Dos Caminos, Un Corazón* come to town."

Sit Down Feed

The next morning, Katie entered The Hen's Nest the moment they opened their door for business at six. She was dressed impeccably and had Henry leashed beside her. He was equally groomed as if they were both seeing royalty later than morning. The look on her face suggested she wanted someone to challenge her dog sitting beside her in a booth. Most everyone in the café had gone to school with Katie or was familiar with her in some other way and wisely pretended as if the *No Pets Allowed, Service Dogs Welcome* sign didn't apply to Henry.

"Would you like to order, honey?" an older waitress asked.

Katie had been sitting in the booth for more than five minutes, staring straight ahead as if she were in a trance. She barely turned as she spoke. "Six slices of bacon, Frannie."

"That's your breakfast, Katie?"

"It's for Henry."

"Now I haven't said anything about your dog coming in, but he cannot eat at the table. We can't let that get started in town or everyone will bring their pets in here and we'll have a zoo." The woman searched Katie's face, her expression showing her sincere hope her words were the end of the subject.

"Restaurants are places of public accommodations under *Title III of the Americans with Disability Act*," Katie said. Her countenance came alive with the possibility of conflict to release the stress she was feeling.

"Honey, why would *you* suddenly need a service dog?" The woman tilted her head, simultaneously showing kindness and firmness with her tone. She had daughters a few years younger than Katie and was not fearful of facing her.

"Because, Frannie, my mother is visiting. If I didn't have this *service* dog, I'd have been in jail by now," Katie said. "He is my emotional support, so I don't choke my mother. I'd say he's earned some bacon at the booth."

"Julia is back in town?" Frannie took the order pad out of her apron and scribbled on it as she spoke. She reached over and patted the dog on the head. "That's some fine servicing you're doing, Henry. How about we add a little whipped cream on top for you, old man?" She winked. "Be right back."

Katie scratched behind her dog's ears. "You're already wonderful, Henry. I simply need you to swallow two early rising birds and you'll be a legend in my book."

Henry licked his lips and nodded.

"I'm kidding," Katie said. "Don't chomp the parakeets." She paused. "Yet."

The door to The Hen's Nest jingled as Theodore and Percy entered, talking animatedly with one another. They took a few steps in and searched for a place to sit before both startled in happy recognition of Katie.

"My favorite cousin," Theodore said, arriving at her booth with Percy. "Mind if we join you?"

"Be our guests," Katie nodded. The café was full of regular patrons, each in their daily claimed spots, the only two seats available in the entire restaurant were across from her.

"Do you feel like company this morning or need some time

to think things through?" Theodore asked, raising his eyebrows. "And by *things*, I mean *Aunt Julia*."

"You probably shouldn't leave me alone with my thoughts." Katie grimaced. "They're grim for early morning hours." Their faces dropped in concern. "I'm mostly kidding. I'm probably tired from my never-ending drive home yesterday."

Both men slid in the booth, Percy grabbing menus from behind the stainless-steel napkin holder and holding one out for Theodore, moving about with the synchronicity of a senior couple who had spent decades together.

"Do you two come here every morning?" Katie asked.

"Yes, nearly every day, since I've come to town," Percy replied.

"I didn't even know you two were friends."

"Why would you assume we were weren't friends?" Theodore asked.

"I've never seen you talk to one another."

"We talk outside Bear Bailey's."

"And why aren't you on the initial, small committee? An attorney would be a good addition to the community group," Percy said.

"I'm married to the owner of Bear Bailey's. Mary thought it would be weird."

"Full of integrity. I love that about you and Mary." He smiled across the table at Katie. "And you too."

The pair of men engaged in happy, early morning conversation as Katie studied them in silence. The bell on the door to the café rang again. The restaurant regulars were used to the sound and regarded it as background noise. Only Katie turned to see who had entered.

Riven stood at the entrance, scanning the café for an empty seat. The chatter in the restaurant came to an abrupt pause as whispers could be heard, sprouting up in place of discernable conversation. Looking around and finding no empty spaces to sit, he turned around to leave.

"Riven!" Theodore said, his voice friendly and excited. "We have room at our booth."

"No, we don't," Katie whispered.

"Can you scrunch over and let Riven sit with you and Henry? I'll explain later." Theodore motioned like a soccer mom giving direction to fit extra children into the back seat of a van.

"Explain now." Katie's face drained of color as she spoke in a hushed tone.

"He needs friends," Theodore replied, all the while keeping his face smiling as he continued to wave the man over. "We can show him a better way to behave. It's the Bear Bailey way."

Riven appeared at the head of the booth as Frannie brought Henry strips of bacon arranged on a plate like a face, whipped cream eyes and nose added for effect. "Whose order is that?"

"The dog's." Frannie was clearly amused.

The old man nodded his head, straining to be friendly. "Of course. Henry asked for the same thing the morning he stayed with me," he said, addressing Katie directly and smiling. He reached out and scratched the dog's head.

While Katie's gaze focused on Henry, Theodore mouthed the words, "*That was good*," as he gestured for Riven to take a seat beside Katie. She scooted to the wall of the booth, putting her arms around Henry, and pulling him closer to make room for Riven.

"What a coincidence, Riven. I think you'll love today's special," Frannie said, putting her hand on the man's shoulder, a sincere smile on her face. "It used to be one of your favorites back in the day. When you—"

"What's the special?" Riven interrupted, glancing around the table nervously.

"Mulligan Stew. You're just a little early. It's simmering right now."

"What is Mulligan Stew?" the younger woman asked.

Every time, Katie spoke, Percy came alive in delight. Her asking a question so open-ended with trivia potential had him nearly whistling in response. "It's of Irish origin as the name suggests. But after the Great Depression, hobos adopted it as their own. A hearty soup made up of whatever each member who was eating could bring to contribute to the meal."

As everyone else was occupied, Theodore looked over at Riven who was clearly antsy. Small beads of sweat were forming over his brow. He smiled to encourage the older man, taking a deep breath to demonstrate calmness. He gently blew the same breath out of his mouth, nodding as Riven mirrored his actions.

"So, really Mulligan Stew is a community soup?" Katie asked. Percy nodded, smiling. "Exactly."

"I love that. It's perfect," Katie said.

"It is?" Riven looked puzzled with her interest. "How?"

"For Bear Bailey's. How did we never put that together for the Grab-and-Go at the co-op?" She kissed the top of Henry's head.

Frannie smiled at the younger woman. "I'd be happy to share a recipe an old friend who worked in the kitchen years ago passed onto me, Katie. I think you might like it too."

Riven cleared his throat. "Why don't you bring these people some breakfast, Frannie? I'll just have coffee."

"Have a look at the menu, Riven," Frannie said. "Your food is on the house today." She took Theodore and Percy's order, promising to return with coffee.

"Last night's episode was a doozy," Theodore said, addressing Percy. "Did you watch it?"

"*Dos Caminos, Un Corazón?*" Percy replied. "Oh, yes. Wouldn't have missed it for the world."

"What are you two talking about?" Katie asked.

"The *telenovela* Lupe has us all hooked on," Percy replied. "*Two Roads, One Heart*. It's riveting television," he said, laughing. "I tried to explain it to my family back home."

"They don't get *MexiVision* back in Vermont?" Katie asked. She cut Henry's bacon with her fork and knife and then dipped small pieces in whipped cream before feeding him with the end of a fork as Riven watched her intently.

"I've never heard of the channel," Percy said.

"That's funny," Katie answered. "Everyone here has it."

"I don't," Riven said. "I have no idea what Theodore is talking about."

"They're going on about a ridiculous soap opera they're all hooked on." Katie rolled her eyes. "You've got to make yourself scarce on Thursday mornings or that's all you'll hear about at the co-op."

"Any chance either of you curmudgeons are going to turn on *Dos Caminos, Un Corazón* in the future?" Theodore asked.

"No!" Katie and Riven answered at the same time, both looking at the other in surprise.

"Then let me give a quick run-down of last night's episode so you two grumps see what you're missing." Theodore smiled as he unwrapped his napkin roll and situated his silverware. "Where do I even start?"

"Roberto." Percy lifted his coffee cup in tribute to the name. "It was definitely his show last night." He politely smiled as Frannie approached the table and began pouring coffee for Riven.

"It was the best episode of the entire series so far," Frannie interjected, topping off Percy's coffee. "That poor man had no idea he even had a daughter, and it was beautiful how he reacted to seeing her!"

"Remember how she stood on the dock as he was sanding

a boat? And he gazed into the morning sunrise and there stood Esme." Theodore theatrically wiped a tear from each eye.

"The look on his face when he thought he was dreaming of Margarita, and it was her spitting image—Esme!" Frannie said. "Not many men would be so wonderful when their daughter was hidden from them for their whole lives."

"Next week's episode is the last one of the series?" Percy asked

Theodore nodded in a tragic manner. "I'm going to have to emotionally prepare ahead of time. I hate good-byes."

"Who on earth are the Del Bosques?" Katie paused with a piece of bacon mid-air as Henry snatched it from her fingers.

"Her grandparents," Frannie answered, taking a napkin to wipe Henry's mouth before he drooled on the table. Without even turning, she dropped the napkin ball behind her back in a busboy's tub as he was passing behind her.

"The grandfather is an old *viejo*. A kind old man who has given his life in service to everyone around him. He'd give away the last one of his *frijoles* if he thought it would help someone." He paused looking at Riven. "*Frijoles* are—"

Riven glanced up from reading the menu, his bifocals on the tip of his nose. "I've lived in western Kansas my entire life. I know the Spanish word for beans."

"I have food up. I'll come back when it's calmed down a bit," Frannie said, tapping the table as she left.

Katie crossed her arms and leaned forward. "Are you two finished with your ridiculous *telenovela* recap?"

Theodore's mouth fell open comically while Percy gripped his chest, both feigning horror at her lack of interest in their recap.

"You idiots." Katie wiped her hands on a napkin and placed it on the empty plate in front of Henry. "That is the dumbest thing I have ever heard in my life."

"Which part?" Percy asked.

"The whole damn thing."

"What about you?" Theodore asked. "What do you think?"

Riven lifted his eyebrows and nodded to Katie. "What she said."

"That's what everyone thinks at first. But it sucks you in," Theodore said.

"What does Mary think about all of this? Is she as nuts as you two ding-a-lings?"

"Your cousin loves *Dos Caminos, Un Corazón*," Theodore answered. "Everyone in town loves it, but you two." He widened his eyes for a moment.

"How would you not love a daughter and father finally being reunited—" Percy said, his voice excited. Theodore tried to kick him under the table and missed his leg, loudly hitting the front of their side of the booth.

"What is going on?" Katie asked, crossing her arms.

Henry put a paw on Riven's arm and whined.

She stared at all three men at the table. "Why did everyone stop talking about the ridiculous soap opera after you kicked Percy under the table, Theodore?"

Both men froze in response.

"I feel we should talk," Riven began. "It's not fair that I ask my *friend*, Theodore, to keep a secret for me the way *friends* do for one another."

"Why are you emphasizing the word *friend* like English is my second language?" Katie frowned at Riven.

"You said Theodore was a model of behavior for men. So, I had him out to my house and—"

"Wait. You've been to his house?" Katie narrowed her eyes at Theodore, before turning her attention back to Riven.

"Uh, not here at The Hen's Nest, Riven." Theodore shook his head. "You should know, Katie really values her privacy."

"You better tell me what's going on before I call Mary." She picked up her phone with one eyebrow raised in an almost scary manner.

Theodore opened his mouth as the bell on the door of the café jingled again. An older woman, dressed so grandly she was an eyelash away from being in costume, entered the restaurant, looking around and smiling as if it were everyone's pleasure to see her.

"Who is that?" Percy whispered to Theodore before drinking his coffee.

Theodore brought his mug up to his mouth. "Aunt Julia," he said, barely above a whisper, taking a swig.

Their backs to the door, both Katie and Riven stiffened at the answer.

Katie put her head to the wall. "What idiot mated with her and produced me?" she said as Percy and Theodore sprayed coffee across the table.

Don't Give Up

"How were you and I are the only people in town who were oblivious?" Katie was wrapped in a blanket on Mary's couch later that day. "My mother says everyone knew, and she's surprised it's taken me so long to figure out."

Mary rolled her eyes. "Which would explain why she freaked out on that phone call with you and couldn't get here fast enough."

"Ugh. That phone call." Katie shed the blanket and reached out to grab a pillow. "It's like I'm so brave over the phone and then I get in front of her, and I can't remember things properly." She sunk back into the couch. "What is wrong with me?"

The pair sat in silence for a few minutes before Mary spoke. "I feel protective of you with your mom. *It's taken you so long to figure out?* That puts the weight of the whole situation on you—the last person who should be in the hot seat with this revelation."

"You never had a clue either?" Katie asked, stroking Henry's back.

"That the man who tried to railroad our entire community was my uncle? No idea at all. It's going to take a long time to wrap my head around it."

"Would you have told me if you knew?"

"Yes, I think I would have," Mary answered. "This is one of the times I wish my mother was here so I could ask her what her thoughts were not to let you know."

"Why didn't anyone else tell me for literally decades?" Katie asked. "I'm so mad, I can't see straight." She punched the pillow in her lap, causing Henry to jump. "They were all making fun of me behind my back." Her eyes fired in anger. "I know it. I hate everyone in town right now."

"You're embarrassed, Katie. And you get a little sharp-sticked when you feel self-conscious. Don't let yourself go there. Nobody didn't tell you from bad motives." She stopped and thought for a moment. "I mean, wouldn't it be truer that if they had bad motives, they would have one hundred percent told you your dad is the town's nightmare?"

Katie dropped her chin to her chest before looking up again. "Then what was it?"

"I can't speak for all the people who might have had knowledge of the situation, but I do know this. We go about our lives thinking that when we interact with people, we take center stage."

"Yeah, center stage. That's my mom."

"Hear me out for a moment." Mary patted her cousin's knee. "I think everyone, me included, can sometimes think we take up more space in people's heads than we actually do. Most people are just doing their very best, trying to make ends meet, raising their children and taking care of tasks at home and work. Never mind all the thoughts swirling in each person's head every day of their lives."

Katie scrunched her forehead. "Thoughts of what?"

"Old hurts. The unfinished business of sadness, grief and embarrassments we always mean to revisit when we have more time," she said, leaning into Katie. "Everyone has past experiences playing like forgotten background music, all while trying to get through life."

"What does that have to do with me and my situation?"

"Exactly," Mary said, hitting her own thigh. "Nothing. Everyone is so focused on their own drama that these pieces of information about you go filed way back in their brains, in the unlikely event they even know in the first place. As much as our child ego wants to believe it, none of us are the focus of other people."

"I will be after today.".

"*Maybe*. But not for long. It'll be like a TV episode that everyone gets wired up with the day after and forgets in a week or two."

"This is exactly why I hate that stupid show you all love," Katie seethed. "It's not much fun when your life is the center of the drama."

The pair of them sat in silence as Katie stared at the fire. The day was much too warm, but she'd asked Mary to start one as it calmed her to watch the flames consuming the wood. "Mind if we get some air?" Mary crossed the house and opened the patio door. A gentle spring breeze cooled the room almost instantly.

"When are we finally going to get some rain?" Katie snuggled into the blanket as Mary returned to the sofa. "Everything is so dry. When the wind blows it nearly blinds me with debris."

"There's always rain at the end of every drought."

"Where'd you hear that?"

"Something my mother used to say."

Katie was silent for a few moments before she popped up in anger. "What about people like Cybil? She was a friend I saw every day and she never said anything to me."

"Do you really think a woman of her generation that lived quietly for decades under small-town radar with her beloved partner is going to reveal other people's secrets?"

"I guess you're right," Katie said, rubbing her eyes. "I think she was trying to tell me without *telling* me the last time we went fishing."

Mary's face was puzzled.

"After the phone call with my mom. She said I should focus on knowing everything about myself." She paused as she thought. "And that I needed to hear what she wants to say to me."

"There you go. Cybil's the wisest woman I know. I think she knew you needed to come to this knowledge on your own."

"Our old shop teacher might be psychic too."

Laughing, Mary leaned in. "What are you talking about?"

"Cybil also told me to show grace to my mom's awkward overtures. Do you think she imagined me sandwiched in a booth with Riven when my mom walked in like she's Judy Garland in *Easter Parade*?"

Mary bit her lip. "I don't know whether to laugh or cry. I can picture everything."

"Then continue envisioning Julia casually throwing out she didn't know I was eating breakfast with my father. She could have sang her words like one of her beloved musicals and it wouldn't have been less jarring. The whole café came to a stop."

"I bet not everyone heard the part about Riven. I'm sure they were staring at your mom. She's a beautiful woman and almost enchanting if you aren't personally involved in her drama."

"My mother did not speak her words. She performed them." Katie took her arms and moved them about in a floating manner like a ballet dancer before slumping into the cushions. "Acting like she always does. I'm going to have a raging case of claustrophobia. I was stuck in the booth as she scooted into Mr. Chapowits, Riven or whoever he is. Henry and I were scrunched into the wall like she hadn't just dropped a bomb. Trapped by my mother's actions once more."

"I'm so sorry. I can't imagine."

"Wait. Did you know Theodore knew?" Katie asked, sitting up. "How did *you* not know if he knew?"

"I think Theodore wanted to tell me. A few days ago, he was

practically bursting. Even Bear was suspicious of him. I dismissed the whole thing as *telenovela* excitement."

"What is with this town's fascination with *Dos Palominos, Un Corazón?*" Katie asked. "Even you, Mary."

"*Dos Caminos, Un Corazón*," Mary corrected. "*Two Roads, One Heart.* But *Two Horses, One Heart* would have been a good title too."

"Or *Two Dogs, One Heart*," Bear said to Henry. "It's practically begging to be written."

Mary's phone rang. She glanced at the screen. "Give me one second. I'll be right back."

Katie sat alone in the room with the dogs. There was a light knock at the patio door and Reyna opened the screen just enough to poke her head in. "Tia? Tia Mary?"

Bear jumped up and ran to the young woman and barked, his entire backside wiggling with excitement as he made his way to her. He stood on his back legs and put his front paws around Reyna's waist. "I love this girl!" he barked to Henry.

"Mary's taking a phone call, Reyna but she'll be back." Katie took a deep breath, attempting to smile in the young woman's presence.

"I'm locked out of our apartment in the barn. I came to see if Tia Mary had her keys." Reyna stopped hugging Bear and looked at Katie with concern. "Are you sick? Do you need something?"

"See what I mean?" Bear said. "She's a senior in high school and she still looks out for others. Just like her mamá."

"She's going to be moving on soon," Henry said. "I sense it."

"*No*," Bear said, emphatically. "She's going to stay here and live in the barndominium forever with us."

"I keep telling you—nothing lasts forever," Henry replied. "No matter how much we want it to."

"I'm fine, Reyna. Really. How are your college applications coming?"

"Slow."

"Really?" Katie asked. "You're always so ahead of the track on everything with school."

"As it seems with all snarls in my life—a lack of money gums things up," Reyna said. Bear had come to her side with eyes so full of sadness at Henry's prediction of her impending departure, he was almost cartoonish in his expression.

"What about scholarships?"

Reyna shrugged her shoulders. "I wasn't born here, and my mom is still waiting on her papers. No Federal Aid for me but there's other state and local scholarships I'm trying to work through. I can always go to the community college here in town for the first couple of years."

"But you want to be an attorney and go to Theodore's alma mater in Chicago," Katie said. "Your dream isn't Merivelle Community College."

Reyna tilted her head and smiled. "Not too long ago, MCC would have been my wildest dreams come true. I want to remember that through this college process."

"She's staying in Merivelle," Bear said with finality. "Where we can all keep our eyes on her to keep her safe." He licked Reyna's hand.

"Perhaps you're right, Bear. A myriad of things each day can change the direction of a person's journey." Henry sighed and closed his eyes.

"Where's your dad?" Katie asked abruptly.

The young woman was puzzled, almost alarmed. "Is my mother here? Did we hear something about him?"

"Oh, Reyna. I'm so sorry," Katie said. She sat up on the edge of the couch. "I only wondered if anyone ever thought to ask you where he might be."

Bear leaned into Reyna, feeling the weakness in her legs. He guided her to a chair across from Katie and set guard beside her as her pulse began to slow.

"I shouldn't have asked you. It really slipped out."

"It's all right, Tia. It's just that he's become a ghost in our lives." Reyna's voice was quiet and soft. "It actually feels nice to hear someone ask about him."

"Do you miss him?"

Reyna kissed the top of Bear's head. "Sometimes. The idea of a father maybe more than him."

"You don't have to say anything else."

"My mother's husband isn't *my* dad."

"But I thought—"

"He's Pablito's dad. I have no idea where my own is. In Mexico? But he could be here somewhere in the States. I could pass him every day and not know it's him. I don't even know if we'd recognize one another after all this time."

"Have you asked your mother?" Katie said. "She could answer a lot of things for you."

"My mother used to cry every day and night before Bear showed up and saved Pablito." Reyna looked at the dog, tenderly tracing the scar where the snake had struck when Bear had stepped between it and the young boy. "We were starving most days after the coyotes ate our chickens—no more eggs. We were literally at the end of our beans when Tia Mary and her wonderful dog visited us the first time."

Bear smiled at Reyna. As she spoke, the smells of the summer day years before mingled in his memory. Coffee and simmering pinto beans had wafted from the Posada's mobile home as he played in the dirt outside with Pablito. He panted in happiness recalling his first friends in Merivelle.

"And then we were part of Mary's world. She fought for us. We weren't isolated anymore. We finally had a home where we didn't panic with a car driving by slowly or jump at a knock on the door. The thought of my father was filled in with other things; school, extracurricular activities, helping Pablito however I can while my mom works at the co-op. Sometimes I realize it's been weeks since I've thought about either of our dads. I'll feel a little guilty. But mostly, I'm so happy to have a place to call home."

Katie sat lost in thought for several moments. "You're very wise, Reyna. I wish I had your thinking and grace when I was nearly eighteen."

"It comes mostly from my mamá. And perhaps doing without things other people take for granted. I might not have seen it that way without a lack first. Or at least that's what I tell myself."

"And you have no daydreams about fathers who may be boat-builders in faraway ports who dream about meeting you again?"

"Wait, I never said that," Reyna said, laughing. "I think about things like that all the time! A good *telenovela* episode keeps my heart open to the possibility of the unexpected."

Tears formed in Katie's eyes. "I don't think we would have been friends when I went to high school and that makes me sad. What a gift it would have been to have someone like you nearby during my teen years."

"But we're friends now. And I'll tell you something about the show you roll your eyes at and suddenly leave when we're all settling in with popcorn on Wednesday nights."

Katie leaned toward the young woman to listen.

"You can never take a wrong turn with a *telenovela*. There is no dead end."

"Having never seen an episode, I'm going to take your word for it, Reyna."

"It's true. No matter how wild the episode, how unbelievable the characters, we're simply one set of twins or a mask reveal away from being on a forward moving course again," Reyna said, grinning. "You never know how things can turn and help you in the way you least expect it. And sometimes in the most ridiculous, funny way possible."

Dry Town

Katie returned home, leaving Mary and Theodore's house well past what she supposed her mother's bedtime to be. The afternoon she'd spent at Mary's had drifted into an evening when Theodore explained, with Riven's blessing, he had been summoned to the man's home only that week and had reluctantly agreed to help Riven make friends in Merivelle. All in aim at building a bridge with Katie.

Hearing the story for the first time, Mary was floored. A fact that gave Katie satisfaction, not feeling alone on an island of naiveté about her own history. Percy had appeared sheepishly at the Bailey's front door during the evening hours, explaining his own knowledge of her parentage had not been of his own volition.

Pondering the new information as she put her key in the lock of her front door, she realized her mother had left it slightly ajar. She entered, nearly turning around instantly. "Katherine, I've been waiting—"

"No."

The older woman's mouth was frozen open. She closed it

when seeing her daughter's face stripped of anger, revealing raw hurt, like bark stripped from a sapling.

"I don't want you to speak."

"But—"

"No words."

"But I really want to—"

"No."

"I can't keep quiet. When something's on my mind, I have to say something. Better out than in my therapist tells me."

Katie hands began to shake. "Can you really sit in my house and say those words considering your inability to speak to me about a subject that would have cleared up a lot with how my life has gone?" Katie clenched her fists to still them. "Please give my regards to your idiot therapist. You're still the same."

Steering clear of Julia, Henry jumped onto the opposite side of the couch and settled into his blanket left from the morning. He faced Katie as he listened, a grave expression on his face.

"Should the dog really be on such nice sofa?"

Katie's eyes widened.

"Forget I said something. I rather like your open policy with pets," Julia said, making two quick kissing sounds as Sonny and Cher flew from their open cage in the guest bedroom and onto her outstretched fingers.

"You're doing what you always do when you know you've made a mess of things."

"And what's that, Katherine?"

"You dance to the next subject with so much absurdity you hope people forget your recent messes." She turned to the door. Henry hopped off the couch and went to her side. "I'm going back to Mary's."

"No, *I* can stay with my niece." Julia sat up, balancing a bird on the forefinger of each hand.

"You haven't seen her since she was in high school. You

missed her mother's funeral. I wouldn't dream of sending you to spend the night."

"Mary and I got along fine in her driveway. She said for me to let her know if I needed anything. Remember?"

Katie unclenched her fists. "You've sucked me into talking. You love not talking about important things. Now I'm going to make sure we do a lot of not talking."

Julia sat the birds on her knees and began gesturing.

"What are you doing?"

"I'm learning sign language with an online course."

Katie threw her hands in the air. "Of course you are."

Her mom signed—*Please don't be mad at me*—as she said the words in a heavy whisper.

"Stop that!"

"Katie, do you have a problem with sign language?"

"*I have a problem with you*! You are a caricature. Over the top. Too much!"

"I'm an original."

"Acting unhinged is not *an original*, it's an embarrassment," Katie said, her face flushing.

"You know, your ungrateful behavior is really my own fault—"

"At least you're taking responsibility for something. That's a first."

"You had too much growing up. We spoiled you rotten."

"You and the man who I *thought* was my father. Until the day he was arrested at my party. You ruined my birthday!"

"You've had a ton of other birthdays. Stop with the theatrics."

Katie was paralyzed by the irony of her mom's words. Julia—dressed in a floor-length pink peignoir with feather trim at her wrists and neckline, gestured as she spoke, sending bits of fluff into the air.

"You're different, Katherine. And I don't know if that's a good thing."

"For the last time, my name is not Katherine."

Henry felt Katie's legs begin to shake. He leaned in and whined to remind her of his presence. Her hands fell to his head. The dog almost seemed to nod in encouragement, his eyes full of what could be taken as wisdom and understanding.

"I'm unclear what you want from me."

Katie took a breath. "I don't want anything from you. But I *need* you to start taking responsibility for your actions. I'm so exhausted from feeling screwed up. At the rate I go through relationships, I don't even think I'll ever have my own family. And for the first time in my life, I feel I might miss out on something very important. The sadness of it keeps me paralyzed. Most of the time, I can't even feel my feelings. I'm so scared I'll be dramatic."

Julia kissed the top of Sonny and Cher's heads, rose from the couch and returned them to her cage, locking the door. When she returned, she sat on the edge of the couch and cleared her throat. "My drinking has left its mark on you."

Her daughter backed into the chair behind her and sat, her face weary with the jet lag of unspoken history. Henry stepped to her side.

"You don't drink. At all."

Crossing her arms, Katie raised her eyebrows. "I made it a guiding crux in my life not to make other people clean up my actions."

"Was it that bad for you?"

"No."

Julia picked up a magazine from the coffee table and fanned herself. "Thank goodness," she murmured.

Katie eyes practically bugged out of their sockets. "It wasn't bad. Your drinking was a freaking nightmare. You left me to fend for myself. Sometimes, I was so young, I tiptoed to reach the counter looking for food."

"I didn't always leave you to drink," Julia whispered, looking at the front door, her face stricken as if a phantom crossed the threshold. "I wanted to go out." Her gaze returned to her daughter. "But most of the time, I stayed. For *your* sake."

"Do you seriously want me to seem grateful for that? Sometimes you sat with empty bottles piling up while soap operas ran non-stop during the day. You'd shake an empty glass at me when I walked in from school as you stared catatonically at the television. Kudos for at-home drinking under the heading of responsible childrearing."

"I know I was sick, but I still tried to think what was best for you. I didn't ever bring anyone into our home after your father was arrested."

"You can't help it, can you? That man was not my father. You realize being a parent isn't like being presented with a pageant sash and crown and you begin your parenting reign."

Her mother crinkled her eyebrows. "I never said it was."

Katie stopped like a lightning bolt had hit her. "Were you even married?"

"No, of course not. We just said that, so people didn't get judgy about our living arrangements. Which came in handy when he was arrested. I wasn't responsible for anything he'd done."

Images from the muted television flashed a late-night talk show, the host and guest talking animatedly, catching Julia's attention for a few moments. Glaring, Katie snatched the remote, turned it off and slammed it back onto the glass table. "You never told me what my fake dad did that got him arrested."

"He stole money."

"From whom?"

"That's the thing. I don't know if Lance really did."

Katie jumped forward from her seated position, nearly ejecting Henry from his resting place. Her eyes went to the door.

Deep breaths.

Puzzled by how strongly she felt she almost heard Alicia's calming yoga voice in her ear, Katie stopped. Though one part of her brain mocked her for doing so, she closed her eyes and breathed in, holding it for several counts before releasing it slowly. When she was finished, she opened her eyes and said, "That's not what I asked. Who did he steal from?"

"Riven," Julia answered. "Your real father had your stand-in father arrested. He worked for Riven and apparently took a large sum of cash from one of his businesses."

"This is *Riven* we're talking about. Are you sure?"

"I don't really know," Julia said, shrugging. "I wouldn't be surprised either way."

Katie grabbed the back of her neck. "Do you mean to tell me, thanks to you and Riven Chapowits, there's a possibility an innocent man has a larceny charge on his record?"

"He was gifting things that were above his pay." Julia shook one of her wrists, extending it in her daughter's direction. "Like this diamond bracelet watch." She lifted her eyebrows in a hopeful manner. "It'll be yours when I'm gone."

"I'm not interested in ever having that piece of jewelry on my person."

"But no one loves sparkle and bling more than you."

"And thanks to you, I'm starting to hate it. I can't believe how shallow you can be."

Soften your gaze and notice what you observe.

Katie relaxed the space between her eyebrows and took another breath. "Who else knew that Riven was my father?"

Her mother's fingers trembled. The two women's eyes met as Julia clasped her hands together to stop from shaking. "Not many people. I was at the end of high school and Riven had graduated two years before. Only one teacher knew the real reason I disappeared after my senior year."

"Cybil."

Her mother nodded. "She has always been a real friend to me. Especially when I returned home with a baby and a flimsy story." Even in the low light of the room, it was obvious Julia's face paled. "I don't know what I would have done without her and Honey's kindness."

"What do you mean you returned with a story?"

"My absence was explained as an impulsive, youthful marriage gone bad. I stayed with some far-flung relatives for a year. My parents were so mad at me, they didn't visit me once."

"What about Riven?"

"I told him as soon as I found out I was pregnant. We wrote to each other the whole time I was gone."

"And?"

"He was eager for us to get married. He was head over heels for me," Julia said, the memory of it giving her pleasure as she sat up and wriggled in place with a smile on her face. Her daughter's piercing gaze drained her nostalgia.

"What did saner heads have to say? Aunt Margaret, for instance."

"I wanted her to be an ally. She'd always praised Riven's work ethic. He was so thankful she saw what other's missed in his scrawny stature." She paused, her expression perplexed. "Then Margaret surprised both us. She was furious with Riven for ruining my life. She was much older, already expecting Mary while running our parent's farm with her husband. The entire time he was growing up, I could tell Riven thought my sister walked on water. It crushed him that she was so disappointed with our news."

Katie turned on a lamp beside her. "You mean to tell me somehow my birth is what has caused Mary a world of trouble."

"No, of course not." Julia shook her head. "Mary has nothing to do with this story."

"Clearly, Riven has been evening a score with her dead mother."

Be open to signs from the Universe.

Katie recalled the phrase and her own rising anxiety from the corpse pose during savasana. "We both know our actions are never only about us. Whatever we do today, inevitably spills into tomorrow, next week or month or even years down the road."

Her mother cocked her head, a mindless habit she'd picked up from years with her parakeets. "That doesn't sound like how you talk, Katie. See how you've changed?"

"Who paid for my college?"

Julia's body jerked like she'd been randomly pushed by a passing stranger. Her chin jutted out in defiance. "What does that have to do with anything?"

"How did I get a degree without any student debt?"

"Let me explain." A tiny pink feather was blowing in the air in front of Julia. She held out her hand, letting it land in her palm. "Riven was so excited when he found out *I* was pregnant." She placed a protective hand over her stomach. "We were *both* so thrilled with our future. That's not say we weren't in a real jam being in a small town and unmarried. Riven had always been alone—" She stopped. "Or would you like me to start calling him your dad?"

Katie blinked in the slowest motion possible. "Too soon. If ever."

"Riven never had any family. We even had him to Sagebrush Farms for a few holidays."

At the thought of a young Riven eating in the home that was now Mary and Theodore's, Katie felt a sudden rush of emotion so strong, she associated the sensation with panic, though she couldn't name it. Henry opened his eyes and put a paw on her arm, nudging her with his snout.

"To say he was excited was an understatement. Before you

were born, Riven brought a tri-fold cardboard savings book from a bank for children to put coins in and learn how to save. He'd already filled up all the quarters, dimes and nickels for you. It was a small amount of money—maybe twenty dollars when it was completely filled but he was so proud to do it for you."

Henry scooted in and put his head on Katie's thigh, sighing. The story had caused tears to form in her eyes and she felt her breath stop as if she couldn't take any oxygen in. She started to panic.

Let the emotions crest and allow—

Clearing her throat to interrupt her own recollection of Alicia's words, Katie sat resolutely and uncrossed her arms as her mother continued, her legs beginning to shake in place.

"I was frustrated at Riven for not putting financial matters together as fast as I imagined it could be done. After you were born, I started dating other men, thinking it might really light a fire under him. Looking back, I realize he was already working around the clock. Jealousy was not the answer to accelerating the arrival of my dreams."

Really? That emotional disaster of a plan didn't work? Katie thought.

"Everything spiraled after that. Riven became distant and withdrawn. By the time Lance arrived in Merivelle, there was a huge chasm between Riven and I. He was never the eager young man excited to bring coin portfolios to share. We stopped outlining plans for college funds and big houses. It was the exact opposite of what I had hoped to achieve.

"I've got to hand it to him. Riven never ran away. Instead, he worked like he was haunted. Saving money like he wasn't sure of his next meal, taking any job that was available. He actually slept in the backroom of the grain elevator during harvest season. He must have brought in a small fortune working so many hours in the summertime. Everyone marveled at his strength and tenacity despite his skinny stature. I think the respect of those summer harvests opened up some real doors for Riven. His life changed very rapidly after a few seasons of backbreaking work."

"A farming community doesn't care where you come from—only how hard you work," Katie said, her face etched in deep thought.

Sensing her daughter's diminishing anger, Julia reached for her hand, but Katie's eyes were glued to her car keys on the coffee table. The older woman pulled back and quietly waited.

In the distance, the evening Amtrak train approached the station, and though half a dozen city blocks away from Katie's home, the wind carried the sound of the horn to her open front door causing her to turn at the sound. Henry sniffed the air and wagged his tail eagerly, invigorated by the sound.

"You still didn't answer my question. Who paid for my college?"

Fluttering her hands, Julia said, "Riven and I had fallen out with one of our more colossal fights. And in front of a lot of people at the summer county fair. It was a spectacle, for sure. My parents were mortified when they heard about it." She was amused at the recollection.

"You're smiling?" Katie was horrified.

Julia fluffed her bangs before running her hands through the rest of her hair. "Two men fighting for my attention. I know it's wrong, but it was such a delicious feeling. Though as my therapist points out—any unhealthy validation-seeking behavior benefits will be fleeting."

Henry put a paw on Katie's arm and groaned. She cleared her throat. "Back to how that relates to this conversation."

"After that last fight, and all of Merivelle talking, Margaret told me to end it with Riven because nothing good ever came from our interactions. Our parents were getting older and stressed with the drama. When I told Margaret I needed to keep in touch with Riven for you financially, she insisted on paying for your college—I just had to cut all ties to stop all the drama."

Katie held a hand up. "So, to be clear, you trained me to resent a woman that gifted me a free college education?"

"You don't know how Riven and I might have worked it out had it not been for Margaret interfering. She may have created the monster she tried to steer me away from!"

"Mary had student debt after she finished college."

"It's on Mary if she wanted out-of-state tuition. Her father had passed by then, and she would have known the farm wasn't the same."

"When will you ever take your share of responsibility when a situation go sideways?" Katie's voice was strong and heartfelt. "I need a clear picture of my history, so I have a guide how to behave better. At least, give me the courtesy of owning your mistakes so I have the truth."

Julia paused with no words for several moments. "I do want to acknowledge Margaret kept her word for your education, even when I'm sure she could have used the money in other ways." She bowed her head and Katie was unsure if she was praying. When she looked up, her face was semi-triumphant. "Remember—Mary was awarded scholarships from almost everywhere she applied to pay for her college. She was just out-of-pocket for her master's degree."

"That's not the point," Katie said, barely above a whisper. "I never had the opportunity to thank Aunt Margaret properly."

"Oh, no. She never wanted you to feel indebted. Margaret made me promise that I'd never tell you."

"And yet, you have."

"She's gone. I don't think our oath extends beyond death."

"There's a certain nobility to keeping your word even if the other party isn't present to insist it's carried out." Henry went to the slightly ajar door. He turned back to gaze at Katie. She rose and followed him, opening the interior door wide so he could look out into the dark evening.

She turned back to her mom. "I was almost always a rebellious brat to her."

"That's just what teenagers do, Katie. Margaret never thought a thing of it."

"I have a feeling there were probably a lot of gaps that she covered so I wouldn't feel left out. Am I right?"

Julia bit her lip and nodded.

"I'm mortified." Katie sat and put her head in her hands. "I went after Mary with a vengeance in high school. Mocked her any chance I could get; I was so jealous of how different her life seemed to be from mine."

"She was kind of a book nerd, if you remember," Julia interjected. "You were always the star, and she was merely the wind beneath your wings," she said, her voice melodious with the words.

Katie ignored her mother's singsong inflection. "Had it not been for Bear Bailey's, Mary would have lived in Chicago. And I'd have had an ugly hatred eating me up whenever I thought of her. Thank goodness for Bear."

"You two would have worked it out. Mary's dog gets too much credit."

"I wouldn't expect you to understand Bear. He brings people *together*. You should spend some time with a few good dogs."

Henry turned around from the door and barked as Katie's phone rang. She answered it, standing up and turning her back to her mom. "It's okay, Theodore. I made it home." She paused as she scanned the floor while listening. "Thanks, I want to come back but—"

You are the Universe in ecstatic motion.

The words had such force, Katie turned around. Her mom was still sitting on the couch, flipping through a magazine, folding the top of a page down for further perusal later.

You are the Universe in ecstatic motion.

In the distance, the earlier arriving train had unloaded passengers. A horn blew again signally the continuation of its night route past Merivelle. Henry jumped up and pushed the handle of the door open as Katie hung up her call and grabbed her car keys, following Henry like a compass out into the night.

WELL-GUARDED HOUSE

A FULL MOON illuminated the blueish-green leaves emerging from the branches of the sagebrush bushes surrounding the sandy hills of the Bailey's house. Sitting in the darkness of her car with Henry beside her, Katie stared into the distance. She sat with her door partially opened and the engine still going. She'd removed her seatbelt and stepped her left leg out of her car but had frozen in place with the movement. Caught between wanting to drive across the country until she ran out of land and walking into Mary's house to sleep for days, she sat listening to the far-off call of coyotes. White night clouds took turns tagging the moon before blowing eastward.

Pawing at the steering wheel, Henry whined at Katie before turning his head in question.

"Hard to believe, but at this moment I'm more exhausted than angry," Katie said, pulling her leg back into the car and turning off the engine. "I need to sleep before I drive myself as far away from here as I can." She put her head on the steering wheel and tried to cry as she breathed heavily, though no tears formed. The door of her car was still open, and a gust of chilly wind blew through the car causing her to shiver.

Henry whined.

Coyotes howled again, the wind carrying the sound to the car so that Katie couldn't tell if the animals were a mile away or merely over the nearest sandhill. She listened seeming confused. "Do you know American Indians believed that if you heard a coyote howl, something was about to die or be born?"

Henry pushed his body closer to Katie. Her trembling lessened with his gesture.

"I feel it's true, Henry. I just can't tell which is about to happen in my life. Birth or dying. Dying or birth. Or both. It all seems the same to me." Her face was creased with worry. She shook her head. "I just need sleep to figure it out."

A light in the house turned on and in crisp night air, one of the Bailey's patio doors opening could be recognized, if one was familiar with the sound. In a few short moments, Bear came galloping around the house. With his eyes wide and ears alert, the Great Pyrenees looked ferocious. His focus was on the eastern night sky and the sound of the wild coyotes in the distance. Bear ran to the frontage of the property and then on to one of the taller sandhills. His white coat reflected the moonlight as he surveyed the land. At his presence, coyotes ceased howling, only yipping in sporadic spurts as they started to run away. For good measure, Bear tilted his head back and bellowed at the moon. One by one, dogs in the surrounding area joined Bear as the wind carried their howls and barks into the night, a community canine chorus protecting the humans they loved.

Sitting up in the car, Henry crawled over Katie's lap to join his voice to the canine chorus, his voice frail but full of heartfelt vigor.

"Good grief, Henry. Settle down," Katie said, jumping in place at the sound. She felt his bones vibrating with the exertion of his howls and noticed a proud smile on his face that he was able to join, despite his age and health. "Never mind. You howl at the moon and coyotes with Bear all you want, good boy."

In a short time, the coyotes were silenced and moved on with the night wind. Bear's attention snapped to the circular drive. His eyes widened for a split second before his ears relaxed and he trotted to the car, his tongue hanging out in happy panting at the unexpected guests. He approached the open car door, his ears dropping when he sensed Katie's countenance. "What's happened?"

Henry's eyebrows knitted in worry. "She thinks she's irretrievably lost. She doesn't realize the feeling happens when a person isn't moving forward like their heart is telling them. But she won't travel on past Merivelle, no matter what I try."

Taking a step closer to Katie, Bear dropped his head on her knee. "She smells like rain." He closed his eyes for a few moments before opening them again. "Rain and the scent of a flower I don't know." Bear hooked a paw onto Katie's arm and tugged gently. He nudged toward the direction of the house. "Mary will know what to do."

The porch lights came on. Theodore opened the front door as Mary appeared behind him, pulling on a robe as she rushed through the doorway.

"We need to get going," Henry said, his eyes once again drooping with his age. "I feel it in my bones."

"She shouldn't travel now. She needs Mary," Bear said. "Don't separate them yet."

Her face alarmed, Mary was down the front steps in an instant. Theodore followed right behind. "Are you hurt?" Mary grabbed Katie's hands.

"So tired." Katie's words came out like a small child limited by vocabulary and emotion. "Sleep. Lots of sleep."

Without a word, both dogs jumped from Katie as Mary

and Theodore each took a side to usher her into the cocoon of their home.

⚜

Everyone at Sagebrush Farms was worried. After coming home from work at the co-op, Lupe had quietly gone in to Katie's bedroom. "Her heart is very tired," she said, later in conversation.

"Gah, I needed a two-hour nap once she was done trying to explain the conversation with her mom," Theodore said. "I'd never seen her so panicked trying to get it all out."

Bear whimpered and began to pant. The thought of anyone in their own Dark Den hurt his heart.

"*Todo está bien, Ángel Oso.*" Lupe leaned down to kiss the scar on his face. "Everything is good."

"I'll circle the wagons around her to keep her safe," Mary said. "Like you do for us, Bear."

Henry wandered past the group gathered in the kitchen on his way out for a bathroom break. Standing at the patio door, he shook his head at the Pyrenees. "Mary can't always protect Katie any more than you can keep me in Merivelle."

"We'll see," Bear said. He pushed his snout into the small open gap of the sliding patio door, making it wide enough for the pair to trot outside. "I can get as clever as I need to be."

Help If You Are Hurt

Two days later, Riven drove through the gravel circle drive and sat in his pickup. His focus shifted between the windshield and the front door of Mary's home. Alerted by the sound of a visitor, Henry opted to return indoors to Katie. However, Bear rushed to the front yard, around to the driveway, growly deeply when he saw who was seated in the vehicle. The front door opened as Mary came to the porch and waved the man forward.

"Come on in, Riven. I promise Bear won't hurt you." The early evening spring air had a warmth to it; the scent of sandy soil mingled with the hint of sagebrush. Doves cooed in the distance as a cricket or two sang for the first time in the season.

Bear squinted in confusion. With an encouraging smile on her face, Mary motioned Bear to enter the house from the back patio doors, giving the Great Pyrenees a wide berth from the old man.

Handing his hat to Mary's outstretched hand, Riven murmured his thanks as he entered the house. He cleared his throat when he saw Lupe and Theodore at the island in the kitchen.

Lupe stood in front of the stove, as a tortilla rose on a hot iron cast skillet. "*Buenas noches*, Riven," she said, pressing the air out of it with a kitchen towel. "You've just missed class." She picked up the tortilla and fanned it in the air for a few seconds before passing it to Theodore.

Riven's face was curious.

"We have a deal, Riven. I just have to speak in Spanish while she's cooking. It's hard but I'm trying." He rubbed his forehead and thought for a moment. "*Estoy embarazado*—"

Mary giggled.

"Wait. What did I say?"

"That you're pregnant," Riven replied.

"*Embarazado* isn't the masculine word for embarrassed?"

"*Avergonzado* is the word, I believe," Riven answered.

Theodore turned to Lupe. "Is this true?"

"Yes, *mijo*." Lupe began cleaning a bowl she'd used to mix the dough. "No more tortillas for you this evening." She rinsed the bowl under warm water. "Riven can speak, so Riven can eat."

Motioning with a drying towel, Mary reached for the bowl. "You've done enough for us tonight. No more spoiling Theodore."

Lupe folded her apron and then smacked Theodore on the backside in a congenial manner, before going to the patio door.

"Stay for coffee with us, Lupe. I'll do something for you," Theodore said, holding a percolator in the air.

"Too soon," she answered, making eye contact with the guest. "Perhaps one day."

Riven cleared his throat and ran his hands through his thinning gray hair. "How are your children, Lupe?" The words were unnatural in their deliverance, though the man's eyes were sincere.

"They're very good. Thank—" Lupe paused. "*Gracias*."

"Good." Riven nodded his head. "*Muy bueno*."

Lupe met her former landlord's gaze with quiet dignity. "I need to look at homework and evince my children if there's anything they need to change."

"Word of the Day?" he asked with a smile. "Don't you mean *convince?*"

"I would if I were trying to make them believe something, but here in this instance, I want to show them, so *evince* is a more fitting word for my job as a parent," Lupe said, opening the door, her face the picture of serenity. "I think all children's hearts, no matter their age, are reached by a parent showing rather than telling." She gave a slight nod to the bedroom where Katie slept, pausing halfway out the patio door.

Riven nodded. "I think I understand what you're saying."

Smiling, Lupe looked to Mary. "Leave a little breeze? Like always?" At Mary's nod, Lupe left the door open a few inches. A pleasant gust of wind moved through the kitchen as the trio watched her walk down the path to her children.

Mary and Riven met each other's gaze.

"It's because of me, isn't it?" The heel of his cowboy boot began to tap rapidly under the table before he held his knee to stop it.

"What?" Theodore asked.

"Lupe's raising her children in your barn."

"A renovated barn. Much better than the shell of a mobile home you rented out to her." Mary's face was flushed with the memory.

At his wife's pause, Theodore jumped in. "Don't forget. You wouldn't fix a toilet until they were caught up on their back rent. I'll never forget Pablito coming out of the sagebrush with a roll of toilet paper the night I first visited the Posadas."

"We got them out of there that same night but who knows what would have happened to them had I not been walking my dog one random summer day months before?" Mary took a breath and settled herself as Bear began a low growl. "I'm good, boy."

The wind blew through the opened patio door with a whistling sound that startled Riven. "Without boring you with tales of my own youth, I want you to know that I'm more ashamed than you would believe in how I treated the Posada family."

Mary raised her eyebrows. "And you're suddenly coming to this conclusion now for what magical reason?"

Bear and Theodore turned to Riven. The percolator gave a quick gurgling sputter in the background, though neither turned at the sound.

"Old age slows your body down while simultaneously turning your mind up. Runaway thoughts make me feel caught in my own body. Many nights it's pure hell."

"You want to do the right thing, so it eases your *own* mind?" Mary asked. "I don't know if that's going to open a lot of the doors you've slammed shut over your lifetime. It has to be for something more than avoiding consequences that you've created through your actions."

"I want Katie to be proud of me."

"There's a fantastic start," Theodore interjected, clapping his hands together. "A father trying to reach out to his daughter."

Mary was not dissuaded. "It doesn't feel clean to me."

"It doesn't?" Theodore asked, his face incredulous.

"It's understandable that you don't trust me, Mary. I have a lot of work ahead of me," Riven answered. "You're the person closest to my daughter, so I'm keenly interested in your viewpoint."

"*Your daughter*," Mary began—a small shiver involuntarily moved through her body before she began again. "Katie is not here to make you, or Julia, feel better. Nor to fix your nighttime anxiety or to provide you proud moments." She stopped. "I just realized that I know nothing about you to speak further."

Clearing his throat, Riven murmured, "If it's all the same to you, I'd like if Katie could know the history of my family first. I feel she's had enough information shared without her consent."

Mary studied the man, noting his hands were shaking and

he'd swallowed nervously waiting for her response. "If your motive is really to help Katie, then I'm all for it."

The sweeping wind outside died down as the sun fully set for the evening. A chill filled the room as Theodore stood up and went to the percolator. "Do you like cream or sugar?"

"Black, please."

"Like your heart?"

"Theodore!"

"We're teasing, Mary," Riven said, though his voice was slightly uneasy. "Your husband is showing me the finer points of friendship."

"You might say I'm evincing him how to make and sustain relationships not motivated by financial gain." Theodore clinked his cup to Riven's as he sat at the table.

Bear sat next to Mary's chair and faced Riven, his eyes still and focused on the man. He did not growl but he did pull his lips back from his teeth, looking goofy to Mary and Theodore but with an entirely different effect on their visitor.

"That dog of yours. He always has me uneasy."

"What do you mean?" Mary said, sitting down as she stirred creamer in her coffee.

"I get the feeling he would tear me to pieces if he could."

Mary pulled Bear close to her. "Only if he thinks you're going to hurt someone he loves. Then he's a sight to behold in the moonlight as he fights coyotes back from the farm, aren't you boy?" She nuzzled into the top of his head for a moment. "But Bear can also be twice as gentle and even more astute understanding someone's true motives. I rely a lot on his intuition when I'm around people I've only just met."

The Great Pyrenees's tail began to thump the floor in joy at Mary's words. Riven cleared his throat and took a drink of coffee. "Is Katie able to talk?"

"She's been in her room for the better part of three days," Mary said.

"Is she all right?" The old man's hands began to tremble. He set his coffee cup down.

"Nothing to be alarmed by. Mary has a close eye on her."

Riven took a breath and began to speak before abruptly closing his mouth.

"It is a conversation about your daughter. You get to share your thoughts," Mary said.

"Why is it such a bad thing for Katie to find out I'm her father?"

Theodore was in the middle of drinking his coffee. He swallowed hard, wincing when the hot liquid burned his throat. "I'm going to let you handle this one, Mary," he choked.

Bear whined and laid down under the table, putting his paws on top of Mary's feet in protection.

"The dog too?" Riven asked.

"Riven," Mary replied. "How could I put this in a way you understand without setting fire to the bridges you're attempting to mend?"

"Go on," he said, leaning into the table.

"Do you want the white glove version or right between the eyes?" Theodore asked. "She always asks me that."

"Is there a third option?" Riven reached into his inner pocket and pulled a tablet out of a small tin and put it on the end of his tongue and swallowed. "Maybe something more in the middle?"

"I'll do my best, but no promises. Especially since the people you've hurt over the years never got a third option," Mary said. "Let's start with someone not even in the picture anymore, Clara Lamb."

Riven stared at the floor like he wanted it to open up and swallow him.

"You remember then. Franklin's tools being purchased for

next to nothing after you scared everyone off from buying them, lest they face your wrath. And had it not been for their honest real estate agent—"

"Katie was the real estate agent," Theodore interjected.

"Without your daughter's help, Clara might have undersold her home to be done with the stress of you just so she could be closer to her grandchildren," Mary continued, her voice stern. Bear's low growling under the table reminded her to remain calm.

Riven dropped his head.

"The darling, kind and lovely Lambs," Mary said, her eyes filling with tears. "I miss them every day. Why was the property so important to you?"

Theodore reached for Mary's hand and squeezed it, their eyes meeting as he nodded his support to her.

"If I'm honest, and I don't know if you want me to be," Riven began, eyeing Bear as the Great Pyrenees lifted his head. He cleared his throat. "I wanted the property to get close to your dog."

"Why?" Mary asked, forehead creased.

"You were so determined with the co-op and nothing I was doing was stopping its progress. I thought if I could cripple you where it would hurt the worst, it might give you enough pause, I could have figured out what else to do," Riven said. "I'm sorry. I really am."

The only sound was the percolator giving a single gasp on the counter. Mary held onto Bear; her arms wrapped around his neck protectively as she glared at Riven.

After a few moments, Theodore cleared his throat. "You didn't think hurting me would hurt Mary most?"

Mary shook her head at Theodore. Her expression was clear—*Are you kidding me?*

"Harming a dog doesn't carry a murder charge like it would if I hurt you, Theodore," Riven mumbled.

Mary's face was aghast. "I... I don't know if I can actually keep talking on this subject."

"As I said those words out loud, I'm clear how diabolical I've been in the past."

"Diabolical? I lost my mother, and all I had was my husband and a wonderful dog that literally saved me. You went after the trifecta of goodness—Bear, the Posadas and the Lambs."

"I want to change. For Katie."

"As much as I want to help Katie by being peaceful with the man who is her father, I'm having a real hard time finding a way to do that given how mean and uncaring I just heard you speak," Mary said.

"I know this isn't an excuse, but I didn't have a father to show me things when I was growing up; he was gone a lot." Riven's eyes moved back and forth, his face draining of color. "I was bullied and tried to be tougher because I didn't know a different way. You have to believe me if I could go back and be different, I really would." He gripped the table to steady his shaking hands. "I'm trying new things you wouldn't believe."

Thank God, I know about the yoga lessons, Mary thought. *Or I'd strangle him with my own hands. With or without Katie's DNA.*

Bear whined and searched Mary's face. His friend, Jiff had shown him how she would have turned out to be the twin of Mr. Chapowits had he not been in her life. And though he couldn't fathom his beloved Mary ever acting in an unkind way, he left her side of the table and slowly went to stand in front of Riven. He bowed his head, touching his nose to the man's shaking knees.

"What's this?" Riven said, his voice choking. He held his hands back from Bear, his eyes wide in fear.

Hooking his paw into the crook of Riven's elbow, Bear whimpered as the man had tears forming in his eyes. He nudged the man with his snout before putting his paw on his thigh so Riven knew he was not alone.

Mary's face melted the same way it had when Bear had brought her abandoned, springtime bunnies onto the porch. "He's trying to help you, Riven. He's saying you're not a coyote anymore. I wouldn't believe it any other way."

Great Place for a Handout

Katie and Mary walked with great speed in the middle of the day. The balmy spring afternoon was a gift from the soon arriving summer and both women used their lunch hour to soak it up. The dogs trotted behind as they exited the co-op and began walking through the tree-lined city blocks of Merivelle.

"Why is it that sometimes being active in the sun will do you just as good as deep rest?" Mary asked.

Katie removed her sunglasses for a moment, pausing mid-stride to let the light warm her face.

"You had me slightly worried at the end of yesterday when you still hadn't emerged your room."

"I was ready to come out for dinner but somehow hearing the three of you talk while I was tucked around the corner made me feel very child-like. It felt good to stay suspended in happy memories of when we were young. Do you remember how we liked to eavesdrop on our moms talking late at night?"

"Us dogs do that all the time, don't we, Henry?" Bear put a paw on the older dog who had unexpectedly stopped for a moment. "Are you all right? You seem even weaker today."

"I need a quick break," Henry said, wheezing.

The two women began to walk again.

"Do you need me stop them for you?"

The old dog shook his head. "I can do it. No need to bother anyone."

"Imagine my surprise when I wake from my coma-like sleep and hear Riven in your kitchen. I thought I was dreaming. Or possibly dead, returned as a ghost to overhear mourners."

"Oh, no, Katie. Do not ever talk like that. I couldn't bear to be without you."

They walked in silence for parts of two blocks, the two dogs following behind as Bear sniffed the slower-moving Henry.

"Do you think you could ever run the co-op without me?" Katie asked, her words spoken in a quiet voice.

Mary's eyes were focused forward, powerwalking as she always did – her brainstorming sessions, as she liked to call them. "Absolutely not. I couldn't and wouldn't want to do it without you. All the impeccable grant paperwork you put through for all of us? Thank, *thank* God for you, Katie. May abundant blessings from every source always be with you and all the generations of your loins," she said, gesturing dramatically as if rain were pouring down on her cousin.

Katie nodded and smiled weakly, but still kept up with Mary's pace.

"Hey, that's supposed to be funny."

"It was."

"I don't actually know," Mary said, slowing her pace. "Do women have loins? And are they blessed? Or is that something to do with men's descendants?" She smiled and waved to an elderly couple on their porch.

"Do you and the dogs have time to join us?" The man on the porch stood up and gestured at the two empty chairs next to him and his wife.

"Another time, maybe!" Mary shouted out, waving. "Out on our afternoon break."

"Hold on. I love these people," Bear said, beginning to pant with excitement. "Follow me, Henry." The Great Pyrenees ran up the porch to the delight of the couple who greeted him as they would any human.

"Apparently Bear has time!" Mary laughed and waved.

Bear stood beside the pair and gently turned so his backpack was within easy reach for them.

"Look at that," the woman said to her husband, laughing. "Bear Bailey's now has a cookie delivery service!"

"We're supporting the Prairtisserie—make sure to drop in and see their lovely bakery!" Mary shouted. "Bear's job is to hand out all their samples today!"

"Just the thing we need for our little party here on the porch, Bear," the woman said. She waved her thanks as Bear lumbered down the stairs to join Henry.

"It makes me happy when we can bring people what they need," Bear said. His pace was brisk and his face happy as the pair of dogs re-joined the women already halfway down the block. "Don't you love when the co-op helps people, Henry?" He stopped and turned his head, puzzled by the old dog's ragged breathing. "You doing okay?"

Henry's tongue dangled out of his mouth. His nose began to bleed heavily, dripping all over the sidewalk. "I'm fine. Let's just keep going." The blood from his nose began to flow and pulse with every step he took.

Bear began howling, causing Mary to spin in her tracks, with Katie mirroring her actions. Henry was struggling to breathe, clear panic in his eyes.

"Do you feel you're going to pass out?" Bear asked, his dark eyes moving back and forth rapidly as Henry swayed in place. "Lean into me."

"Let's keep moving forward. Used to happen to me all the time before I got to Katie's."

"Please lay down, you've lost a lost a lot of blood."

"Leave my old carcass. It's my time to move on. I'm sure of it." The dog dropped to the ground.

"Are you chucking a dummy, Henry? Please tell me this is you just pretending to faint," Bear cried.

The old dog's gums were dry, keeping his lips pulled up and stuck in place. His tongue hung over his mouth as he tried to raise his head.

"Please, no. Katie won't be able to take it. Not now. Hold on, buddy," Bear said, his face horrified as Henry laid still on the sidewalk.

Katie dropped to her knees and pulled Henry close, examining his face as blood smeared all over her. "Get help!"

Mary nodded, already on the phone directing Lupe to where they stood.

"Hang in there. Help is coming." Bear adjusted his tone to soothe the dog, saying the words as gently as he'd ever spoken. He laid on the ground next to the old dog, putting his paw on his leg to let Henry know he was not alone.

"She's been an angel—hobo speak for a kind woman who goes above and beyond," Henry said, closing his eyes and sighing. "She treated this old wanderer like a king. When I'm gone, make sure you always give her a hand when she needs it, Bear."

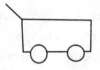

Trolley Stop

"Henry." Josephine stood at the entrance of the Rainbow Bridge. Her expression was joyful as the old dog stared in astonishment.

"I knew it was time to move on. I felt it."

"You're a wise and humble soul, Henry. It's wonderful to see you."

Henry marveled at the light prisms around Josephine while she spoke. His eyes followed the varied colors as they danced in the light. He wiggled his nose curiously and sniffed. "You smell like my favorite flowers."

"And what might those be?" Josephine asked, though she already knew his answer.

"Violets." With Henry's answer, the fields of blowing gold and green grass began to fill with purple flowers. A canopy of branches grew rapidly as a grove of oak trees surrounded the pair. A gentle breeze blew through the boughs as Henry's nose went upward, followed by a long and relieved howl. "Forests and flowers. Two of my favorite smells. Just missing the sounds and smells of the railroad—all three together are my dream of heaven."

Josephine smiled. "I love your imagination, Henry."

"Imagination?" He turned in head in confusion. "This isn't the Rainbow Bridge?"

"It is, but every dog will imagine it differently as they wait for their owner to join them."

A small cricket jumped in front of the old dog and began to rub its front wings together in a happy song. Touching the small creature with his nose, Henry was confused. "Where are all the other dogs?"

"It's not your time, Henry."

The old dog huffed, his droopy jowls filling with air and indignation. "My bones say it's time. Are you sure?"

"We have a way to tell the difference between a dog's soul visiting and one whose time on Earth is complete and they've crossed the Rainbow Bridge. It never fails us," Josephine answered.

"How's that?" Henry asked mournfully.

"Almost immediately, once a dog's paws touch the Rainbow Bridge, everything in them is made new again. It doesn't matter if it's a bruised part of their body or a broken heart from mistreatment. Or *'old bones'* as you like to say," she said, winking. "Along with missing teeth, worn fur and groaning joints—with each passing moment, every step brings a dog back to a healed state. And they become the version of themselves when they were most joyful."

Henry searched the gaps in his mouth, his tongue still spilling between the spaces. His ears fell in disappointment. "I'm only a visitor?"

"For now." Josephine reached out and caressed the dog's head with the care of handling a newborn baby.

A breeze blew through the trees again, swaying the violets with the movement. Though it was clear Henry was disappointed, he closed his eyes and took a deep breath, smiling in the sunlight. "I've traveled more than the average dog and still, I can't recall such a wonderful scent."

The sun seemed to grow brighter, though the area still maintained the temperature of the loveliest spring afternoon. As the light turned brighter and brighter, until there was only white background, Lea appeared out of nowhere, a big smile on her face. "I thought I sensed you up here, Henry. What's our favorite wanderer up to?" She put her cheek next to Henry's. "Here for a quick visit before getting back to Merivelle?"

"I thought it was my time."

"You just needed a little Rainbow Bridge nudge to keep you going. I think Katie still needs you more than we do," Lea answered. Her attention snapped to mayhem in the distance, though nothing could be seen from the bright background. "I was in the middle of refereeing an epic tug-of-war when I sensed you, Henry." She leaned down and breathed into the top of Henry's head. "Safe travels, my friend." She began walking, fading with each step as Henry's forest and violets reappeared.

"I never thought I'd say it, but I want to rest. I'm tired of wandering," Henry said, his cheeks blowing in and out in emotion. It began to rain in the grove of trees, though the rest of the Rainbow Bridge was sunny.

Josephine knelt to him. "Then don't wander anymore."

"I want to stay with Katie but there's this feeling I have that I should always be moving on."

"You can change any feeling you sense you've outgrown," Josephine said, her robes moving in the wind like shimmering water. She massaged Henry's ears as she murmured a few words and moved back to face him. "I have every confidence in you."

"Even if I want to stay to help her, I'm an old dog and as they say, no new tricks."

Josephine gazed to Earth and then to Henry, a look of sincere fondness on her face toward the old dog. "Behave in the way your heart wants to be. Shed anything that no longer serves you. It's that simple."

"I understand." Henry turned to begin his journey back.

"One more thing. A small favor if you'd be so kind," Josephine said.

Behind her in the distance, a hazy figure with a black Labrador stood at the far end of the meadow as majestic mountains appeared for a few brief moments and then disappeared like the pigment swirling off a paintbrush in water.

The old dog raised his eyebrows, waiting for Josephine's request.

"Tell my old friend, Bear Bailey, hello."

11

The Sky's the Limit

"He has a severe case of heartworm. Dr. Luke said it was the worst he'd ever seen. He was surprised Henry was still able to go on walks at all. I think he's seen the last of his adventuring days."

Bear began to howl and shake his head, knowing how much his friend loved to roam.

Mary reached down under her desk, scratching behind the dog's ears. "Poor Bear is in such a state not understanding what's going on with Henry."

"How's our best cousin?" Theodore asked, sitting down in front of Katie's desk at the back of the co-op.

"As you might imagine her to be with her beloved dog at death's door."

Bear let out another howl, hitting his head on the top of her desk. He whined and began to huff, laying down as Mary smoothed the top of his head.

"He's going to be okay, Bear. Dr. Luke said Henry needed to rest and let the medicine work."

Theodore spread out brochures on Mary's desk. "Thank goodness for that. Can you imagine everything going on with Katie right now and then she loses her dog?"

"It was the oddest thing. I sat in the backseat of Lupe's car with Katie. Henry was not breathing at all. Katie was hysterical. It was a scene at the vet's office. Then, when Henry was laying there with barely a pulse, Dr. Luke was talking to her about worst-case scenarios, and Henry popped up like a gopher. He went to the door of the exam room, scratching that he was ready to go home."

Bear wagged his tail, hitting the side of the desk like a drum, a joyful cadence showing his relief at Henry's prognosis. He yelped in happiness.

"Are those travel brochures?"

"Yes!" Theodore responded, his face lighting up as he picked up one with the Leaning Tower of Pisa on the front. "The co-op seems more self-sufficient, and I thought we could steal a few weeks away to make up for lost travel time."

Mary shook her head. "Not now, Theodore. Especially after today with Henry."

"Then when?"

"Our grant funding still isn't secure. Percy's very encouraging but he's not giving anything away about our chances. And besides that, if I'm honest, the co-op isn't self-sufficient. It's Katie-sufficient."

"Meaning what, Mary?"

"Her knowledge of grants and the never-ending paperwork associated with them is what's going to keep the co-op going in the foreseeable future. I swear the paperwork the Rural Initiative needs is like never-ending handkerchiefs out of a magician's hat."

Theodore clapped his hands together. "That's great!" He held a victory fist into the air. "Yay for Katie! She can handle it all while you travel for a bit."

Mary leaned forward. "Today before Henry collapsed, Katie wanted to tell me something. I didn't catch it at the time because

I was so happy to be outside walking but playing it back in my head, I think she wants to leave Merivelle."

"No. You do this every time we're close to getting a break from the co-op," Theodore said. "It's only a quick little vacation. You're the one who always wanted to travel, Mary."

"Wait, what do you mean I do this every time?"

"When I look for opportunities to help you travel, you find ways it won't work. Only long weekends since Bear Bailey's opened."

Bear groaned apologetically.

"Look—you've gone and upset Bear." Mary cocked one eyebrow in warning.

Theodore ruffled the top of the Great Pyrenees' head. "Nothing personal, Bear." He looked to his wife, eyes loving and concerned. "Life is short. Remember you told me that your mom always wanted to publish a book but got caught up with anything in Merivelle but writing."

"What does that have to do with anything?" Mary said. Her voice started out defensive, but her eyes were immediately sad.

"It's great to help. But don't sacrifice your passions under the heading of service. Your dream is to travel. Your mom's was to write a book. And neither has happened. One of you is still here."

Mary bit the inside of her cheek and took a deep breath. Bear closed his eyes and nodded, putting his paw into her hand. She looked up to see Katie behind Theodore, a welcome diversion from the conversation at hand.

"Let's just take a break and enjoy a vacation that's longer than a three-day weekend. And you've just said yourself, Katie can handle everything! She's a genius!"

Mary tried to hide her smile as her gaze met Katie's.

"She's so smart and can run this place probably better than you can," Theodore said, effusively.

"Agreed! She's always been the smarter cousin."

"She's become a complete joy around here. Everyone loves her. And if Percy has half a brain, he'll marry her. They'd be a perfect yin and yang couple."

Katie emerged from behind the doorway. "Settle down, *Dos Caminos, Un Corazón* man."

"How long as she been there?" Theodore asked, looking at his laughing wife.

"Long enough, you big dork," Katie said, sitting beside him instead of behind her desk. "You know, you're the brother I never had."

Theodore reached out and gently punched her upper arm. "A true *telenovela* sibling relationship. And to think I couldn't stand you when I first arrived."

"Aww, Theo. The feeling was quite mutual." Katie made a sappy face.

Theodore clutched his chest as if he'd been mortally wounded.

Mary rolled her eyes. "What's going on with Henry?"

Bear emerged from behind the desk, trotting to Katie's chair, gently nudging her hand with his snout.

"Henry's with my mom. He was too tired to come with me. Didn't even try and get up from his bed when I left."

Bear gave a desperate bark and rested his head on Katie's thigh, looking up at her with concerned eyes.

"He just needs to rest, Bear," Katie said, putting her hands on top of his head. "Everything will work out."

The phone rang on Mary's desk, the extension beep that it was being transferred from the main line. "You'll never guess who's on the other line for you, Mary," Lupe said. "It's going to make your whole day."

Mary picked up and listened. "Clara?" Her voice choked in happy emotion.

Bear went to Mary's side, sitting up in excitement as he tilted his head at the name.

Theodore and Katie waved their greetings like happy mimes. "I'm in my office with some extra visitors. Theodore, Katie and Bear look as excited as I am. We all miss you so much." She waited, nodding her head. "They can't hear you, but I could put you on speakerphone if you like." She smiled. "One sec, Clara."

"Are they there? Hello, Theodore and Katie! And my wonderful friend, Bear Bailey!" Clara's voice had the lilting tone it always had, although it carried a weariness it had taken on after Franklin's death. "I miss you all so very much."

A few moments of silence waited to be filled. Mary took a deep breath as her face softened in remembrance. "And of course, we all miss Franklin deeply. There's not a drive home each night where I don't picture you both waving in the distance."

"Franklin." Clara sighed on the other end of the call. "I love hearing his name spoken aloud. He's also spoken of here, of course. But as Dad and Grandpa. Those are lovely titles, but somehow hearing his given name spoken far away by people he loved profusely gives me great peace."

Bear whined, nodding his head toward the sound of Clara's voice.

"I have a dog here who wants you to know he misses Franklin too."

Gently tugging at Mary's arm, Bear whimpered and gave a little bark.

"And Jiff. He also misses his other friend."

Satisfied his salutations had been properly passed on, Bear sighed and nestled his head alongside Mary's leg.

"That precious corgi came at the right time, didn't he? And then he disappeared into thin air," Clara said, her voice curious. "I think I'll always say a prayer of thanks every time I see one of those wiggle-bottom dogs." She cleared her throat and paused for several moments before continuing. "But that is not the reason I called today."

Mary exchanged glances with Theodore and Katie.

"It's very *Dos Caminos, Un Corazón.*"

"Not you too, Clara?"

"Now, Katie—don't miss out on all the fun."

Theodore tilted his head to Katie, a *tried-to-tell-you* look on his face.

"Did you know they're extending the original program for a Christmas special?" Clara asked. "*Dos Parentes, Una Navidad.*"

"*Two Parents, One Christmas?*" Katie groaned. "Could this show be anymore grating on my nerves?"

"We did not know that!" Theodore slapped Mary's desk, causing Bear to jump. "You've made our day!"

"I was going to call you just on that news alone but no, that's not it. I'm calling about Riven Chapowits. What is going on in Merivelle?"

Katie's eyes widened as she shook her head furiously at Mary.

"We're pretty busy around here," Mary said, simultaneously confused by her cousin's actions. "Maybe you could give us a hint?" She hit the mute button. "*What is it, Katie?*"

"Don't say anything." Katie's neck and chest began to blotch. "About him being my dad."

"It's not my business to tell." She motioned she was unmuting the phone. "I wouldn't even know where to begin with Riven."

"You don't call him Mr. Chapowits anymore, Mary."

"Riven seems to be trying harder these days," Theodore interjected.

"No '*El Chapo*' either?" Clara asked, her voice teasing but curious.

"I gave my word I'd stop using it. Which is a real shame. It was a really good nickname," Theodore said, shaking his head.

"What about you, Katie? What are you calling Riven these days?"

"I don't call him *dad*," Katie blurted out.

Mary's face dropped in horror as she pointed a dramatic finger at Katie. "Calm down," she whispered.

"Well, whatever a person feels like they're compelled to call him these days. I can't tell you how angry I've spent these last few years anytime Riven sprung to my mind. I think I might have hit him with my car, or worse, if I still lived in Merivelle. I'd imagined scenarios of hurting the old coyote and it helped me get my nose above my drowning grief. Like I could still advocate for Franklin somehow through my obsessive thoughts about revenge."

"We're so sorry, Clara," Mary said, as Theodore and Katie nodded their heads in agreement. "I think that's totally understandable."

"But in the past few weeks the mental pictures of revenge have started to dissipate. I realized my thinking could bring me no joy because it couldn't ever bring back Franklin—the kindest man, no matter what anyone else's actions were. After that, I had the most vivid dream about Riven. We stared at one another on Main Street in Merivelle. I gave him a wave I'd extend to any stranger and continued walking. And at the next corner, Franklin was waiting for me with the black Lab, Jiff, from his childhood. He extended his hand and smiled at me with great pride and love. I've felt complete peace on the matter since then."

Bear sat up at Clara's words and though he rarely did it because of his size, he sat on his rear behind and held his paws up in the air with great joy, sighing contentedly.

"May we all be as gracious, kind, and forgiving as Franklin and you have always been, Clara," Mary replied.

Theodore and Katie murmured in agreement.

"After that final dream, I haven't given Riven two thoughts until earlier this afternoon. I got a phone call out of the blue with his voice on the other end. It has a distinct sound to it, and I knew immediately who it was. I had to pinch myself to make sure I wasn't imagining things."

"What did he say?" Katie asked, so softly Mary wasn't sure if Clara heard or was merely continuing on.

"He asked if there was an account I felt comfortable having him wire money to."

Mary sat up taller in her chair. "Why was he offering that?"

"For the money he shortchanged Franklin for all his tools. He offered the difference based on nearly new equipment values. Plus, interest and penalties. Can you imagine? I was shocked at the amount he proposed."

There was a long bit of silence before Theodore asked, "What did you tell him?"

"I accepted his offer. The funds came at the most perfect time. My grandson can pay the last of his civil engineering tuition. Would you believe he wants to build bridges? He can accomplish anything now without the stress of worrying about money and school." She paused for a moment, sighing in a happy manner. "All of this possible because of the building tools his grandfather had used over a lifetime. It feels as close to a miracle from my Franklin as I'd ever hoped to feel."

Keep Away

Upon hearing the news of Henry's health, Percy showed up at Katie's front door, groceries in hand, offering to make dinner as she rested with her dog. A short time later, Mary and Theodore unexpectedly arrived, Bear in tow. In a few minutes time, Percy had served up extra plates of food with both dogs under the table watching for any fallen morsels.

"I don't know why thinking about Riven's conversation at your house is making me feel worse." Katie dropped her fork, splattering tomato sauce on her white tablecloth .

"It's new. You have to give yourself some time to see how you really feel," Percy said. "No need to rush your emotions. You're the one in the driver's seat."

Mary glanced at Theodore, tilting her head toward Percy with her eyebrows lifted. It was clear she was delighted at the man's thoughtfulness toward her cousin.

Picking up a piece of baguette, Katie began tearing it into small pieces. "At first, I liked the idea of Riven at your house. Now I'm feeling weird again." She brushed breadcrumbs off the table, knocking her fork onto the floor in the process. "And I don't know why that is."

Mary bent down to gather the utensil before pushing herself up. "Like the chef said—you need time to process this." She rose to place the fork in the sink, retrieving a new one to place in front of Katie.

"It's a lot, for sure." Theodore twirled spaghetti onto his fork and began gesturing with it. "Mary even had to stop Riven at one point. He spent an hour telling her almost everything about his past, ranging from not returning extra change to trying to get the Lamb's property so he could murder Bear."

"He was going to kill Bear?" Katie stood, pushing her chair back with such force it nearly hit the wall.

"Theodore. Really?"

"Is that what Riven said?" Percy asked.

"Umm... yes. And while the mere thought of that could give me nightmares, I can't explain why I don't think he would have actually gone through with such a diabolical plan," Mary said.

"Oh, he would have, Henry. My friend Jiff showed me what Mr. Chapowits would have done. He would have—" Bear stopped and shook his head. "I need to remember Riven is trying to be different. But it's hard with the memory. I don't even really like to think about it."

"Then stop talking about it," Henry said, closing his eyes. "Behave the way your heart wants to be. That's what Josephine told me."

"*Who?*" Bear raised up in surprise, hitting his head on the table.

"I forgot to tell you. She also said, '*Tell my good friend, Bear Bailey hello.*'"

Bear sighed heavily. "I've never met her, but I love Josephine. Please, tell me something more." He began panting so hard that Mary looked under the table to check on him.

"There are specks of light that surround her when she talks.

Like when the sun's rays hit little drops of rain at the end of a spring shower." Henry thought for a moment. "She's very mesmerizing."

"And she said I was her good friend?"

"That's it. Nothing more."

"That makes me want to try harder. To make Josephine proud. Like I want Mary to be," Bear said. He came up from under the table. He sat up tall with a dignified and focused look on his face.

Katie began drumming her fingertips on the table, looking toward the door nervously.

"It's really fascinating when you think about it," Theodore began, chuckling. "Riven—"

"*My life is not a telenovela for your enjoyment, Theodore!*" Katie slapped the table, her eyes firing in anger. "If you're like that, then imagine everyone else in town. They'll all mock me!"

Mary placed her napkin on her plate. "No one here would ever make fun of you behind your back."

"Promise, Katie. I'd be too scared to," Theodore answered. "But mostly because you're very beloved. We couldn't do without you."

"Being here only a short time, I've only ever heard love and respect when your name comes up in conversation," Percy said, an encouraging expression on his face. "I'd imagine people would rather throw you a heartfelt party than a charivari."

"Percy, what on earth is a *charivari*?" Katie sighed. She was teetering on irritation, though she tried to maintain a curious tone with the gentle man.

Theodore held his hand up in an excited way. Like he was a very motivated pupil on the front row of a favorite class. "Charivari—an old European and North American folk custom, a charivari was a mock parade staged to shame a member of a community."

Mary shook her head. "Not now."

"I never win Word of the Day. I thought you'd be proud."

The front door was open to the screen door. Shadows passed on the sidewalk in front of the house. Bear barked in warning before an extended growl.

"Are you expecting someone?" Mary asked.

"My mom must be home."

"Where'd Julia go?" Theodore asked.

Katie's gaze met Mary's. "She said she was going on a date."

The front door opened. Julia peeked her head in like a neighbor popping by for sugar. "Oh," she said, her voice dropping. "You have company." Sonny and Cher began to chirp in their cage in the adjoining bedroom.

"Is that a problem in my own house?"

"*And* you're in a prickly mood. Another time then," Julia said, though she did not move. "I've brought someone with me, and I was hoping we could talk."

Katie got up and began quickly clearing the table as Percy joined her. "No, please. Let's meet my new father, I'm sure. Then you can move back to Merivelle, and we can all live happily ever after," she muttered under her breath. She turned her back and began to furiously rinse the dishes, clanging silverware on the plates as she scraped them clean. She flipped the switch to the garbage disposal as the door opened and her mom entered with her guest.

"Oh, dear God." Theodore put his head in his hands.

Mary jumped from her chair and went to Katie's side, taking a knife she was rinsing out of her hand before her cousin glanced up.

"What are you doing, Mary?" Katie asked, shaking soapy suds off her hands. "I am not a child."

Mary took a step into her, their shoulders touching as she nodded to the door.

Everyone in the room froze as if they were awaiting stage direction. Even the parakeets silenced in the background.

"Katie's heartbeat is through the ceiling." The old dog strained as he rose and joined the women at the sink. He pushed Katie's legs in support.

"I'll handle the door," Bear said, taking a few steps. He faced Katie's parents with solemn eyes.

"Is your co-op dog going to bite us, Mary?" Julia asked.

"Bear doesn't—"

Katie cut her off. "He's been known to grab coyotes by the throat and rip them to pieces just because he doesn't like the way they look. Isn't that right, Bear?"

Julia's arms flew up in alarm and she took a step into Riven, nearly toppling them both as she did so.

Taking two strides forward, Mary said, "He will not bite either of you. Besides, we're just leaving."

"No, *I'm* leaving." Katie threw a dish towel on the counter.

"When are you returning?" Julia asked.

"Maybe never. And then, only to burn the house down."

"Perhaps this will be less awkward if I go," Percy offered.

Katie turned to him, speaking quietly. "I'm sorry, Percy. I've been a grump and your dinner is ruined. I'm mortified."

Speaking in a hushed tone between the two of them, Percy said, "Don't forget—every family has their moments. One day, I'll tell you how a llama ended up in our pool after a family fight over a shattered heirloom vase." He took off his apron and calmly put it on the counter.

"Your family has llamas?"

"The neighbors do. It was quite the ordeal," Percy said, buoyed by her elevated tone of interest. "Take a breath. You have this."

She nodded, turning to her parents.

"I can go. Really. I had no idea you had guests," Riven said.

Katie's eyes were on the door before she met Percy's gaze. She nodded and took a deep breath in. "Go ahead. Let's hear what you have to say. I want my friends around me to keep me from doing something criminal."

Riven's quizzical gaze went to Theodore, who mouthed, *Be brave!*

Clearing her throat and looking pleased, Julia blurted out, "Your father and I would like to co-parent you."

Mary held the counter to steady herself. Percy and Theodore's mouths formed twin O's.

"You what?" Katie's voice shook.

"I think there's a better way we could express our motives, Julia," Riven interjected. "Katie *is* a grown woman. It's not her fault we're both late to the parenting party."

"Nonsense. She's still living in the house that you paid for."

All color drained from Katie's face. "I thought an old friend gave you this house."

Julia went to the couch and patted the seat beside her for her daughter to sit. "Riven used to be a friend. I realize it was a bit duplicitous. I can't help when you assume things, Katie."

"Yes, you can!" Mary practically shouted as Theodore put his head in his hand and Percy winced. The energy of the room shot through both dogs who began barking in earnest until Mary shushed them.

Riven's focus was squarely on his daughter. "Katie, I never wanted your school years to be disrupted with housing uncertainty. It's yours for as long as you wish to remain here. No strings attached."

"That's basically what I was trying to say," Julia said. "I just didn't get a chance to finish."

"I didn't mean to throw you for another loop coming to see you this evening. Just to make myself available for any questions you may have. With your mom present too. I didn't want you to feel any duplicity between us."

Henry went to sit beside Riven. He looked up and panted. "He's trying. I'll give him that."

Going up to sniff him, Bear nudged Riven's hand. "There is no coyote here tonight."

At the dogs' attention, Riven knelt and spoke softly to each of them, as he waited for Katie's answer.

Bear put his snout to the old man's cheek and gave him a sniff and the smallest of licks as he looked the man in the eyes. "He just wants what every dog does, Henry."

"What's that?" The old dog leaned into Riven, lowering himself onto the man's feet.

"To find his place in a pack."

Mary's face softened watching the dogs interact with Riven. "We're going to go and let the three of you talk. The smaller the circle, the easier to sort things out."

"Don't go on our account, Mary. You're family. Please spend some time with us."

"Another time, Aunt Julia."

Hearing Katie's mom's name, the Great Pyrenees got up and followed his owner out the door and groaned. He couldn't help himself.

Tell a Pitiful Story

"The long and short of it, my sister is the one who ruined Riven's life. And our only chance for happiness as a family. And now, look how it's spilled over to Katie. She was fit to be tied when we spoke to her last night. I thought she'd never calm down. And all because of Margaret."

"That is not true, and you know it, Julia." Cybil pushed away a half-eaten piece of peach pie on her plate. The Hen's Nest was nearly empty, everyone else having vacated for the evening. "You look for every reason to implicate your sister in your affairs. Perhaps you miss her more than you let yourself admit. Take it from me—there would have still been huge problems between you and Riven, even without Margaret involved."

"She wasn't the wonderful saint everyone thought she was." Julia sat up straight, arms crossed like a stubborn child refusing to eat vegetables.

"You have this grand idea of perfection which none of us can fulfill. Your sister always tried to look after you," Cybil replied. "Margaret may have been strong-willed, but she was never unkind."

"She didn't let Riven and I be together."

"Those were much different times, big age gaps didn't seem

to come across our radars like they do today," Cybill said. "Still, Margaret had me keep an eye out for both of you. Riven was six years older than you when you took up with him for the first time. You were barely in your freshman year of high school."

"He was a senior."

Cybil thought for a moment. "That poor kid had some real circumstances. It took him extra time to finish high school." She cleared her throat. "But he didn't give up getting a diploma. Even without parents."

"How on earth do you remember all of that?"

"I think any teacher can remember remarkable details of their first years of teaching." Cybil began to rearrange the silverware on the table in front of herself. "Merivelle was such a tiny school district. All you hooligans fit into four years of a small and memorable high school." She glanced up as Frannie moved over from wiping down the booth next to them.

"As long as we're reminiscing here—" Frannie put her hands on her hips and glared at Julia. "—I'd like to share some things that might refresh some memories at the table."

With wide eyes, Julia slowly pushed herself into the corner of her booth. The sudden change in Julia's demeanor brought a bemused smile to Cybil's face as she searched between the two women.

"You haven't been gone that long, Julia. And my recollections are fresh on your past dealings in Merivelle."

The bell on the front entrance door rang as a customer popped their head in. "Any coffee left? I need a quick to-go for my evening shift."

"I've already torn down the coffee service," Frannie said. "If it's an emergency, I can start a fresh pot." Her hands were shaking as she tried to smile.

"Wouldn't dream of it. See you tomorrow," the man said, waving.

"Could you flip the sign for me, Smitty?"

The man peered at the three women with Julia still huddled in the corner and nodded. "Sure thing, Frannie," he said, turning the small placard over as he left.

"You were saying." Cybil raised her eyebrows.

"Julia likes to think of herself as everyone's victim," Frannie began, looking to Cybil before continuing to speak. "When you were quite the opposite in school. Your parents spoiled you rotten. You had no empathy."

"I think you're being a bit overreaching." Julia sat up in defiance for a few seconds before withering under Frannie's steel glare.

"Maybe I imagined serving you over there at the soda fountain?"

"You waited tables and the counter all during high school," Julia replied. "You've worked here forever."

"I remember you would show up here and start running me around in service to you. A little princess with all your demands."

"That was your job. To *wait* on me. I did nothing wrong."

"Most people can reach in front of themselves for straws and napkins from a dispenser a few inches away instead of calling a waitress from across the restaurant to do it for them."

Julia's eyes went to the utensil and napkin caddies that had sat on every table and counter for decades, wincing at the close proximity.

"Do you remember the time you *accidentally* dropped a milkshake all over the front of my apron when we were in high school? In front of a large and rowdy group that came in after a Friday night football game?"

Julia put her head down.

"And then announced one day you'd live in the biggest house in town, and I'd be your maid."

Wrinkles in Julia's forehead deepened as she listened.

"And to further make everyone laugh, you pointed your

dainty little foot out to have me clean off some of the shake that got on your shoe. You said you'd have me fired if I didn't do it."

"I did?"

"I was desperate to keep a job to help my family. Do you have any idea how those kinds of antics set a person's life in a small town?"

"Not at the time," Julia said, barely above a whisper.

Frannie dropped the rag she was clutching onto the table and stared at Julia. "Would you like to know who did help me that day?"

"Probably my sister," Julia whispered.

"Wrong again." Frannie put her hands on the table and leaned in. She stared pointedly at Julia. "Riven Chapowits. The skinny, poor kid who worked in the kitchen as he tried to put himself through high school. He came out and helped mop it up while you and your friends threw straw wrappers and salt at us. So don't you dare sit here and act like you were some sort of…" She paused. "Cybil, what's the female equivalent to a knight?"

"A dame."

"Don't you dare come in here after decades of hoping people forget your bratty teenage behavior that didn't change after high school and try and act like you were Riven's dame in shining armor and Margaret messed it all up."

Julia cleared her throat and held a finger up meekly. "There are things you don't know."

"Let me guess. He got you pregnant. I put that much together when you returned from your *marriage gone bad* after high school."

"You knew?" Julia asked.

"An easy guess. Riven seemed over the moon once you graduated. Then devastated when you left Merivelle. And briefly happy again when you came back to town with a baby. Do you know he never outed you?"

"He's always been good at secrets," Julia replied. "I never worried he'd tell anyone."

"I remember one day he was practicing what he was going to tell your parents. How he could provide for you and your grand tastes, but your family wouldn't have it. I actually don't blame them. You didn't behave in a way to show them you two would have worked. Much more dramatic if you act like the victim, string him along for a few years, and then take up with a real scoundrel. Can you imagine how it felt for Riven to stay in town and see another man raise the daughter he desperately wanted? I expect that would cause a lot of men to turn as mean as a rattlesnake."

"He didn't have to become what he did," Julia said, meekly. "No matter what I did."

Cybil cleared her throat, and then spoke quietly. "Because you're hurt doesn't make it a given that you'll turn cruel. Ideally, you let the pain soften you. But it takes real strength not to let life's disappointments harden you."

The palpable pain from Cybil's words momentarily paused the electric energy at the table. "I'm so happy Bear Bailey's has given you a showcase for all your talents," Frannie said.

Julia rolled her eyes. "Always with the dog store." She stopped and took a deep breath. "Can I ask you a question, Frannie? And an honest one. Not one where I'm trying to be unkind. Only a sincere ask."

"Go ahead," Frannie answered.

"Why are you still here after all these years?"

"In Merivelle? Do you mean why didn't I move away like you did?"

Julia shrugged her shoulders. "I don't understand why you still work here. It was your high school job and you're still here decades later."

Frannie grabbed the rag again, wiping two small circles on the table, leaving behind liquid reside of her motions. "I'll let you in on a little secret. I tell Cybil almost everything and even she doesn't know."

Moving from the wall and closer to the center of her side of the booth, Julia's eyes were wide. "I'm listening."

"I've worked here day and night for the past thirty years. I've done everything there is to do at The Hen's Nest. Hired and fired employees, done all the accounting and was even on the back food line for more than a few meals when cooks didn't show up for early morning shifts."

Julia sunk back in the booth; like a re-run of her favorite show was showing instead of an anticipated new episode. She shuffled around in her purse for a tube of lipstick and mirror, nodding half-heartedly for the story to continue once she was holding an item in each hand.

"And now I own this profitable establishment free and clear."

With only her bottom lip painted bright pink, Julia paused in surprise.

Frannie held her shoulders back. "And would you like to know how I was able to secure the original loan for it, despite my husband dying in a harvest accident and leaving me with two small children and no insurance money?"

Cybil had tears in her eyes. "Your clever and handsome husband was always one of my favorite students," she said, her voice exceedingly kind.

For a few moments all was silent except for a lone, unseen employee in the back washing dishes and the sound of passing traffic.

"Who helped you?" Julia asked, breaking the silence as she finished applying her makeup. She rubbed her lips together as she put the tube and mirror back in her handbag.

"The same boy who rushed out from the kitchen and helped me clean up your mess. He gave me the loan to buy The Hen's Nest when the original owner moved away and wanted to close it."

"Riven?" Julia was aghast.

"The very one. And Riven being Riven, the loan was at a high interest rate. But no other lending institution was interested in listening to a young and recent widow with no college experience—despite my pleas that I'd work my fingers to the bone to pay back any loan so I could provide for my young family. Riven was my last and only hope. He gave me a stern warning letting me know he'd take the restaurant back the first chance he got if I was ever late on a payment. Which made me highly disciplined. I sometimes wonder if I'd been as successful without that old coyote at the door."

"Why didn't you ever let anyone know before? I'd have told everyone in town, so they didn't think I was just a waitress."

At Julia's tone-deaf words, Cybil's head fell forward as she closed her eyes.

"The one non-negotiable from the transaction—Riven said I couldn't tell anyone. He said he couldn't have every Tom, Dick and Frannie running to him trying to get a loan, armed with sad stories. And so, out of enormous gratitude for the ability to provide for my kids and not have them worry about losing their home after they'd already lost their dad, I never let it slip."

"Your children? That's why they were always here clearing tables and doing their homework at the back booths?" Cybil asked.

"The Hen's Nest taught them hard work and helped them set aside a substantial portion of their college funds," Frannie said, a clear look of satisfaction on her face as Julia sat with her mouth wide open. She pulled her order pad out of her pocket, ripped the top sheet off and tore it in half, setting it in front of the other woman. "Your tab is clear, Julia. Try and behave in a way that shows we've all been given plenty to make our lives successful despite the stories we like to tell ourselves."

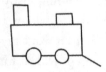

Good Place to Catch a Train

"I'm going home."

Katie heard the voice but did not look up from her paperwork, scanning the spreadsheets in front of her. "Henry and I will be at the house in a bit."

Julia leaned in the doorway as vendors in the co-op were tidying up their stalls from the day's activities. Lupe moved around the space like a bumblebee making sure everyone had what they needed for the following day. Pablito sat in the middle of the space, in front of the dormant fireplace. His homework was spread out in front of him. He eyed the papers, cupping the back of his head with his hands, leaning back on his chair.

"Is there something you need, Mom? Get some food from the Grab-and-Go cooler. I'm too tired for anything else."

Henry was at Katie's feet. He yawned loudly and repositioned himself closer to her. She reached down, thankful for the buffer of his presence.

"You know, I always expected if you ever got an animal, it would be a cat. A large white Persian with a pink bow in their hair." Julia stepped into the office with an expectant look on her face as she sat down.

Katie shrugged. "That sounds like me when I was a kid."

"And if I ever pictured you with a dog, it would have been a little one you could slip into a purse." She smiled at her daughter, tapping her fingers lightly on the desk. "But you always do things your own way, Katie Kat. Look at the hobo dog at your feet. The two of you don't match at all but somehow you do."

"*Katie Kat?*"

"I'm trying to wean myself off from Katherine. Like you said you wanted me to," she said, expectantly. "I'll keep trying until I find something."

"Katie would be fine." Her daughter put her pencil down, clearly agitated at the interruption. She startled. "You don't have on makeup."

"I washed my face off before I laid down for a quick nap. You still weren't home when I woke up."

"You don't go out without makeup. Ever. Like my whole life." Katie paused for a moment, turning the paperwork over, her focus solely on her mother. "Are you dying?"

Julia shrugged, her eyes wide with the hunger of her daughter's rapt attention. "I haven't been feeling myself lately…"

Katie stood up and went to the other side of the desk. "Is that why you're here in Merivelle?" Her heart began to accelerate, and she put her hand to her mother's cheek, searching for a temperature.

Julia reached for Katie's hand and leaned into her for a moment, breathing in the younger woman's scent—a French perfume she'd loved when her daughter was just a child. Her face softened with the connection.

"How exactly have you been feeling, Mom?"

Taking another inhale of the fragrance, Julia stopped and shook her head. "No, Katie. I can't do this to you anymore."

"Do what?"

"What I always do. Act theatrical. Blow things out of

proportion in hopes I center myself in the middle of everyone's attention."

"That was extremely self-aware." Katie pulled back from her mom. "You're sure you aren't seriously ill?"

With a loud vocal groan, Henry rose and went to sit beside Julia. He lifted a paw and set it on her knee.

Julia reached into her bag and sprayed her hands and the air with anti-microbial.

"You can't catch heartworm from dogs, Mom."

Her hand was suspended in the air over Henry's head. "Even a little?"

Katie rolled her eyes and returned to the work on her desk.

"I was actually on the Google—"

"You were on the internet Googling," Katie corrected.

"Whatever you kids say," Julia said, waving her hand. "I was *Googling* heartworm to see what we could come up here to help Henry."

"You did?" Katie stopped and pushed her papers forward to make room for her elbows on the desk, resting her head in the cradle of her hands.

"Did you know there's another meaning?"

Henry closed his eyes, a small grin beginning to form as Julia scratched his ears. He leaned into her as she continued to scratch down his neck and back as she spoke, his whip-like tail thumping the concrete floor.

"A heartworm can also mean a relationship you can't get out of your thoughts."

"Kind of like an earworm?"

"No, a *heart*worm," her mother corrected.

"Similarly, an earworm is when you can't get a song out of your head once you hear it. It won't go away." The lights to the co-op went out and Lupe and Pablito's footsteps could be heard in the darkness as they made their way to the front door. "Why are you bringing up alternative heartworm definitions?"

Looking up from Henry, Julia said, "I've had a case of heartworm my whole life."

Groaning, Katie said, "Mom, you make everything about yourself." She pushed away from her desk and walked to the darkened doorway.

"See you mañana, Tia!" Pablito slung his backpack over his shoulder as he followed Lupe out the door.

She waved and signaled her request for Lupe to lock the door and set the alarm.

Turning her attention back to her mother, Katie said, "I've got to hand it to you. I don't know how—but you've found a way to make my dog's condition something about you."

"That wasn't my motive, honey."

The look of sincere regret on her mom's face softened her. "I'm probably being sensitive. Go on. How does someone who loves the finer things in life self-diagnosis their *own* heartworm infestation?"

"I think I have a lot of relationships in my heart that aren't finished. Like the songs you mentioned that don't leave your head when you hear them."

"I can't decide if you're being wise or nonsensical." Katie closed her eyes for a moment. "*Wisensical*," she said, under her breath. She opened her eyes again to find her mom patiently waiting.

"I haven't always taken responsibility for my actions, and you've been the main recipient of those mistakes, Katie. I desperately want a relationship with you. Then I set it on fire every chance I get. I panic when things aren't going well between us, and then I do what I've always done."

"What's that?"

"When I feel out of control, I play the victim. I act like

everyone's hurt me. So, no one will hurt me," Julia said. She reached down and scratched Henry's back. "And then I run away so I'm not held accountable for my part in relationships fracturing."

Still as a statue, Katie hadn't taken a breath since Julia began speaking in earnest.

"And my biggest regret in not taking responsibility for my actions is sitting in front of me," Julia continued. "Because of me not taking accountability for my own choices, I've heaped tons of messes on my only child to sort out."

Katie began to cry. Like an old engine without oil, the sobs came dry and angry as she hit a fist on the surface.

"Katie," her mother said, jumping in surprise. "I want nothing more than to start fresh between us—"

"*No*! You don't get to Google and make a grand speech with astute connections and then think we're fine." Her breath came in short, dragon-like spurts.

"You have every right to not trust a thing coming out of my mouth. I understand this is a result of your history with me."

"What has got into you suddenly?" she choked.

"At lunch with Cybil today, I spoke with someone so free of self-pity and noble in their behavior, it provided me a stark and shocking contrast with my own behavior. I deserve every bit of suspicion and fire that comes from you, Katie. That's what I came here to say—I'm going home."

"Home? Where?"

"My home. Back to Cincinnati. I need to sort this. Away from you. I don't want you lifting a finger to get me straight, Katie."

The cell phone on Katie's desk rang. Without looking, she sent the call to voicemail. "When are you leaving?"

"Soon. Tomorrow. I booked an Amtrak ticket. A long train ride to think about things here."

"You detest the train."

"My first gesture that you don't need to always go out of your way to right my world."

"You said you were coming for Easter."

"I think you're a little old to be heartbroken that I won't be here to hunt pastel-colored eggs."

Katie furrowed her brows. "You don't think it's running to come to these big revelations and vacate town?"

"I think as much as I would love to speak to Riven about the past, it would be easier for both of you to figure out a relationship without me. Especially since I'm not cured of my tendency to dramatize or victimize." Julia rose from her chair, her eyes searching the darkness outside of the office. "That will take time on my part." She patted Henry before exiting the office. "I expect a part of me will always love theatrics."

A wave of strong emotion hit Katie as she followed her mom to the front door. With each step, the feeling of panic grew stronger, starting at her stomach and then slowly, winding up to her chest, filling it with such a force of fear, she felt her heart would explode.

"Everything okay, Katie?"

Though feeling like her head was the weight of a watermelon, Katie nodded.

"Good, because I don't want you to feel bad after this discussion. I only want a fresh start with you."

Nothing with Katie's senses was sharp. Her hands felt overinflated and unreal as she pushed the front door open for Julia. She searched for something to say but there were no words.

"Don't work too late, honey," Julia said as she exited.

From the back of the co-op, the store's alarm began beeping rhythmically with the opened door. Julia waved goodbye from the other side of the glass door.

At the same time, Henry whined and scratched at the door

frantically. More energy than she'd seen in him since he'd come to live with her.

Katie put her hands on her knees and tried to catch her breath. "Henry, please hang on for a minute."

More determined, the dog continued.

"I can barely keep my balance." She backed away from the door, feeling as though the room was tilting, the sickening feeling that she might slide off of it. *All in your mind*, she thought, trying to calm herself down. "I need to call Mary. I think I'm dying," she said aloud.

Henry hurled the side of his body into the door, opening it by force. A chilled wind blew through the store with such power, it knocked down items from display tables all over the co-op, shocking Katie with swirling force of it. Taking a deep breath of the fresh air to steady herself, she ran in pursuit of Henry, already halfway down the block.

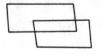

AFRAID

THE DOG CAME to rest in front of Alicia's studio, sitting at the entrance as calmly as if he were a decorative statue placed to welcome guests. Katie pounded on the yoga studio door, her breath coming in panicked gasps. She grabbed onto the front of the door handle to steady herself before cupping her face as she peered inside. The studio was dark behind the partition, blocking the view from Main Street when classes were in session, but Katie could see the flickering light of the battery-operated candles.

"I think I'm having a heart attack, Henry," she said, holding onto her chest with one hand and the crossbar of the door with the other. "I need Mary. Why did you run here, in the other direction?"

The old dog looked up at her, nodding in reassurance.

"What if I die here on Main Street in the same town I've never left? I barely saw the world past these city limits." Her eyes were wide, and her face was flushed red in the dwindling evening light.

Henry whined and turned his head to the door.

Katie began speaking rapidly to distract herself. "What if my mom was right about leaving Merivelle? Why would the right advice come from the wrong person?"

At the sound of her words, Henry stopped and howled a mournful and heartbreaking sound of homesickness.

"You sound like a sad horn blowing, Henry. Please stop. You scared me to death.'"

She pounded on the door again. An entire block of empty parking spaces suggested no scheduled classes.

A serene looking woman peeked from behind the partition, her face relieved when she saw Katie. "One second!" She held a finger up and vanished for few moments, before appearing again, a sheer kimono duster over her yoga pants and top as she put a key in the door to unlock it. "I'm sorry, Katie. I thought you were one of the kids who pass by in the evening who love to knock like little maniacs and run."

"Something's wrong with me," Katie's choked.

"I have a private client tonight, but—"

"I think I'm having a heart attack. It feels like I'm dying," Katie blurted.

Alicia's face creased in concern. "Come in," she said, opening the door wider. "What makes you think you're having a heart attack?" She locked the door once they'd entered, placing an arm around Katie's shoulders.

"I'm about ready to come out of my skin. And my heart is beating so loud, I can hear it in my ears. I want to run," Katie said, tears welling in her eyes. "Look at my hands. They're shaking like leaves." She held them out to Alicia like a terrified child.

"Do you have a history of heart issues?"

"Only the romantic kind," Katie said, trying to smile as tears began to slowly escape the sides of her eyes.

"No heart murmur or mitral valve prolapse in your medical history?"

Katie shook her head.

"When's the last time you had your blood pressure checked?"

"The fire department was at Bear Bailey's this week doing inspections and they checked all of ours as a courtesy," Katie answered, following Alicia around the partition.

"And how was it?"

"They said my heart was perfect."

"We don't have heart issues in our family," a voice said, coming from a place on the floor.

Katie's eyes widened. "*This* is your client?"

"Alicia has helped me with my own panic attacks. Really big ones, if I'm honest." Riven rose, though he nearly fell back down on his yoga mat.

"How have I been without parents for large parts of my life and now they're crawling out of the woodwork?" Katie asked, taking a few steps back and bumping into Henry, who was keen to stay close to her.

"I only want to—"

"I think I'm going to be sick," she said, holding her stomach. "Oh, God. I hate to throw up." Her eyes searched the room.

"The bathroom is in the back, Katie," Riven said, his voice gentle and kind. "I know when I'm gripped with anxiety, it seems to hit my stomach. Alicia has taught me to sit with my feelings and they'll pass much quicker than if I give in to worry about the physical symptoms."

Katie gawked at Riven as if he were an extraterrestrial alien giving her advice.

"I want to help you."

"*You*? You're the cause of my impending heart attack!"

"I've been trying…"

"You've been trying? Wow! How many days now?"

He put his head down. "I'm new to this."

"You've been here in Merivelle my entire life. You've never taken a step forward to fix anything between us. Do you know how much the odds improve for a girl's future success when she has a father behind her giving her confidence?"

"Would you have taken help from the town villain?"

"You didn't have to be one. Don't you see? You knew you had a daughter and could have simply tried to be better. For my sake. Look how different Mary's life is because she had sane parents!"

Riven cleared his throat and put his head down. "That hurts me more than you realize."

"That's not the point. I'm a mess! *I can't even save this dog!*" As the desperate words came out, tears poured from Katie's eyes. "I'm so, so... *furious*, I just want to punch something!"

"Here?" Riven asked, his eyes wide with surprise.

"Yes! Do you see how screwed up and messy I am? I want to lose my marbles in a *yoga studio!*"

Henry began to howl again, joining his voice to Katie's. She sank her knees onto the floor and convulsed in sobs as the dog pushed into her, his worry accelerating her emotion until she sat exhausted on the mat. She leaned forward over her thighs, stretching her back and arms forward.

Alicia knelt to Katie. "That's an excellent child's pose you've naturally moved into," she said, her hand on Katie's back. "How are you feeling?"

"Suddenly very tired."

"And your anxiety level?"

Still stretched forward, Katie peered at Alicia from under her arm. "Very little, if any at all."

"Anxiety is only ever an emotion wanting to be recognized." She patted Katie's back and stood up. "Once the emotion has been expressed, it moves on leaving you space for new growth."

Rain began to hit the windows of the studio. At first, random drops on the glass and then rapid and generous rain pouring from the sky—the season's first substantial rainfall. Katie sat up, turning her head toward the sound as her shoulders relaxed.

"I'm going to go check out what sounds like a welcome deluge," Alicia said. "You two stay and talk for as long as you need."

Alone in a room with her dad for the first time in her entire life, Katie squirmed and opened her mouth to speak before abandoning the idea, too tired to form words to express herself properly.

"You know you were also so many other things."

"What do you mean?" Katie's voice was weary.

"You recounted only the lower points in your life that everyone has. You've accomplished so much more."

Katie clutched Henry. "You weren't close enough to know anything about me. The only link we had was the day you had the man I thought was my father arrested."

Pulling a handkerchief out of his pocket and handing it to Katie, Riven went to the wall of the studio. He searched through his jacket before going back to where Katie sat.

"What are you doing?"

Opening his wallet, he pulled out old newspaper clippings, yellowed with age and began to unfold them in his hands. Smaller fragments rained to the floor in front of Katie.

"Local Girl Scout Saves Injured Rabbit at Easter," Riven read, holding up the newspaper print with the accompanying photo of a pre-teen Katie, holding the small animal to her cheek with a smile of braces.

Katie reached for the newspaper articles with her name and photos in them, examining them carefully.

"You won your school spelling bees in fourth, fifth and sixth grades, had a 4.0 grade average through your entire school career, and won every sash and crown available. Not to mention you were on the debate team. State champions all four years when you were in high school," Riven continued. "I loved every one of the snippets of your life I came across."

Katie was dumbfounded. "How do you know all of that?"

"You've been…" Riven trailed off, his face flustered.

"I've been what?"

Clearing his throat, he continued. "A great joy to me. Though I haven't shown it."

"You haven't." She shook her head. "The way you've treated Mary—"

"But search your mind and heart. Can you recall when I was personally unkind to you?"

Katie took a deep breath in, her cheeks full of air before she blew out a deep breath of air. "That's the thing." Henry whined at her side, putting a paw on her thigh as they sat in solidarity. "You've hurt my family."

"You mean your mother?"

"I mean, everyone who helped build Bear Bailey's."

"Always with the co-op," Riven said under his breath, though his tone was regret.

"We're a team. We've built something in spite of all the bureaucratic nonsense you had Mary crawling through to get it started."

"How can you say it's your family though? It's a store. *I'm* your family."

"Bear Bailey's is the heart of Merivelle. It's the hub where everyone brings their talents, and we weave them all together to create something the whole community can benefit from." Her voice was clear and calm as she squared her shoulders, sitting up tall. "It's the proudest accomplishment of my life, so far."

"You're the sparkle—the real star of Bear Bailey's. I've seen it with my own eyes since Percy's been here."

"We all shine at Bear Bailey's."

"But think what you could do on your own."

"Coyotes hunt alone. Dogs love to share," Katie said.

"Call me a loner coyote then. I accomplished a lot more on my own than trying to fit in with people who didn't appreciate me."

She put her hand on his forearm. "Every dog has a bit of coyote in him. And every coyote has a dog in him."

"Meaning?"

"We both get to choose which we are by how we show up in our community," Katie answered. "Alone or for everyone's benefit."

Mary's head popped around the partition with Bear right beside her. He barked and his tail wagged when he spotted Katie and Henry, clearly happy at his beloved owner's changed demeanor. "Are you all right? I've been scared to death since the alarm to Bear Bailey's went off and you were nowhere to be found. I'm so relieved to find you." She put her head down and breathed deeply before looking up and smiling. "We couldn't do without you, Katie."

The Owner is Out

Percy was sitting on Katie's front porch steps when Mary pulled up outside the house to drop her home. Windchimes with a violet bow were hung on the lowest branch of the tree beside her house, a gift from Percy the previous day. He gave a polite wave with one hand, while cupping something in the other.

"Is his hand all right?" Mary asked. "He's holding it like its injured."

"He's probably examining some bug he remembers the Latin name for, along with a literary reference that correlates to a quantum physics theory that somehow ties it all together." Katie watched him with a tender expression as he put an index finger near his cupped hand and let a winged insect alight on it.

"Is that a dragonfly?"

"Maybe," Katie shrugged. "Possibly a damselfly."

"I can't tell if you're teasing."

"I am. A little." She continued to explain. "Percy gets people excited about seeing simple things in a new light. Did you know dragonflies and damselflies are often confused? It's a cinch to distinguish between the two—eye shapes, how the wings are positioned at rest and the comparative shape of both insect's bodies."

"When did you go to Dragonfly University?"

Though still weary, Katie laughed. "He told me when he joined Cybil and I fishing one evening. They were flying around the cattails at the Round Pond. I've never known someone who loves learning like Percy. He's curious and passionate about almost everything he encounters. The world is his classroom."

"He looks really serious. Do you have any idea what he might want?"

"Non."

"I'm sorry, what?"

"The French word for no," Katie said. "Percy said it the first time we met. I made fun of him for it. Now it's kind of a thing we tease about. His goofy portmanteaus and linguistic quirks are rubbing off on me." She opened the car door and pulled the front passenger seat forward so Henry could pass. "Kind of a miracle of sorts I'd find someone like him. Who knows, maybe I've grown? He says he has a million things to show me one day."

Mary took a deep breath and reached back to Bear to steady herself. "You're leaving us, aren't you?"

"I am not," Katie said, shutting the door and leaning in through the rolled down window. "You and I are the best team I've ever been a part of. Look at all we've accomplished together."

Tears formed in Mary's eyes. "You have to go, Katie."

"I wouldn't ever leave you when you need me the most. Ever since I jumped in to help Bear Bailey's, you always say you can't do without me."

Mary wiped away a tear. "I've always meant, I couldn't do without you in my story. But you still get to live your own life full of experiences and people you love. I wouldn't ever ask you to give up your own dreams to make mine bigger." She was full-on crying but in a happy way as she leaned over to hug her cousin.

Bear watched Henry with great thought. A serene feeling came over him. Like when Mary gently ran her fingers through his fur at the end of a particularly good day, praising him while she said his name affectionately. Suddenly, Bear's instinct changed. "You know, tonight, for the first time since I met you, I can feel what you've always told me, Henry. It is time for you to go. With Katie. Neither of you will be alone. And I think that's just the best thing in the whole world for a dog to accomplish." He reached a paw out to Henry in friendship. "It was nice to have a buddy to hang out and talk with again."

"I'll always remember to lean in with love, thanks to you, Bear." He nodded to the Great Pyrenees. "I'm puzzled though. Why aren't you worked up? I've never seen you so calm when Mary's upset."

His face lit up when Mary turned her gaze to meet his own, smiling through her tears. "Because even though she's sad, she smells like rain in springtime," Bear replied. "And we've got miracles and old dogs around."

Courthouse

"It's our last meeting before Percy heads home tomorrow," Katie said, looking around at the group assembled at the co-op. "And it's come on the Friday before Easter Sunday. We'll make the meeting short so everyone can get on their way."

Bear sat beside Mary with a headband of floppy bunny ears. Sighing, he said, "Around here, the days before a holiday throws gasoline on the fire that is women dressing dogs, Henry."

The old dog laid on the floor. He scratched behind his ear, knocking his own matching bunny ears to the floor. Percy got up from where he sat and knelt down to Henry, picking the item up off the floor. "Can you wear this a little bit longer?" he said quietly, holding the headband up for the dog's inspection. "It sure makes your mom happy."

Lupe leaned into Katie sitting next to her. "He's *muy guapo*," she whispered. "And so kind."

With Henry settled, Percy adjusted his tie and stretched his neck in a nervous manner.

"We've loved having you here," Mary said. "I think Theodore is at home packing his own bags to join you. He hates goodbyes."

She smiled before switching back to business. "Katie said you wanted to talk to us about something important?"

He nodded, looking around the table. "First, I want you to know, Merivelle lives up to its French word origins. It is a wonderful story." He took a ragged breath in.

"Whatever it is, go ahead," Cybil said. "We're all made of tough stuff, Percy."

"I tried everything I could. But the Rural Initiative board has decided to pass on funding for the co-op."

Everyone at the table was stunned, not sure if they'd heard his words correctly.

Percy was stricken. "I want to stress your ideas were compelling. We hope we might use them to help other communities across the country."

"You're going to swipe the women's ideas but not fund them?" Riven crossed his arms. "At another time of my life, I might have found that move impressive. Now, after knowing all the hard work that goes into the co-op, I find it offensive."

"No, of course not. I could have explained that portion better."

"Did you advocate properly? Do they know how hard Katie has worked to help Merivelle?" Riven slammed his fist on the table, shaking everyone in surprise.

Percy cleared his throat. "I'd be happy to discuss the matter with you in private. After the meeting. Especially given both of our personal contributions that led to this decision."

"I have nothing to hide from the group." Riven stopped, turning his head in wonder. "That's a new feeling."

"What is going on?" Mary whispered to her cousin.

Shrugging her shoulders, Katie was clear that she also was in the dark.

"Percy's legs are shaking. I can sense them from over here," Bear said.

"He tried to talk to Katie last night, but she was too tired.

She told him to please tell her with everyone else." Henry yawned and put his head down.

"I assure you, I will work as hard as I can to come up with other solutions," Percy said. "I'm as invested in Bear Bailey's and the desire to help the rest of Merivelle as you are."

Katie's posture was straight and poised. "You were here to observe and see if our interests aligned. You were under no obligation. What can we learn going forward?"

"*Learn going forward*? What about now?" Riven asked, his face incredulous. "I'm sorry, Katie, but you all have worked too hard. We should know the problem so we can try and fix it."

"Should it scare me that everything out of Riven's mouth is what's in my brain right now?" Bear asked.

Henry chuckled. "Maybe you've both changed."

"You and I, Riven—*we* were the problem," Percy said.

"What do you mean *we*? We have nothing in common with this project outside of the group."

Percy's eyes went to Katie before directing his words at Riven. "Again—let's talk and then fill the others in."

"No, please." Katie crossed her arms. "Enlighten us."

Henry sat up and then leaned into Katie, soothing her momentarily with the action.

"I'll help Riven," Bear said, belly scooching toward the old man. Riven reached down and patted the top of the Pyr's head in thanks.

"We've all made mistakes, Percy. Added an extra zero to a column. Forgot to mail a check," Mary said, grimacing as she looked at Katie, remembering the time her mistake had been a financial catastrophe for the co-op building at Christmas.

"I chewed up a check once, Henry. I was a nervous wreck. It caused a whole mess," Bear said, whimpering, He put his head down in regret, the bunny ears sliding off and onto the floor. "It wasn't really Mary's fault."

"She's a human. With thumbs to write another check," Henry said. "And the co-op's still standing."

Percy nodded in appreciation of Mary's words. "If I could go back and think of how my words would impact Merivelle, I would say the same thing but perhaps with different timing." He shook his head. "I don't know where to start. Let me think of the quickest way to say this."

"Let's all give Percy a moment to catch his breath and gather his thoughts." Katie's face was kind as she locked eyes with him. "Go ahead when you're ready, Percy. Or we can even take a break."

Percy held the back of his neck. "The issue is—my family runs the Rural Initiative."

"They do?" Katie asked, her face puzzled.

"Mary and Katie are related and are thick as thieves in here every day. Surely, working with family isn't frowned upon," Cybil said.

"When I say, my family '*runs*' the Initiative, I should have said…" Percy paused. "I didn't mention my family actually funds the Rural Initiative."

There were lines of confusion on Mary's forehead as she glanced from Katie to Percy.

"As a philanthropic endeavor," Percy said, reaching inside his jacket. He pulled out a handkerchief from his pocket and blotted his face. "It's a foundation to help rural areas thrive. My family hails from small towns where they first found opportunities as immigrants generations ago."

"*Your* family were immigrants?" Lupe asked, her face lighting up. She smiled at Percy's nod.

Mary folded her hands and leaned into the table. "Why does it matter that your family *funds* the Initiative's projects? Nothing has changed on our end from when we originally reached out to seek out help."

"I agree," Riven said. "You're absolutely right, Mary."

"I want to take full responsibility for my actions. As I said, I was the problem—"

"You are never a problem, Percy Bourne," Lupe said, shaking her head. "You are a sincere and virtuous man."

Attempting to smile at the woman's generous words, Percy continued. "A few days ago, I didn't think of the import of my words with my mother on a personal call."

Katie's face froze.

"I told her I had feelings for you, Katie. That I didn't even want to come home for Easter. I wanted to stay in Merivelle."

Lupe clapped her hands in triumph. "I knew it!"

"You did what?" Katie whispered, sinking back into her chair.

"I didn't want to tell you like this, Katie. I was so excited to tell my family about you. How smart you are. How you're feisty and think I'm ridiculous and persnickety, but we have so much fun."

"We haven't even gone on a date. We're just *friends*. Hanging out with other *friends*," Katie said, though her expression betrayed her words.

Percy closed his mouth as he thought.

"Look at her! Who wouldn't love that amazing young woman? Why does your family care?" Riven asked. "Why should the project she's put so much time into be penalized because of *your* feelings."

Bear groaned under the table. "Because the ethical ramifications of a relationship between a person seeking money and an individual in a position to give them said funds might be misconstrued as an unfair advantage to other communities not able to offer such a relationship in consideration of financial awards." He stopped, turning his head in wonder. "I don't know how I know that."

"I'm not sure I follow," Henry said. "But it makes no difference to me. I've never had use for money."

Bear saw Katie had pushed her chair out from the table and was eyeing the door. He barked to divert her attention. Her attention snapped back to the table.

"Wait a second." Katie lifted one brow at Percy. "Why do you want to talk to Riven in private?"

The older man shifted in place uncomfortably, reaching for Bear's head to steady himself. He began petting the dog as he waited for Percy's answer.

"Maybe it's best if I read the email correspondence directly," Percy said, picking up his phone, scrolling through his messages and clearing his throat as he began reading.

> "Having someone locally with monies who is keenly interested in the future of their town well beyond their death is remarkable. The Initiative feels with Merivelle in the safe hands of Riven Chapowits's careful shepherding, the funds marked for Merivelle and their charming co-op could be used for another rural area in dire need of funding and direction.
>
> Your time could also be spent better elsewhere where a personal conflict won't call into question our family integrity. You mustn't let your personal feelings wash away generational building with high ideals as the cornerstone."

Foot traffic to and from The Hen's Nest passed by the co-op's front door. A couple of Merivellians tapped the glass in morning greeting as they waved on their way to breakfast.

Riven reached across the table to Katie, his hand shaking. "I'll figure this out. I didn't think past—"

She put her hand up to stop him. "I'm going to say what everyone here is too polite to verbalize."

"No one is thinking anything," Mary said.

"I already told you yesterday, Mary. I'm leaving. This is just a sign that my decision was the right one. I need a fresh start away from Merivelle."

"Please, Katie," Riven said, clearly shaken at her words. "It all began with me. I should have been transparent with my desire to get to know you as my daughter." His voice was shaking with emotion. "I had no idea my actions would propel you away even further."

"Please keep front and center, I let my feelings override my head. And that's not my mother's conversation style," Percy said. "Even without Riven reaching out with an offer to fund the co-op and beyond, my family would have pulled the grant because of my feelings for you."

"Don't leave Merivelle over the bumbling actions of two well-intentioned men," Riven said. "We only wanted to learn more about you in our own ways." He had a pleading look on his face as Percy nodded in agreement, equally remorseful.

Katie looked at the pair of them. "I'm not even angry. Please believe me."

"You have every right to be," Percy said.

She put her hand up and smiled. "I don't want to run, but I definitely want to grow. And more than anything, I want a fresh start while this old dog still has time for adventures."

Henry looked up at her, panting in excitement at her words.

"I'm more scared than you can imagine. And I'm sure I'll feel incredibly lonely without all of you nearby with the familiarity of Merivelle."

The room was quiet except for the ticking of the old grandfather clock in the corner. Afraid of the impact of her words and seemingly sudden decision, Katie still stood resolute, looking to her dad.

Riven cleared his throat. "I want to support whatever it is you want to do. But honestly—I'm not the person to encourage you to leave Merivelle." He put his head down. "We haven't even begun a real relationship."

"Travel is sometimes the wandering medicine we need, Riven." Cybil's voice was rich with warmth as she then looked to Katie. "Trust your intuition. Us old folks can handle ourselves. Plenty of relationships to mend here." She grasped Riven's hand in encouragement.

Mary's gaze was fixed on the back mural that Cybil painted of Bear years before. She nodded at Katie. "Do you remember how you thought I was nuts for buying an old hardware store to start a co-op?"

Laughing through tears that were beginning to form, Katie said, "And then you named it after your dog. That part, I particularly thought you'd gone crazy."

"You still showed up, even when you didn't see my vision. Have the same faith in what's blowing you to explore the world with Henry."

The memories released Katie's tear ducts. "I couldn't summon a single tear for years and now it seems as if all I do is cry. Is that normal when you're just appreciating everything?" she asked, wiping her eyes as she tried to smile. "I'm scared I'm going to feel so alone without all of you. When I think about it, it's almost enough to get me to stay."

A few moments of silence followed before Percy and Katie's eyes met. He nodded at her. "*Do not feel lonely, the entire Universe is inside you.*" The ever-present sincerity of the man caught Katie and everyone else's attention.

"Rumi," Cybil whispered. "I love Persian poetry." Lupe's eyes were glued to Percy as Mary held onto Bear, smiling in friendship to Riven across the table.

"*Stop acting so small. You are the Universe—*"

"*—in ecstatic motion.*" Katie completed his sentence, her eyes glancing at the windows, a hopeful look on her face.

Putting his hand over his heart, Percy's eyes were bright with encouragement. "*Set your life on fire,*" he said, continuing the poet's words. "*Seek those who fan your flames.*"

Henry smiled at Bear as a train blew its whistle on the edge of Merivelle. "Campfire time."

Fresh Water

"You're not gathering Easter eggs with everyone else? Your mother always told me that was one of your favorite things when you were younger." Riven stood beside a log next to his daughter at the Round Pond.

"How did you know I was here?" Katie cast her line into the pond. The hook and worm hit the water, sending out ripples to meet the shoreline.

"A hunch. I wanted to check on you. You've been pretty quiet with everyone the past couple of days."

She adjusted the slack in her line and shrugged. "I wanted to come and fish one last time before I leave."

"Pretty quick exit strategy."

She raised her eyebrows. "One of the benefits of no husband or children. Just readying myself and Henry to hit the road."

"I don't see your car."

"I walked," Katie answered, not taking her attention off her cast.

"After all the downpour the past two days? There are puddles of rain everywhere." Riven let out a low whistle. "That must be three miles from your house one way." He searched around her feet. "With your fishing pole and worms."

"A good early morning walk helps me to think."

"Overalls?" Riven asked, a slight smile on his face.

"Weird habit I've picked up lately," she shrugged.

Henry began to whine and went to sit by Riven.

"Look at this fine and handsome dog," Riven said, tenderly stroking his head.

"I wouldn't have guessed you liked dogs."

His face was puzzled. "I've loved dogs since I was a kid."

"I wouldn't have guessed that the way you treated Bear."

Riven dropped his hands from Henry. His face reflecting his sincere disappointment. He stood up and shoved his hands in his pockets.

Henry groaned and scratched his own ear with one of his hind legs.

"I realize I have a lot of ground to make up with you." Riven shuffled in place, his cowboy boots sinking in the moist sand of the bank. "I don't know what to do or say where you're concerned. Which is disconcerting to me because I'm used to barking orders."

The silence between the pair amplified as Katie reeled in her line, the sound barely louder than the nearby damselfly wings whirring among the spider webs and cattails along the bank. Finally, Henry turned his head and yelped before pawing the air to get their attention.

"Does he know any tricks?" Riven knelt to pet the dog. He winced as his knees popped. He fell backward, landing on his behind onto the moist ground.

"Those boots are going to sink you. It's too muddy and soft out here after the rain."

Riven's face was touched. He pushed himself up into a sitting position and pulled off his boots and socks one side at a time.

Katie turned her attention back to the pond, pulling the line a bit to entice fish by dancing the worm.

"You know the pole you're using to fish was my father's," Riven said, pushing the socks into the boots and off to one side. "You'd never believe it, but Julia and I liked to sneak away and go fish by ourselves."

Nearly toppling over in surprise, Katie blinked to regain her thoughts.

Riven chuckled while rubbing his temples. "One of our last times together, I'd left my father's pole at her house and was too stubborn and prideful to ask for it back. I can show you if you want to see." He pushed himself up to a standing position, much stronger in his stance with bare feet.

Katie reeled in the line, snacked clean by a turtle. She secured the hook before extending the pole to him. Once in his hands, he held it as if it were an ancient relic he was examining for the first time.

Henry pawed Riven on the thigh and whined.

"I'm all right, old boy," he replied. "A bit overtaken with the past."

Katie eyed her swaying father. "Do you need to sit down?"

Henry leaned in to steady Riven's shaking legs. He looked up and whimpered, seeming concerned at the man's emotions.

Softened by her dog's actions, Katie said, "Tell me about the fishing pole."

Riven pulled a handkerchief out of his pocket and blew his nose into it. "It's what I have left of my father."

A gust of wind blew in the area, whipping up enough debris that both Katie and Riven put their heads down, waiting for it to stop. When she opened her eyes, Katie found Riven had tears in his.

"Let me show you something, if it's even still visible." Riven examined the grip with his glasses at the tip of his nose. He grinned. "Here, have a look-see."

Katie leaned over. There were etchings on the handle. "It's a box with a line underneath. Inside a triangle," she said, looking up at Riven. "What is it?"

"Hobo code," Riven whispered. He scratched Henry behind the ears. "My father was a wanderer. Something I was deeply ashamed about my entire life—a hobo in my immediate family."

"*My grandfather?*"

Nodding, Riven continued. "He came back from the Second World War, apparently a much different man than when he left for it. He returned home and couldn't sit still from anxiety. Which made holding down a job nearly impossible."

"I have grandparents," Katie said, softly.

"My mother passed when I was barely in high school. She was exhausted and sick with worry. She missed him terribly when he was gone."

"Who took care of you and your siblings when she was gone?"

"No brothers or sisters. Only me. As I got older, my dad holding down a job in one place became an even greater challenge to him. He'd just disappear for large stretches of time." Riven glanced up, still holding the pole. "Do you know how I'd know he'd taken off again looking for work?"

Katie shook her head.

"He'd leave a note—*Gone Fishing*." He scratched the back of his ear in a nervous twitch. "It was our code between each other. Somehow not calling it what it was made it easier." He paused. "Or perhaps harder now that I think about it."

"How long was he gone?"

"It would depend. As time went on, the gaps between my dad's visits widened. On his last trip home, he gave me his prized fishing pole. I should have known he'd never come home to Merivelle again."

Katie's face was solemn listening to his words. The residue of anger she had been feeling since she'd decided to leave town lessened with the breeze of the morning and Riven's words. She sighed in empathy.

"Does all of this embarrass you? The last thing I want to do is introduce any more drama into your life. And here I go telling you about a hobo grandfather."

"Hobos weren't tramps or bums." Katie lifted her head proudly. "They traveled to find work, not to seek handouts. They were self-governed by a code of ethics that any community would be enriched by adopting."

Riven loosened his grip on the pole, his face surprised at his daughter's kind reaction. He rubbed his thigh in anxiousness. "How do you know all that information?"

"Percy called my wandering dog a hobo, and I let him have a piece of my mind. He was eager to tell me about the nobility of hard-working men who were merely seeking innovative ways to provide for their families."

"Good man—Percy," Riven murmured. "Not many men from his background would have seen my father with such benevolence." He handed the pole back to Katie. "You know there are smaller hobo fishing poles. Ones that you can fit in a pocket. But this one here served another purpose."

"What's that?" Katie was tracing the grooves in the handle of the pole.

"Many people used to turn their dogs loose on my father— one of the kindest men you can imagine."

Katie's face dropped in horror.

"Large, protective dogs were one of the banes of my father's life. Sometimes just walking to another location was fraught with danger. His fishing pole doubled as a stick to protect himself."

"No wonder—"

"That's no excuse for my past behavior with Bear's protectiveness of Mary." Riven shook his head. "My father still loved dogs. Most are like your handsome Henry here."

Gingerly inspecting the pole as Riven spoke, Katie eyes lit up. "I've seen this before. It's your logo! Riven Chapowits has a hobo sign for his businesses!"

Riven began to speak, his face worried at her recognition of the connection.

Katie put her hand on his arm. "I'm strongly intrigued, not in the least bit ashamed."

"Look here then," he breathed out, clearly relieved as he traced his index finger on the box with a line underneath. "This is actually a top hat."

Katie leaned in.

"The hobo sign for a gentleman with money. Something I always thought would be the solution to so many of my family's issues. More money, less problems. No one mocking my absent father, my shabby clothes or where we lived. My youthful mind thought getting ahold of a great deal of money could right all wrongs. Except bringing back my mother. My financial success was too late to lessen her burdens," he said, shivering.

For the first time that morning, clouds passed over the bright sun and the breeze that blew across the surface of the water caused goosebumps to appear on Katie's arms. Without a word, Riven took his jacket off and put it around her shoulders.

"When I was a kid, I always carried a stick and traced top hats into any ground surface I could." He crouched down, tracing the hobo sign into the sandy soil with his finger. "It became somewhat of an obsession for me. I'd even trace them in my mind at night as I fell asleep."

"What about the second symbol—the triangle?"

"I was an abysmal failure with the second." Riven paused for a moment. "A triangle meant a home."

"Why do you think you failed? I don't know of anyone with a bigger house."

"It's simply a house—not filled with people I love."

The truth of his words left Katie without any of her own, despite her mind searching for something to say.

"My father taught me the two marks combined—a top hat with a triangle—meant a kind, wealthy man lived in the house. Someone who could be of compassionate assistance to a person in need." He chewed the inside of his cheek and shook his head. "He'd be so ashamed of many parts of me." Though the wind was warming, it whipped sharply again and Riven shuddered.

"You can still do so much good," Katie said, taking the coat off her shoulders and putting it back on Riven's. "It's not too late."

"*You* could do good. You'd know how to use my resources better than the time I have left to learn, Katie," Riven said. "Please stay here in Merivelle. You belong here."

Katie took the fishing pole from her father's hands and stared at the etchings on it before looking up. "I think my hobo ancestry is awakening."

"Don't say that, Katie. You aren't, and never will be, a hobo. Not my daughter." Riven shook his head resolutely. "That's not why I told you about my past."

"You say it like it's something bad. You've hidden one of the most wonderful things about yourself. You've pulled yourself up by your bootstraps and while I'm still lost on the details of how the son of a hobo amassed what seems to be a fortune, you're hiding the parts of you that are the most interesting and worthy of respect." Katie shielded her eyes as the sun came out from the clouds again. Wisps of her hair, blowing in the breeze, framed her face in a pretty way.

"I can assure you there's nothing interesting about being so poor, you wonder where your next meal comes from. Nothing worthy of respect when classmates make fun you're wearing their hand-me-downs."

Katie held up the fishing pole and gently traced the top hat and triangle. "Who does the code serve if you can't take your painful experiences and make life easier for someone else traveling the same road?"

"That's why, if you stay," he replied softly, "we can fix so many things." He searched for his features within hers, taking solace in her cheekbones and nose as she spoke to him.

Taking a deep breath, Katie put the pole back in Riven's hands. "It's awkward. I don't know what to call you. Father? Dad? Certainly not Daddy." She smiled. "Pops?" She tilted her head in thought. "It's the closest, but not quite."

"Chaps?" His tone was expectant, but his face was humble as he waited for her reaction.

"*Chaps*," Katie repeated. Her eyes sparkled at the sound of it. "Chaps. I like it. We can ease into parenthood endearments starting with an affectionate nickname."

Buoyed by the small victory, Riven took a step forward, extending the pole back to Katie. "Think about staying. It's the perfect season for fresh starts."

"To travel on in spring sounds like heaven to me. And I think the Universe is trying to move me on to make space for you," Katie said. "You have a lot of ground to make up in Merivelle, but it can still be done."

"Everyone in town will hate me without you here to buffer."

"People love a good redemption story and Merivelle is full of the most wonderful people who will help you. Trust me. You have to make things right for you, not because you want something—a relationship with me. Do the good your heart sees needs to be done in Merivelle. That will be the bridge that brings me home one day."

Hit the Road

Shortly after noon, the wind picked up to such a great degree, Katie could not decline her father's offer for a ride home. The sand had begun to blow outside of town, obscuring their vision, causing the pair of them to flee with Henry into the refuge of Riven's pickup.

"Western Kansas wind," Riven muttered. "There's nothing quite like it."

The pair rode in awkward silence for a couple of minutes.

"So, this is what it feels like to have a dad take you home when you find yourself in a jam?" Katie asked, raising her eyebrows. "It feels weird." She paused. "But also, kind of good," she said, a shy smile on her face.

"I'm not sure. My dad never owned an automobile to my knowledge," Riven replied. His voice was one of stating fact, no hint of self-pity. He put his arm around Henry seated between the two of them and smiled.

"I'm learning a lot of people haven't had dads around. One of them in town breaks my heart, and I hope you might remedy that if it's at all in your power." Katie reached to Henry's back as she spoke. The old dog was delighted with the abundance of affection. "Reyna Posada."

At the sound of the surname, Riven returned both hands to the steering wheel, his face solemn as he gripped, waiting for Katie to speak.

"She's a remarkable young woman. Kind, smart, and has had the weight of the world on her since she's been in Merivelle the past few years. She, too, has no father." Katie paused as they approached the first city stop sign on their ride into town. "And her little brother, Pablito, is so sweet. I think he has some real artistic talent. He's equally athletic. It's hard to figure with him, he's so reserved and in his own shell."

"You have to believe me. I haven't done what Theodore says I have."

"Terrify the Posada family? Make them jumpy that they can't make the tiniest mistake as they try and put a life together in Merivelle?" Katie tilted her head. "Just being truthful with what I've seen with my own eyes."

Riven's shoulders slumped forward, his forearms dropping to the steering wheel. He looked at his daughter. "I thought Lupe and I were mending fences at the co-op."

"Only because she's a saint," Katie replied "It's her kids. You've loomed large in their lives. Early experiences shape a child's reality like nothing else."

"Maybe they don't remember. Especially the boy," Riven said, his voice edged in hope.

"You're many decades older than Pablito. Do you remember how it feels when your family was mistreated?"

"I told you this morning…" Riven said, before trailing off. A car had approached the same intersection and had given a polite tap on its horn. He nodded. "Point well taken, Katie."

"Fix things as you can, Chaps," Katie said, as they continued down Main Street at a crawling speed. Every business was closed on the holiday, but their windows were vibrant with colorful Easter decorations.

"There was never any mail."

"What?"

"Theodore has always been on me about taking it. There wasn't ever any mail."

Katie turned from gazing at the storefronts. "Then why didn't you ever tell him any of the times it's come up over the years? You've taken a real beating on the subject."

"You wouldn't believe me." Riven placed his right hand on Henry again.

"Try me. Here I am sitting in the truck of the former town villain on my favorite holiday after hearing our shared family hobo history." Katie scratched her nose, leaving a streak of mud down the length of it. "There's a huge chance I'll be open to belief."

Riven cleared his throat. "I know how it feels to be on tenterhooks waiting for a father to show up. It's why I didn't leave Merivelle for years. What if I left and my dad returned and didn't think I cared enough to wait?" He paused. "You have to believe me. There was no mail. I thought it better to have them think there was, and I was keeping it from them. I was okay with being the villain on that particular situation."

"If what you're saying is true—I don't know if I would have had the patience that you've shown both situations," Katie said. "However, it's still mistaken nobility. Keeping the truth from someone never makes things better."

"I understand. It won't happen again," Riven said, his eyes straight ahead as they drove in silence. He slowed the truck down the last two blocks to Katie's house, clear to both of them he was trying to draw out the unexpected interaction between the two of them.

"And when you're trying to do better, take a lesson from my wonderful dog here."

"How's that, Katie?"

"He can't say a word or explain his own actions, but he's a pretty blowed-in-the glass dog, isn't he?" she asked, recalling the hobo term for a genuine, trustworthy individual told to her and Mary on their recent walk.

The sun shone through the window of Riven's side of the truck while the wind blew shadows of the old elm trees lining the city streets onto the hood. "You know that term?" He closed his eyes as a single tear fought its way from under his lid while he was nodding in joy. "Of course, you know that term." He smiled at her. "I'll try my best. I hope it's good enough to mend some pain I've caused over the years."

"You can never go wrong, doing the right thing, Chaps," Katie said, patting his hand. "Somehow good things will always find you."

You Can Camp Here

A block from home, Katie caught an odd sight in the side mirror. She turned around in the front seat of Riven's truck. "Why is there a line of cars three blocks behind us?"

Henry sat up and followed Katie's gaze out the back window.

"Where are all these people going?" Katie asked. She glanced at her watch. "It's after church. They should all be at home for Easter dinner." Turning her attention to her house, she jumped in place and then froze. "And why does my house look like pastel toilet paper has exploded on the lawn?"

Riven pulled up in front of Katie's home. Every bush and low tree limb was covered in light-colored crepe streamers. A costume Easter rabbit walked around with a basket of eggs, bumping into people. Running right into the character's stomach area, a small child bounced back like they'd hit a trampoline. The contents of the basket spilled on the ground as an apologizing parent helped the fallen rabbit back to their oversized feet.

Mary squinted into the sun as Riven put his truck in park. She waved at the passenger seat. "Katie!" She turned and yelled to everyone on the lawn, pointing at Riven's truck. "Katie's home!"

With the production value of a well-meaning, unrehearsed,

middle school play, Theodore, the Posadas and Cybil took their posts and began to cheer among the rest of the town.

"Did you know about this, Chaps?" Katie asked, sighing.

He tried to hide his amusement. "A general idea."

"I'm in overalls for an Easter parade at my house."

"Let yourself be celebrated," Riven said, clearly proud. With his words, the strong wind of the morning suddenly calmed. A gentle breeze moved about the scene, bringing cool refreshment to all in attendance. Percy's gift of windchimes tinkled with a pleasant sound, music to Katie's ears.

She pulled the visor down and peered in the mirror at the mud schmear on her face. "Perfect." She began to laugh as Riven grinned at her, clearly charmed by everything about her.

Strains of music filled the crisp air. A large homemade cardboard sign bearing the bedazzled words *Sparkle On* was leaned against a tree in the yard.

"Chaps, I rarely say this, but this whole thing might be a bit over the top." Katie rolled her window down as Mary approached the vehicle.

Leaning in and bowing her chin to her chest before looking up again, Mary said, "You once gave me the Hollywood movie version of a Christmas miracle." She sighed. "And I've accidentally orchestrated an Easter extravaganza of gaudy proportions for you."

On cue, a group of teenage cheerleaders waved at Katie. Holding up the *Sparkle On* cardboard sign, they cheered. "S-P-A-R-K-L-E *spells Katie*!"

"Thank you, girls!" Katie shouted out the window. "So very kind of you!"

Happily nodding, they threw confetti in the air before dissipating in the crowd's growing numbers assembling in the front yard.

Katie stared at Mary slack-jawed and then giggled. "You

couldn't have given me a tiny clue?" She pointed at her hair in a messy ponytail.

"I promise, it didn't start out this way," Mary explained. "It was just people from the co-op and a cake from the Prairtisserie. Word got out and everyone wanted to show you how much we appreciate your hard work with the Rural Initiative."

"We didn't get the grant though," Katie said.

"But you put the work in. Something wonderful will happen and everyone feels it," Mary replied.

Bear appeared beside Mary, jumping onto his back legs, and panting when he saw Henry. "Get out! There's all sorts of things to eat around here." People had laid out blankets with picnic hampers and were placing food items out to share with their neighbors. Henry put his nose in the air, closing his eyes and smiling at the variety of delicious scents he took in.

"Easter dinner at your house," Mary said. "Everyone wanted to share one last meal with you. We're walking to Bear Bailey's afterward where the big *Sparkle On* cake the Prairtisserie made for you is waiting." She opened the door, eyes widening when she saw Katie's muddy rubber boots. "Please play along for what's next. Everyone's so excited to thank you," she whispered.

Reyna appeared, a big smile on her face. "To the woman I look up to most in town."

Katie's eyes widened as she nodded to Mary.

"Technically, Mary lives outside the city limits," Reyna replied. "Don't worry, both of you are covered."

"What high schooler thinks like this?" Katie asked, kissing the young woman's cheek.

"We have a crown and sash for the occasion," Reyna said, her voice grand. Pablito followed behind her holding both items as if he were Master of the Robes at a royal event. Lupe was serving food in the middle of the yard. She looked up and blew a kiss to

Katie before turning her attention back to the long line of people waiting for food she'd prepared for the occasion.

"Reyna, look how I'm dressed," Katie whispered, getting out of the truck. She smiled and waved at the people in her yard. "I haven't washed my hair in three days."

"Which makes us love you even more." Reyna took the sash from her brother and placed it over Katie's shoulders. With great care, she secured the crown with bobby pins, straightening it on Katie's head. She backed up to survey her work and nodded her approval. "Remember how much you did getting me ready for my *quinceañera*? I had to return the favor." She hugged Katie tight as she began to cry. "I'll miss you, Tia."

Cybil appeared behind Reyna. "I don't think I've ever seen you more beautiful."

Katie put her hand in the air to protest.

"You could be wearing couture and you'd not be lovelier," Cybil said, smiling. "Your sparkle truly comes from within."

Theodore joined the group. "Well, I'm not in agreement, kiddo." He bearhugged Katie. "You look absolutely ridiculous."

Katie started to cry.

"Theodore!" Riven's voice thundered in warning.

"It's what we do, Chaps." Katie wiped a tear from her eye. "We keep each other real, don't we? I was just overwhelmed with how much I was going to miss this goober."

"*Chaps?*" Theodore raised his eyebrows high in question.

Katie leaned in and hugged him. "I'll explain later. Don't use it. It's mine," she whispered.

"El Chapo it is!"

"I'm going to trust this is your way of teasing me," Riven said.

Theodore pointed his forefinger. "There you go," he said, smiling warmly. "You're getting the hang of what's always made your daughter so fun and loveable."

Down a few city blocks, people dressed in their Sunday best

appeared carrying food trays. Some in pants or pressed jeans, others using the opportunity to dust off elaborate Easter hats, many of which were vintage and of a by-gone era. Katie's lawn soon filled to capacity. Her next-door neighbors appeared and motioned their desire to share their porches and yards for the overflow of visitors. A community camp of sorts appeared before everyone's eyes.

"How did you plan something this big so quickly?" Katie asked when there was a break between people sending her off with hugs and recounting their favorite memories of her.

"You've spent your whole life here, participating, helping and being an integral part of the town. This is a much deserved send off. Unless you've changed your mind?" Mary said, her face soft, already knowing the answer.

"I have to go. And get to the bottom of whatever's out there calling me." Her eyes filled with tears. "But I promise, I'll always be home in Merivelle for the holidays."

"Of course, you will," Mary replied. "All the best souls arrive at Christmas."

Bear began to whine at the sound of the words remembering Katie's part in mending Mary's heart years earlier. "Please look after her," he said, turning to Henry. "She's a sister to Mary."

Henry was sleepy, his stomach full. He sighed in contentment, laying down on the green grass of Katie's yard to begin an afternoon nap. The gathering had lifted the dog's spirits and the promise of moving on a brightness to his eyes. However, his breath was still labored. "I'll try, Bear. But like I told you—nothing lasts forever."

"We're here such a short time. Dog's lives are even more of a glimmer than humans," Bear replied. He'd thought long and hard about Henry's words since the first day they'd met at the co-op. And though he hated the thought of not always being near Mary, for the first time in his six years, he'd begun to imagine himself an old dog like Henry. A lifetime of protection and gentleness his accomplishments. He glanced over to his beloved Mary and then nodded to her cousin. "Keep Katie safe until she finds her way. Enjoy all your adventures together in the time you have left. Just never let her feel alone on her journey. Promise?"

The old dog nodded in agreement. "Hobo's honor. If it's the last thing I do, I'll hang on until I know Katie's finally found her home."

Keep Quiet, Baby Sleeping

The sound of a train approaching a station blew in the background, the misty morning leaving droplets of moisture clinging to every surface. A soft breeze with the gentlest bit of cold nipped at the scene as the sun began to hint at its imminent arrival. An old dog stared in wonder at the high ceilings of the Art Deco style railway station. Rows and rows of ornate carved benches sat unoccupied, the floor of the terminal gleaming so brightly one might think it was glass. An empty ticket booth with a drawn shade was nearby, though there was no sign of anyone coming or going.

As the skinny dog with cloudy eyes of cataracts began to walk, his ribs disappeared. Muscle began to form all over his body and his coat glistened in the pre-dawn light. His sagging jowls tightened and gaps in his teeth filled in as his ears perked up. Full of energy, his tail began to wag. His eyes cleared to a deep amber shade as his sight returned, causing the dog to bark in a melodious way. He turned his head to seek the warmth of daybreak on his full and glistening coat of fur.

"Henry!" Josephine and Lea stood in front of him, the younger angel kneeling to kiss him on the nose.

"We've been waiting for you, good boy. We watched the bridge almost every day for a few human years after you and Katie left Merivelle," Josephine said. "And here you are *today*."

Henry put his head down and began to cry. The mournful sound floated on the air and reverberated into the distance.

"It's normal to be sad for a few moments when you first arrive." Lea put her face next to his, stroking his back with great care. "It's beautiful on the Rainbow Bridge. But it can be overwhelming to your newly restored senses. Give yourself a few moments."

The dog took deep breaths and then howled. He sighed and looked up at the angels. "I love traveling, but this time it's different. I feel homesick for my owner."

Hearing the dog's steadfast loyalty, Lea's expression was full of tenderness. "You fulfilled your time with Katie. You literally changed her life in every way."

"She's the one who took care of me," Henry replied. "I could never repay her kindness."

"You helped Katie start her journey out of Merivelle," Josephine said. "She found her true purpose once she emerged from the safe cocoon she'd always hidden herself in." She lifted her hands and butterflies of every color appeared, fluttering out of nowhere.

Watching the delicate creatures dance in front of him in a playful manner, the dog calmed almost instantly.

"Let me tell you a little secret about some of our friends on Earth, Henry," Josephine said.

A shiver of curiosity went through the dog's body. He took a few steps toward the angel.

"Humans get stuck in their lives out of fear. Even when their heart is telling them to move on."

As she spoke, Henry sat down and gazed at Josephine, his expression puppy-like as he listened.

"They can think of all kinds of noble reasons why they stay in one place longer than they should—duty, responsibility or even love. In actuality, it's fear masquerading as a more noble emotion," Josephine explained.

The same train horn from when Henry first arrived began to blow again, this time with an accompanying locomotive sound. The dog turned around in question and then back to Josephine.

"You were the magic key in her life, Henry. Katie loved you more than her fear of change. Your wandering ways were what she needed to fulfill her dreams. You're Katie's own Wanderful Dog."

"Like Bear is to Mary?" he asked, looking up and wagging his tail. "I always liked that very much."

"Bear brought Mary home to Merivelle and you led Katie on the journey her heart always wanted," Josephine said. "So, yes—like Bear is to Mary. You've both guided the women to their highest purpose."

"Will Katie ever go home to live in Merivelle?" Henry asked. "Now that she's married and has the little one?"

"It's entirely up to Katie," Lea said. "Now she's in touch with the feeling of living her best life. Her heart will always tell her where her home is."

"All from you, Henry," Josephine said. "And the adventures you had together."

The dog watched the Rainbow Bridge fading for the day, his face soft with remembrance as he watched the colors disappear. "I wanted to stay and help with the new baby. Katie was so excited when it was growing inside of her. I loved the smell of the little one getting ready to arrive."

Lea smiled. "What scent was that?"

"Violets. The baby smelled like flowers. I liked to push into Katie on the couch when she read in the evening, resting my head on her belly. When we fell asleep, I would dream of so many fields of violets." Henry sighed.

At the dog's words, the area outside of the train station came alive in purple color, blooms of violets carpeting a field of great expanse, as the sun burned away the fog of the area. A lone figure appeared in the meadow as the train that had sounded at Henry's earlier arrival was entering the station. A burst of strong wind blew through the meadow sending the scent of the flowers through the station.

"Do you think Katie will be all right without me?" Henry sniffed the air, closing his eyes in relaxation at the smell. "I never want her to forget me."

"You know she named her baby after your own vision of heaven?"

Henry opened his eyes. They lit up at Josephine's words. "*Violet*? I thought it was only a funny coincidence."

"There is no such thing as a coincidence, Henry," Josephine said. "Only great love and miracles leaning into one another. Your presence and the birth of her baby brought great happiness to Katie. You'll always be part of her story."

"All the heavenly hobo signs we try to send waiting for humans to read them properly," Lea said, her voice kind. "I wish they knew how many *coincidences* happen so they know they are loved beyond measure, and everything will work out better than they can imagine."

"She was so happy," Henry said, his face affectionate. "I remember her holding the baby up and saying, 'And though she be but little, she is fierce.' Her eyes would sparkle with joy." He turned his head, before then remembering his friend Bear. "She was quoting Shakespeare. But I don't know how I know that."

The angels laughed at his words. "I imagine Katie wants her little girl to be connected to what Percy loves. What a kind gesture to bequeath to her own child when it wasn't done for her growing up. True nobility," Josephine said, her face soft as she spoke.

From the opposite side of the tracks, the man from the field approached the station. He wore striped overalls and tipped an old hat in their direction. "May I?" he asked, before jumping across the tracks at Josephine's smiling nod.

"This is unusual at the Rainbow Bridge. Though not unheard of," Lea said, looking between Henry and the new visitor. "You two have never met."

The man knelt to the dog. "I know who you are, but you have no idea who I am." He smiled with tears in his eyes.

"You both have something beautiful in common," Josephine answered, stepping back to allow more room for Henry who had come alive at the man's touch and attention. "You love Katie. And now this kindhearted gentleman is welcoming you home."

"*You know Katie?*" Henry asked, trying hard not to bark too loud in excitement.

"My granddaughter," the man said, tracing a feline figure with long whiskers on the ground.

"A cat," Henry said, looking up. "Hobo code for a kindhearted woman." He nodded, eyes full of emotion. "Katie was always that to me. And everyone she met."

"I can't tell you the fun of seeing the two of you travel together. I want to extend to you my biggest thanks, Henry. What fun and love you showed Katie when she needed it most."

The dog was torn between sadness and joy. The memory of Katie and the kind words of her grandfather standing in front of him.

Noting the dog's dichotomous emotions, Lea spoke. "Do you know that before you arrived in Merivelle, Katie once told Mary her only wish was for a male to sit quietly with her in loyal companionship, no heartbreak or drama, and lastly, not to hog the covers."

"I never took her blankets." Henry's voice was solemn. "And I loved sitting with her. No words. Just being with her."

"You've fulfilled her wish and even more," Josephine said, turning her attention past the assembled group.

Lea stroked the dog's back again. "You'll always be Katie's daughter's guardian angel from here on the Rainbow Bridge. The scent of violets at random moments will help you to know she could use a heavenly hobo code to help her on her way. You won't believe how close you'll still feel to Katie and Violet when they recognize the connection always existing between you."

The waiting train gave a long exhale of steam as the engine idled like the soft whisper of a lullaby. The window shades opened revealing a carriage of luxurious, velvet upholstered seats, chandeliers in the middle of the aisle, sunlight shining through the individual crystals casting little rainbows all over the station's corridor. A woman was waiting inside. She waved at the group, a serene and happy look on her face.

"My wife, Vi," the man said. "And she'd love to hear all the stories you care to tell her about Katie and her little one."

"You're home, Henry. With Wendell to lead you," Josephine said.

"No more wandering?" Henry asked, his tail drooping for a moment. "I know this is the Rainbow Bridge, but I love to travel. The feeling hasn't left me."

The old man smiled at Henry, tapping his side as a gentle invitation to the dog. "Traveling is our favorite thing to do here. We wander wherever we want. There's never an end to the journeys." He turned to face the train as a platform appeared at the foot of the entrance. Stepping up onto it, Wendell turned to the dog whose nose was in the air, sniffing the silver platters of food that had magically appeared on the tables inside the carriage. "Now where would you like to go first, Henry?"

The handsome dog jumped and barked in joy as the pair boarded their transportation, chatting with excitement as the train began to move again, a slow and gentle rocking leading the loyal dog toward more adventure than could be had in a myriad of human lifetimes.

*Goodbyes are only for those who love with their eyes.
Because for those who love with heart and soul,
there is no such thing as separation.*

-Rumi

About the Author

Keri Salas is a native Kansan, living in Oklahoma with her husband and four wonderful dogs. It's a Wonderful Dog – Easter Eggs is her second novel. She is at work on the remaining two books to finish the "It's a Wonderful Dog series.

www.KeriSalas.com
www.instagram.com/kerisalas
www.instagram.com/itsawonderfuldog

www.ingramcontent.com/pod-product-compliance
Lightning Source LLC
LaVergne TN
LVHW041110220425
809138LV00068B/108/J